HOT
SIX

G·K
Hall
&C°.

Also by Janet Evanovich
in Large Print:

One for the Money
Four to Score
High Five

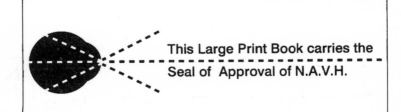

HOT SIX

JANET EVANOVICH

G.K. Hall & Co. • Thorndike, Maine

Published in 2000 by arrangement with St. Martin's Press, LLC

G.K. Hall Large Print Core Series.

The text of this Large Print edition is unabridged.
Other aspects of the book may vary from the original edition.

Set in 16 pt. Plantin by PerfecType.

Printed in the United States on permanent paper.

Library of Congress Cataloging-in-Publication Data

Evanovich, Janet.
    Hot six / by Janet Evanovich.
        p.   cm.
    ISBN 0-7838-9083-4 (lg. print : hc : alk. paper)
    ISBN 0-7838-9082-6 (lg. print : sc : alk. paper)
        1. Plum, Stephanie (Ficticious character)—Fiction. 2. Women
    detectives—New Jersey—Trenton—Fiction. 3. Bail bond agents—
    Fiction. 4. Trenton (N.J.)—Fiction. 5. Large type books. I. Title.
    PS3555.V2126 H6 2000b
    813′.54—dc21   00-040824

ACKNOWLEDGMENTS

Thanks to Eileen Hoffman and Larry Martine for suggesting the title for this book.

PROLOGUE

Okay, so here's the thing. My mother's worst fear has come true. I'm a nymphomaniac. I lust after a lot of men. Of course, maybe that's because I don't actually actually have sex with *any*. And some of my lustings probably aren't going anywhere. Probably it's unrealistic to think I'll ever get it on with Mike Richter, the goalie for the New York Rangers. Ditto Indiana Jones.

On the other hand, two of the men on my list of desirables actually desire me back. The problem being that they both sort of scare the hell out of me.

My name is Stephanie Plum. I'm a bounty hunter, and I work with both these men. Both are involved in law enforcement. One is a cop. And the other takes a more entrepreneurial approach to deterring crime. Neither is very good at following rules. Both outclass me when it comes to lusting *experience*.

Anyway, there comes a time in a girl's life when she needs to take the bull by the horns (or some other appropriate body part) and take charge of her life. And this is what I just did. I made a phone call, and I invited one of the scary men over for a visit.

Now I'm trying to decide if I should let him in.

My fear is that this could be an experience similar to the time when at age nine I got carried away in a Wonder Woman fantasy, fell off the Kruzaks' garage roof, destroyed Mrs. Kruzak's prize rosebush, ripped my shorts and flowered cotton underpants, and spent the rest of the day not realizing my ass was exposed.

Mental eyeroll. Get a grip! There's no reason to be nervous. This is the will of God. After all, didn't I pick this man's name out of a hat tonight? Well, actually it was a bowl, but still, this is a cosmic meeting. All right, so the truth is, I cheated a little and peeked when I picked. Hell, sometimes fate needs some help. I mean, if I could rely on fate to do the job I wouldn't have had to make the stupid phone call, would I?

Besides, I have some things going for me. I'm prepared for the task ahead. Man-eater dress, short and black. Ankle-strap heels. Glossy red lipstick. Box of condoms hidden in my sweater drawer. Gun fully loaded, on standby in the cookie jar. Stephanie Plum, woman on a mission. Take 'im down, dead or alive.

Just seconds ago, I heard the elevator doors slide open, and I heard footsteps in the hall. The footsteps stopped outside my apartment door, and I knew it was him because my nipples contracted.

He rapped once, and I stood paralyzed, staring at the lock. I opened the door on the second knock and stepped back, and our eyes met. He showed no sign of the nervousness I felt. Curiosity, maybe. And desire. Lots of desire. Desire in *spades*.

"Howdy," I said.

He stepped forward into the foyer, closed the door, and locked it. His breathing was slow and deep, his eyes were dark, his expression serious as he studied me.

"Nice dress," he said. "Take it off."

"Maybe some wine first," I said. Procrastinate! I thought. Get him drunk! Then if it's a disaster he might not remember.

He slowly shook his head. "I don't think so."

"Sandwich?"

"Later. A lot later."

I did some mental knuckle-cracking.

He smiled. "You're cute when you're nervous."

I narrowed my eyes. I hadn't been shooting for cute when I'd set this up and fantasized the evening.

He pulled me in to him, reached behind my back, and slid the zipper down on my dress. The dress dropped from my shoulders and pooled at my feet, leaving me in my slut shoes and Victoria's Secret barely-there string bikinis.

I'm five feet seven inches, and the heels added another four, but he still had an inch on me. He had a lot more muscle, too. His hands skimmed the length of my back, and he looked me over.

9

"Pretty," he said.

He seen it before, of course. He'd had his head under my skirt when I was seven. He'd relieved me of my virginity when I was eighteen. And, in more recent history, he'd done things to me that I wouldn't soon forget. He was a Trenton cop, and his name was Joe Morelli.

"Remember when we were kids and we used to play choo-choo?" he asked.

"I was always the tunnel, and you were always the train."

He hooked his thumbs into the waistband of my panties and inched them down. "I was a rotten kid," he said.

"True."

"I'm better now."

"Sometimes."

This got me a wolfish smile. "Cupcake, don't you ever doubt it."

And then he kissed me, and my undies floated to the floor.

Oh, boy. *Oh, boy!*

ONE

Five months later . . .

Carol Zabo was standing on the outermost guardrail on the bridge spanning the Delaware between Trenton, New Jersey, and Morrisville, Pennsylvania. She was holding a regulation-size yellow fire brick in the palm of her right hand, with about four feet of clothesline stretched between the brick and her ankle. On the side of the bridge in big letters was the slogan "Trenton Makes and the World Takes." And Carol was apparently tired of the world taking whatever it was she was making, because she was getting ready to jump into the Delaware and let the brick do its work.

I was standing about ten feet from Carol, trying to talk her off the guardrail. Cars were rolling past us, some slowing up to gawk, and some cutting in and out of the gawkers, giving Carol the finger because she was disturbing the flow.

"Listen, Carol," I said, "it's eight-thirty in the morning, and it's starting to snow. I'm freezing my ass off. Make up your mind about jumping, because I have to tinkle, and I need a cup of coffee."

Truth is, I didn't for a minute think she'd jump. For one thing, she was wearing a four-hundred-dollar jacket from Wilson Leather. You just don't jump off a bridge in a four-hundred-dollar jacket. It isn't done. The jacket would get ruined. Carol was from the Chambersburg section of Trenton, just like me, and in the Burg you gave the jacket to your sister, then you jumped off the bridge.

"Hey, *you* listen, Stephanie Plum," Carol said, teeth chattering. "Nobody sent you an engraved invitation to this party."

I'd gone to high school with Carol. She'd been a cheerleader, and I'd been a baton twirler. Now she was married to Lubie Zabo and wanted to kill herself. If I was married to Lubie I'd want to kill myself too, but that wasn't Carol's reason for standing on the guardrail, holding a brick on a rope. Carol had shoplifted some crotchless bikinis from the Frederick's of Hollywood store at the mall. It wasn't that Carol couldn't afford the panties, it was that she wanted them to spice up her love life and was too embarrassed to take them to the register. In her haste to make a get-away, she'd rear-ended Brian Simon's plain-clothes cop car and had left the scene. Brian had been in the car at the time, and had chased her down and thrown her into the pokey.

My cousin Vinnie, president and sole propri-

12

etor of Vincent Plum Bail Bonds, had written Carol's get-out-of-jail ticket. If Carol didn't show up for her court date, Vinnie would forfeit the walking money — unless he could retrieve Carol's body in a timely manner.

This is where I come in. I'm a bond enforcement agent, which is a fancy term for bounty hunter, and I retrieve bodies for Vinnie. Preferably live and unharmed. Vinnie had spotted Carol on his way in to work this morning and had dispatched me to rescue her — or, if rescue wasn't possible, to eyeball the precise spot where she splashed down. Vinnie was worried if he'd be out his bond money if Carol jumped into the river, and the divers and cops with grappling hooks couldn't find her water-logged corpse.

"This is really a bad way to do it," I said to Carol. "You're going to look awful when they find you. Think about it — your hair's gonna be a wreck."

She rolled her eyes up as if she could see on the top of her head. "Shit, I never thought of that," she said. "I just had it highlighted, too. I got it foiled."

The snow was coming down in big wet blobs. I was wearing hiking boots with thick Vibram soles, but the cold was seeping through to my feet all the same. Carol was more dressy in funky ankle boots, a little black dress, and the excellent jacket. Somehow the brick seemed too casual for the rest of the outfit. And the dress reminded me of a dress I had hanging in my own closet. I'd only worn the dress for a matter of minutes before it had been dropped to the floor and kicked aside . . . the opening statement in an exhaustive night with the man of my dreams. Well, one of the men, anyway. Funny how people see clothes differently. I wore the dress, hoping to get a man in my bed. And Carol chose it to jump off a bridge. Now in my opinion, jumping off a bridge in a dress is a bad decision. If I was going to jump off a bridge I'd wear slacks. Carol was going to look like an idiot with her skirt up around her ears and her pantyhose hanging out. "So what does Lubie think of the highlights?" I asked.

"Lubie likes the highlights," Carol said. "Only he wants me to grow it longer. He says long hair is the style now."

Personally, I wouldn't put a lot of stock in the fashion sense of a man who got his nickname by bragging about his sexual expertise with a grease gun. But hey, that's just me. "So tell me again why you're up here on the guardrail."

"Because I'd rather die than go to jail."

"I told you, you're not going to jail. And if you do, it won't be for very long."

"A day is too long! An hour is too long! They make you take off all your clothes, and then they make you bend over so they can look for smuggled weapons. And you have to go to the bathroom in front of everyone. There's no, you know, privacy. I saw a special on television."

Okay, so now I understood a little bit better.

I'd kill myself before I'd do any of those things, too.

"Maybe you won't have to go to jail," I said. "I know Brian Simon. I could talk to him. Maybe I could get him to drop the charges."

Carol's face brightened. "Really? Would you do that for me?"

"Sure. I can't guarantee anything, but I can give it a shot."

"And if he won't drop the charges, I'll still have a chance to kill myself."

"Exactly."

I packed Carol and the brick off in her car, and then I drove over to the 7-Eleven for coffee and a box of glazed chocolate doughnuts. I figured I deserved the doughnuts, since I'd done such a good job of saving Carol's life.

I took the doughnuts and coffee to Vinnie's storefront office on Hamilton Avenue. I didn't want to run the risk of eating all the doughnuts myself. And I was hoping Vinnie would have more work for me. As a bond enforcement agent I only get paid if I bring somebody in. And at the moment I was clean out of wayward bondees.

"Damn, skippy," Lula said from behind the file cabinets. "Here come doughnuts walking through the door."

At five feet five inches, weighing in at a little over two hundred pounds, Lula is something of a doughnut expert. She was in monochromatic mode this week, with hair, skin, and lip gloss all the color of cocoa. The skin color is permanent, but the hair changes weekly.

Lula does filing for Vinnie, and she helps me out when I need backup. Since I'm not the world's best bounty hunter, and Lula isn't the world's best backup, it's more often than not like the amateur-hour version of *The Best of "Cops" Bloopers.*

"Are those chocolate doughnuts?" Lula asked. "Connie and me were just thinking we needed some chocolate doughnuts, weren't we, Connie?"

Connie Rosolli is Vinnie's office manager. She was at her desk, in the middle of the room, examining her mustache in a mirror. "I'm thinking of having more electrolysis," she said. "What do you think?"

"I think it's a good thing," Lula told her, helping herself to a doughnut. "Because you're starting to look like Groucho Marx, again."

I sipped my coffee and fingered through some files Connie had on her desk. "Anything new come in?"

The door to Vinnie's inner office slammed open, and Vinnie stuck his head out. "Fuckin' A, we got something new . . . and it's all yours."

Lula screwed her mouth up to the side. And Connie did a nose wrinkle.

I had a bad feeling in my stomach. Usually I had to beg for jobs and here Vinnie was, having saved something for me. "What's going on?" I asked.

"It's Ranger," Connie said. "He's in the wind.

16

Won't respond to his pager."

"The schmuck didn't show up for his court date yesterday," Vinnie said. "He's FTA."

"FTA" is bounty-hunter-speak for "failure to appear." Usually I'm happy to hear someone has failed to appear, because it means I get to earn money by coaxing them back into the system. In this case, there was no money to be had, because if Ranger didn't want to be found, he wasn't going to be found. End of discussion.

Ranger is a bounty hunter, like me. Only Ranger is *good*. He's close to my age, give or take a few years; he's Cuban-American; and I'm pretty sure he only kills bad guys. Two weeks ago some idiot rookie cop arrested Ranger on carrying concealed without a license. Every other cop in Trenton knows Ranger and knows he carries concealed, and they're perfectly happy to have it that way. But no one told the new guy. So Ranger was busted and scheduled to go before the judge yesterday for a slap on the wrist. In the meantime, Vinnie sprung Ranger with a nice chunk of money, and now Vinnie was feeling lonely, high off the ground, out there on a limb all by himself. First Carol. Now Ranger. Not a good way to start a Tuesday.

"There's something wrong with this picture," I said. It made my heart feel leaden in my chest, because there were people out there who wouldn't mind seeing Ranger disappear forever. And his disappearance would make a very large hole in my life.

"It's not like Ranger to ignore his court date. Or to ignore his page."

Lula and Connie exchanged glances.

"You know that big fire they had downtown on Sunday?" Connie said. "Turns out the building is owned by Alexander Ramos."

Alexander Ramos deals guns, regulating the flow of black market arms from his summer compound on the Jersey shore and his winter fortress in Athens. Two of his three adult sons live in the United States, one in Santa Barbara, the other in Hunterdon County. The third son lives in Rio. None of this is privileged information. The Ramos family has made the cover of *Newsweek* four times. People have speculated for years that Ranger has ties to Ramos, but the exact nature of those ties has always been unknown. Ranger is a master of keeping things unknown.

"And?" I asked.

"And when they could finally go through the building yesterday they found Ramos's youngest son, Homer, barbecued in a third-floor office. Besides being toasted, he also had a large bullet hole in his head."

"And?"

"And Ranger's wanted for questioning. The police were here just a few minutes ago, looking for him."

"Why do they want Ranger?"

Connie did a palms-up.

"Anyway, he's skipped," Vinnie said, "and

18

you're gonna bring him in."

My voice involuntarily rose an octave. "What, are you crazy? I'm not going after Ranger!"

"That's the beauty of it," Vinnie said. "You don't have to go after him. He'll come to you. He's got a thing for you."

"No! No way. Forget it."

"Fine," Vinnie said, "you don't want the job, I'll put Joyce on it."

Joyce Barnhardt is my archenemy. Ordinarily, I'd eat dirt before I'd give anything up to Joyce. In this case, Joyce could take it. Let her spend her time spinning her wheels, looking for the invisible man.

"So what else have you got?" I asked Connie.

"Two minors and a real stinker." She passed three folders over to me. "Since Ranger isn't available I'm going to have to give the stinker to you."

I flipped the top file open. Morris Munson. Arrested for vehicular manslaughter. "Could be worse," I said. "Could be a homicidal rapist."

"You didn't read down far enough," Connie said. "After this guy ran over the victim, who just happened to be his ex-wife, he beat her with a tire iron, raped her, and tried to set her on fire. He was charged with vehicular manslaughter because according to the M.E. she was already dead when he took the tire iron to her. He had her soaked in gasoline and was trying to get his Bic to work when a blue-and-white happened to drive by."

Little black dots danced in front of my eyes. I sat down hard on the fake-leather couch and put my head between my legs.

"You okay?" Lula asked.

"Probably it's just low blood sugar," I said. Probably it's my *job*.

"It could be worse," Connie said. "It says here he wasn't armed. Just bring your gun along, and I'm sure you'll be fine."

"I can't believe they let him out on bail!"

"Go figure," Connie said. "Guess they didn't have any more room at the inn."

I looked up at Vinnie, who was still standing in the doorway to his private office. "You wrote bail on this maniac?"

"Hey, I'm not a judge. I'm a businessman. He didn't have any priors," Vinnie said. "And he has a good job working at the button factory. Homeowner."

"And now he's gone."

"Didn't show up for his court date," Connie said. "I called the button factory, and they said last they saw him was Wednesday."

"Have they heard from him at all? Did he call in sick?"

"No. Nothing. I called his home number and got his machine."

I glanced at the other two files. Lenny Dale, missing in action, charged with domestic violence. And Walter "Moon Man" Dunphy, wanted for drunk and disorderly and urinating in a public place.

I tucked the three folders into my shoulder bag and stood. "Page me if you hear anything on Ranger."

"Last chance," Vinnie said. "I swear I'll give his file to Joyce."

I took a doughnut from the box, gave the box over to Lula, and left. It was March and the snowstorm was having a hard time working itself up into anything serious. There was some slush on the street, and a layer of ice had accumulated on my windshield and my passenger-side windows. There was a large blurry object behind the window. I squinted through the ice. The blurry object was Joe Morelli.

Most women would have an orgasm on the spot to find Morelli sitting in their car. He had that effect. I'd known Morelli for most of my life, and I almost never had an on-the-spot orgasm, anymore. I needed at least four minutes.

He was wearing boots and jeans and a black fleece jacket. The tails of a red plaid flannel shirt hung under the jacket. Under the flannel shirt he wore a black T-shirt and a .40-caliber Glock. His eyes were the color of aged whiskey and his body was a testament to good Italian genes and hard work at the gym. He had a reputation for living fast, and the reputation was well deserved but dated. Morelli focused his energy on his job now.

I slid behind the wheel, turned the key in the ignition, and cranked up the defroster. I was driving a six-year-old blue Honda Civic that was perfectly good transportation but didn't enhance my fantasy life. Hard to be Xena, Warrior Princess in a six-year-old Civic.

"So," I said to Morelli, "what's up?"

"You going after Ranger?"

"Nope. Not me. No siree. No way."

He raised his eyebrows.

"I'm not magic," I said. Sending me after Ranger would be like sending the chicken out to hunt down the fox.

Morelli was slouched against the door. "I need to talk to him."

"Are you investigating the fire?"

"No. This is something else."

"Something else that's related to the fire? Like the hole in Homer Ramos's head?"

Morelli grinned. "You ask a lot of questions."

"Yeah, but I'm not getting any answers. Why isn't Ranger answering his page? What's his involvement here?"

"He had a late-night meeting with Ramos. They were caught on a lobby security camera. The building is locked up at night, but Ramos had a key. He arrived first, waited ten minutes for Ranger, then opened the door for him. The two of them crossed the lobby and took the elevator to the third floor. Thirty-five minutes later Ranger left alone. And ten minutes after that, the fire alarm went off. Forty-eight hours' worth of tape has been run, and according to the tape no one else was in the building with Ranger and Ramos."

"Ten minutes is a long time. Give him three

more to ride the elevator or take the stairs. Why didn't the alarm go off sooner, if Ranger started the fire?"

"No smoke detector in the office where Ramos was found. The door was closed, and the smoke detector was in the hall."

"Ranger isn't stupid. He wouldn't let himself get caught on videotape if he was going to kill someone."

"It was a hidden camera." Morelli eyed my doughnut. "You going to eat that?"

I broke the doughnut in half and gave him a piece. I popped the other into my mouth. "Was an accelerant used?"

"Small amount of lighter fluid."

"You think Ranger did it?"

"Hard to say with Ranger."

"Connie said Ramos was shot."

"Nine millimeter."

"So you think Ranger is hiding from the police?"

"Allen Barnes is the primary on the homicide investigation. Everything he's got so far leads to Ranger. If he brought Ranger in for questioning, he could probably hold him for a while based on priors, like the carrying charge. No matter how you look at it, sitting in a cell isn't in Ranger's best interest right now. And if Barnes has Ranger nailed as his number one suspect, there's a good chance Alexander Ramos has reached the same conclusion. If Ramos thought Ranger blew Homer away, Ramos wouldn't wait for justice to be served by the court."

The doughnut was sitting in a big lump in my throat. "Or maybe Ramos has already gotten to Ranger. . . ."

"That's a possibility, too."

Shit. Ranger is a mercenary with a strong code of ethics that doesn't necessarily always correspond to current popular thinking. He came on board as my mentor when I first started working for Vinnie, and the relationship has evolved to include friendship, which is limited by Ranger's lone-wolf lifestyle and my desire for survival. And, truth is, there's been a growing sexual attraction between us which scares the hell out of me. So my feelings for Ranger were complicated to begin with, and now I added a sense of doom to the list of unwanted emotions.

Morelli's pager beeped. He looked at the read-out and sighed. "I have to go. If you run across Ranger, pass my message on to him. We really need to talk."

"It'll cost you."

"Dinner?"

"Fried chicken," I said. "Extra greasy."

I watched him angle out of the car and cross the street. I enjoyed the view until he was out of sight, and then I turned my attention back to the files. I knew Moon Man Dunphy. I'd gone to school with him. No problem there. I just had to go pry him away from his television set.

Lenny Dale lived in an apartment complex on Grand Avenue and had listed his age as eighty-two. Big groan on this one. There is no good way to apprehend an eighty-two-year-old man. No matter how you cut it, you look and feel like a creep.

Morris Munson's file was left to read, but I didn't want to go there. Best to procrastinate and hope Ranger came forward.

I decided to go after Dale first. He was only about a quarter-mile from Vinnie's office. I needed to make a U-turn on Hamilton, but the car was having none of it. The car was heading for center city and the burned-out building.

Okay, so I'm nosy. I wanted to see the crime scene. And I guess I wanted to have a psychic moment. I wanted to stand in front of the building and have a Ranger revelation.

I crossed the railroad tracks and inched my way along in the morning traffic. The building was at the corner of Adams and Third. It was redbrick and four stories high, probably about fifty years old. I parked on the opposite side of the street, got out of my car, and stared at the fire-blackened windows, some of which were boarded over. Yellow crime-scene tape stretched the width of the building, held in place by sawhorses strategically positioned on the sidewalk to prevent snoops like me from getting too close. Not that I'd let a detail like crime-scene tape stop me from taking a peek.

I crossed the street and ducked under the tape. I tried the double glass door, but found it locked. Inside, the lobby seemed relatively unscathed.

Lots of grimy water and smoke-smudged walls, but no visible fire damage.

I turned and looked at the surrounding buildings. Office buildings, stores, a deli-style restaurant on the corner.

Hey, Ranger, are you out there?

Nothing. No psychic moment.

I ran back to the car, locked myself in, and hauled out my cell phone. I dialed Ranger's number and waited through two rings before his answering machine picked up. My message was brief: "Are you okay?"

I disconnected and sat there for a few minutes, feeling breathless and hollow-stomached. I didn't want Ranger to be dead. And I didn't want him to have killed Homer Ramos. Not that I cared a fig about Ramos, but whoever killed him would pay, one way or another.

Finally I put the car in gear and drove away. A half-hour later I was standing in front of Lenny Dale's door, and apparently the Dales were at it again because there was a lot of shouting going on inside the apartment. I shifted foot to foot in the third-floor hall, waiting for a lull in the racket. When it came, I knocked. This led to another shouting match, over who was going to get the door.

I knocked again. The door was flung open, and an old man stuck his head out at me. "Yeah?"

"Lenny Dale?"

"You're looking at him, sis."

He was mostly nose. The rest of his face had

shrunk away from that eagle's beak, his bald dome was dotted with liver spots, and his ears were oversized on his mummified head. The woman behind him was gray-haired and doughy, with tree-trunk legs stuffed into Garfield the Cat bedroom slippers.

"What's she want?" the woman yelled. "What's she want?"

"If you'd shut up I'd find out!" he yelled back. "Yammer, yammer, yammer. That's all you do."

"I'll give you yammer, yammer," she said. And she smacked him on top of his shiny skull.

Dale wheeled around and clocked her square on the side of her head.

"Hey!" I said. "Stop that!"

"I'll give you one, too," Dale said, jumping at me, fist raised.

I put my hand out to ward him off, and he stood statue still for a moment, frozen in the raised-fist position. His mouth opened, his eyes rolled into the back of his head, and he fell over stiff as a board and crashed to the floor.

I knelt beside him. "Mr. Dale?"

His wife toed him with Garfield. "Hunh," she said. "Guess he had another one of them heart attacks."

I put my hand to his neck and couldn't find a pulse.

"Oh, jeez," I said.

"Is he dead?"

"Well, I'm no expert . . ."

"He looks dead to me."

27

"Call 911 and I'll try CPR." Actually I didn't know CPR, but I'd seen it done on television, and I was willing to give it a shot.

"Honey," Mrs. Dale said, "you bring that man back to life and I'll hit you with the meat mallet until your head looks like a veal patty." She bent over her husband. "Anyway, look at him. He's dead as a doorknob. A body couldn't get any deader."

I was afraid she was right. Mr. Dale didn't look good.

An elderly woman came to the open door. "What's happening? Lenny have another one of them heart attacks?" She turned and yelled down the hall. "Roger, call 911. Lenny had another heart attack."

Within seconds the room was filled with neighbors, commenting on Lenny's condition and asking questions. How did it happen? And was it fast? And did Mrs. Dale want a turkey noodle casserole for the wake?

Sure, Mrs. Dale said, a casserole would be nice. And she wondered if Tootie Greenberg could make one of those poppyseed cakes like she did for Moses Schultz.

The EMS unit arrived, looked at Lenny, and agreed with the general consensus. Lenny Dale was as dead as a doorknob.

I quietly slipped out of the apartment and did a fast shuffle to the elevator. It wasn't even noon, and already my day seemed too long and cluttered with dead people. I called Vinnie when I reached the lobby.

"Listen," I said, "I found Dale, but he's dead."

"How long's he been like that?"

"About twenty minutes."

"Were there any witnesses?"

"His wife."

"Shit," Vinnie said, "it was self-defense, right?"

"I didn't kill him!"

"Are you sure?"

"Well, it was a heart attack, and I guess I might have contributed a little. . . ."

"Where is he now?"

"He's in his apartment. The EMS guys are there but there's nothing they can do. He's definitely dead."

"Christ, couldn't you have given him a heart attack after you got him to the police station? This is gonna be a big pain in the ass. You wouldn't believe the paperwork on this kind of thing. I tell you what, see if you can get the EMS boys to drive Dale over to the courthouse."

I felt my mouth drop open.

"Yeah, this'll work," Vinnie said. "Just get one of the guys at the desk to come out and take a look. Then he can give you a body receipt."

"I'm not dragging some poor dead man off to the municipal building!"

"What's the big deal? You think he's in a rush to get embalmed? Tell yourself you're doing something nice for him — you know, like a last ride."

Ugh. I disconnected. Should have kept the whole box of doughnuts for myself. This was shaping up to be an eight-doughnut day. I looked at the little green diode blinking on my cell phone. Come on, Ranger, I thought. Call me.

I left the lobby and took to the road. Moon Man Dunphy was next on my list. The Mooner lives in the Burg, a couple blocks from my parents' house. He shares a row house with two other guys who are just as crazy as Moon Man. Last I heard, he was working nights, restocking at the Shop & Bag. And at this time of the day I suspect he's at home eating Cap'n Crunch, watching reruns of *Star Trek*.

I turned onto Hamilton, passed the office, left-turned into the Burg at St. Francis Hospital and wound my way around to the row houses on Grant. The Burg is a residential chunk of Trenton with one side bordering on Chambersburg Street and the other side stretching to Italy. Tastykakes and olive loaf are staples in the Burg. "Sign language" refers to a stiff middle finger jabbed skyward. Houses are modest. Cars are large. Windows are clean.

I parked in the middle of the block and checked my fact sheet to make sure I had the right number. There were twenty-three attached houses all in a row. Each house sat flush to the sidewalk. Each house was two stories tall. Moon lived in number 45 Grant.

He opened the door wide and looked out at me. He was just under six feet tall, with light brown shoulder-length hair parted in the middle. He was slim and loose-jointed, wearing a black

Metallica T-shirt and jeans with holes in the knees. He had a jar of peanut butter in one hand and a spoon in the other. Lunchtime. He stared out at me, looking confused, then the light went on, and he rapped himself on the head with the spoon, leaving a glob of peanut butter stuck in his hair. "Shit, dude! I forgot my court date!"

It was hard not to like Moon, and I found myself smiling in spite of my day. "Yeah, we need to get you bonded out again and rescheduled." And I'd pick him up and chauffeur him to court next time. Stephanie Plum, mother hen.

"How does the Moon do that?"

"You come with me to the station, and I'll walk you through it."

"That sucks seriously, dude. I'm in the middle of a *Rocky and Bullwinkle* retrospective. Can we do this some other time? Hey, I know — why don't you stay for lunch, and we can watch ol' Rocky together?"

I looked at the spoon in his hand. Probably he only had one. "I appreciate the invitation," I said, "but I promised my mom I'd have lunch with her." What is known in life as a little white lie.

"Wow, that's real nice. Having lunch with your mom. Far out."

"So how about if I go have lunch now, and then I come back for you in about an hour?"

"That'd be great. The Moon would really appreciate that, dude."

Mooching lunch from my mom wasn't a bad idea, now that I thought about it. Besides getting

31

lunch, I'd get whatever gossip was floating around the Burg about the fire.

I left Moon to his retrospective and had my fingers wrapped around the door handle of my car when a black Lincoln pulled alongside me.

The passenger-side window rolled down and a man looked out. "You Stephanie Plum?"

"Yes."

"We'd like to have a little chat with you. Get in."

Yeah, right. I'm going to get into the Mafia staff car with two strange men, one of whom is a Pakistani with a .38 tucked into his Sans-A-Belt pants, partially hidden by the soft roll of his belly, and the other is a guy who looks like Hulk Hogan with a buzz cut. "My mother told me never to ride with strangers."

"We aren't so strange," Hulk said. "We're just your average couple of guys. Isn't that right, Habib?"

"That is just so," Habib said, inclining his head in my direction and smiling, showing a gold tooth. "We are most average in every way."

"What do you want?" I asked.

The guy in the passenger seat gave a big sigh. "You're not gonna get in the car, are you?"

"No."

"Okay, here's the deal. We're looking for a friend of yours. Only maybe he's not a friend anymore. Maybe you're looking for him, too."

"Uh-huh."

"So we thought we could work together. You know, be a team."

"I don't think so."

"Well, then, we're just gonna have to follow you around. We thought we should tell you so you don't get, you know, *alarmed* when you see us tailing you."

"Who are you?"

"That's Habib over there behind the wheel. And I'm Mitchell."

"No. I mean, who *are* you? Who do you work for?" I was pretty sure I already knew the answer, but I thought it was worth asking anyway.

"We'd rather not divulge our employer's name," Mitchell said. "It don't matter to you anyway. What you want to remember is that you don't cut us out of anything, because then we'd be annoyed."

"Yes, and it is not good when we become annoyed," Habib said, wagging his finger. "We are not to be taken lightly. Is that not so?" he asked, looking to Mitchell for approval. "In fact, if you annoy us we will spread your entrails across an entire parking space of my cousin Muhammad's 7-Eleven parking lot."

"What are you, nuts?" Mitchell said. "We don't do no entrails shit. And if we did, it wouldn't be in front of the 7-Eleven. I go there for my Sunday paper."

"Oh," Habib said. "Well, then, we could do something of a sexual nature. We could perform amusing acts of sexual perversion on her . . . many, many times. If she lived in my country she would forever be shamed in the community. She would be an outcast. Of course, since she is a decadent and immoral American she will undoubtedly be accepting of the perverse acts we will inflict upon her. And it is most possible that because *we* will be inflicting the perversions upon her, she will enjoy them immensely. But wait — we could also maim her to make the experience unpleasant in her eyes."

"Hey, I don't mind about the maiming, but watch it with the sexy stuff," Mitchell said to Habib. "I'm a family man. My wife catches wind of anything like that, and I'm toast."

TWO

I threw my hands into the air. "What the hell do you want, already?"

"We want your pal Ranger, and we know you're looking for him," Mitchell said.

"I'm not looking for Ranger. Vinnie's giving him to Joyce Barnhardt."

"I don't know Joyce Barnhardt from the Easter Bunny," Mitchell said. "I know you. And I'm telling you, you're looking for Ranger. And when you find him, you're gonna tell us. And if you don't take this to be a serious . . . responsibility, you'll be real sorry."

"Re-spons-i-bility," Habib said. "I like that. Nicely put. I teenk I will remember that."

" 'Think,' " Mitchell said. "It's pronounced 'think.' "

"Teenk."

"Think!"

"That is what I said. Teenk."

"The raghead just came over," Mitchell said to me. "He used to work for our employer in another capacity in Pakistan, but he came over with the last load of goods, and we can't get rid of him. He don't know much yet."

"I am not a raghead," Habib shouted. "Do you see a rag on this head? I am in America now, and I do not wear these things. And it is not a nice way that you say this."

"Raghead," Mitchell said.

Habib narrowed his eyes. "Filthy American dog."

"Blubber-belly."

"Son of a camel-walla."

"Go fuck yourself," Mitchell said.

"And may your testicles fall off," Habib responded.

Probably I didn't have to worry about these guys — they'd kill each other before the day was over. "I have to go now," I said. "I'm going to my parents' house for lunch."

"You must not be doing so good," Mitchell said, "you gotta mooch lunch from your parents. We could help with that, you know. You get us what we want, and we could be real generous."

"Even if I wanted to find Ranger, which I don't, I couldn't. Ranger is smoke."

"Yeah, but I hear you got special talents, if you get my drift. Besides, you're a bounty hunter . . . bring 'im back dead or alive. Always get your man."

I opened the door of the Honda and slid behind the wheel. "Tell Alexander Ramos he needs to get someone else to find Ranger."

Mitchell looked like he might hack up a hair-ball. "We don't work for that little turd. Pardon my French."

This had me sitting up straighter in my seat. "Then who *do* you work for?"

"I told you before. We can't divulge that information."

Jeez.

My grandmother was standing in the doorway when I drove up. She lived with my parents now that my grandfather was buying his lotto tickets directly from God. She had steel-gray hair cut short and permed. She ate like a horse and had skin like a soup chicken. Her elbows were sharp as razor wire. She was dressed in white tennis shoes and a magenta polyester warm-up suit, and she was sliding her uppers around in her mouth, which meant she had something on her mind.

"Isn't this nice? We were just setting lunch," she said. "Your mother got some chicken salad and little rolls from Giovicchini's Market."

I cut my eyes to the living room. My dad's chair was empty.

"He's out with the cab," Grandma said. "Whitey Blocher called and said they needed somebody to fill in."

My father is retired from the post office, but he drives a cab part-time, more to get out of the house than to pick up spare change. And driving a cab is often synonymous with playing pinochle at the Elks lodge.

I hung my jacket in the hall closet and took my place at the kitchen table. My parents' house is a narrow duplex. The living room windows look out at the street, the dining room window overlooks the driveway separating their house from the house next door, and the kitchen window and back door open to the yard, which was tidy but bleak at this time of the year.

My grandmother sat across from me. "I'm thinking about changing my hair color," she said. "Rose Kotman dyed her hair red, and she looks pretty good. And now she's got a new boyfriend." She helped herself to a roll and sliced it with the big knife. "I wouldn't mind having a boyfriend."

"Rose Kotman is thirty-five," my mother said.

"Well, I'm almost thirty-five," Grandma said. "Everyone's always saying how I don't look my age."

That was true. She looked about ninety. I loved her a lot, but gravity hadn't been kind.

"There's this man at the seniors club I've got my eye on," Grandma said. "He's a real looker. I bet if I was a redhead he'd give me a tumble."

My mother opened her mouth to say something, thought better of it, and reached for the chicken salad.

I didn't especially want to think about the details of Grandma tumbling, so I jumped right in and got to the business at hand. "Did you hear about the fire downtown?"

Grandma slathered extra mayo on her roll. "You mean that building on the corner of Adams and Third? I saw Esther Moyer at the bakery this morning, and she said her son Bucky drove the hook and ladder to that fire. She said Bucky told her it was a pip of a fire."

"Anything else?"

"Esther said when they went through the building yesterday they found a body on the third floor."

"Did Esther know who it was?"

"Homer Ramos. Esther said he was burned to a crisp. And he'd been shot. Had a big hole in his head. I looked to see if he was being laid out at Stiva's, but there wasn't anything in the paper today. Boy, wouldn't that be something? Guess Stiva couldn't do much with that. He could fill up the bullet hole with mortician's putty like he did for Moogey Bues, but he'd have his work cut out for him with the burned-to-a-crisp part. Course, if you wanted to look on the bright side, I guess the Ramos family could save some money on the funeral being that Homer was already cremated. Probably all they had to do was shovel him into a jar. Except I guess the head was left since they knew it had a hole in it. So probably they couldn't get the head in the jar. Less of course they smashed it with the shovel. I bet you give it a couple good whacks and it'd crumble up pretty good."

My mother clapped her napkin to her mouth.

"You okay?" Grandma asked my mother. "You having another one of them hot flashes?" Grandma leaned in my direction and whispered, "It's the change."

"It's *not* the change," my mother said.

"Do they know who shot Ramos?" I asked Grandma.

"Esther didn't say anything about that."

By one o'clock I was full of chicken salad and my mother's rice pudding. I trotted out of the house to the Civic and spotted Mitchell and Habib half a block down the street. Mitchell gave me a friendly wave when I looked his way. I got into the car without returning the wave and drove back to Moon Man.

I knocked on the door and Moon looked out at me, just as confused as he had been before. "Oh, yeah," he finally said. And then he did a stoner laugh, giggling and chuffing.

"Empty your pockets," I told him.

He turned his pants pockets inside out, and a bong dropped onto the front stoop. I picked it up and threw it into the house.

"Anything else?" I asked. "Any acid? Any weed?"

"No, dude. How about you?"

I shook my head. His brain probably looked like those clumps of dead coral you buy in the pet store to put in aquariums.

He squinted past me to the Civic. "Is that your car?"

"Yes."

He closed his eyes and put his hands out. "No energy," he said. "I don't feel any energy. This car is all wrong for you." He opened his eyes and ambled across the sidewalk, pulling up his sagging pants. "What's your sign?"

"Libra."

"You see! I knew it! You're air. And this car is earth. You can't drive this car, dude. You're a creative force, and this car's gonna bring you down."

"True," I said, "but this is all I could afford. Get in."

"I have a friend who could get you a suitable car. He's like . . . a car dealer."

"I'll keep it in mind."

Mooner folded himself into the front seat and hauled out his sunglasses. "Better, dude," he said from behind the shades. "Much better."

The Trenton cop shop shares a building with the court. It's a blocky redbrick, no-frills structure that gets the job done — a product of the slam-bam-thank-you-ma'am school of municipal architecture.

I parked in the lot and shepherded Moon inside. Technically, I couldn't bond him out myself, since I'm an enforcement agent and not a bonding agent. So I got the paperwork started and called Vinnie to come down and complete the process.

"Vinnie's on his way," I told Moon, settling him onto the bench by the docket lieutenant. "I have some other business in the building, so I'm going to leave you here alone for a couple minutes."

"Hey, that's cool, dude. Don't worry about me. The Mooner will be fine."

"Don't move from this spot!"

"No problemo."

I went upstairs to Violent Crimes and found Brian Simon at his desk. He'd only been promoted out of uniform a couple months earlier and still didn't have the hang of dressing himself. He was wearing a yellow-and-tan-plaid sports coat, navy suit slacks with brown penny loafers and red socks, and a tie wide enough to be a lobster bib.

"Don't they have some kind of dress code here?" I asked. "You keep dressing like this and we're going to make you go live in Connecticut."

"Maybe you should come over tomorrow morning and help me pick out my clothes."

"Jeez," I said. "Touchy. Maybe this isn't a good time."

"Good as any," he said. "What's on your mind?"

"Carol Zabo."

"That woman's a nut! She smashed right into me. And then she left the scene."

"She was nervous."

"You aren't going to lay one of those PMS excuses on me, are you?"

"Actually, it had to do with her panties."

Simon rolled his eyes. "Oh, crap."

"You see, Carol was coming out of the Frederick's of Hollywood store, and she was flustered because she'd just gotten some sexy panties."

"Is this going to be embarrassing?"

"Do you get embarrassed easily?"

"What's the point to all this, anyway?"

"I was hoping you'd drop the charges."

"No way!"

I sat down in the chair by his desk. "I'd consider it a special favor. Carol's a friend. And I had to talk her off a bridge this morning."

"Over panties?"

"Just like a man," I said, eyes narrowed. "I knew you wouldn't understand."

"Hey, I'm Mr. Sensitivity. I read *The Bridges of Madison County*. Twice."

I gave him a doe-eyed, hopeful look. "So you'll let her off the hook?"

"How far off the hook do I have to let her?"

"She doesn't want to go to jail. She's worried about the out-in-the-open-bathroom part."

He bent forward and thunked his head on the desk. "Why me?"

"You sound like my mother."

"I'll make sure she doesn't go to jail," he said. "But you owe me."

"I'm not going to have to come over and dress you, am I? I'm not that kind of girl."

"Live in fear."

Damn.

I left Simon and went back downstairs. Vinnie was there, but no Moon Man.

"Where is he?" Vinnie wanted to know. "I thought you said he was here at the back door."

"He was! I told him to wait on the bench by the docket lieutenant."

We both looked over at the bench. It was empty.

Andy Diller was working the desk. "Hey, Andy," I said. "Do you know what happened to my skip?"

"Sorry, I wasn't paying attention."

We canvassed the first floor, but Moon didn't turn up.

"I've gotta get back to the office," Vinnie said. "I've got stuff to do."

Talk to his bookie, play with his gun, shake hands with Mr. Stumpy.

We went out the door together and found Moon standing in the parking lot, watching my car burn. There were a bunch of cops with extinguishers working on it, but things didn't look too hopeful. A fire truck rolled down the street, lights flashing, and pulled through the chain-link gate.

"Hey, man," Moon said to me. "Real shame about your car. That's mad crazy, dude."

"What happened?"

"I was sitting there on the bench waiting for you, and I saw Reefer walk by. You know Reefer? Well, anyway, Reefer just got let out of the tank, and his brother was coming to pick him up. And Reefer said why didn't I come out to say hello to his brother. So I walked out with Reefer, and you know Reefer always has good weed, so one thing led to another, and I thought I'd just relax in your car for a minute and have a smoke. I guess a pod must have jumped, because the next thing your seat was on fire. And then it kind of spread from there. It was glorious until these gentlemen hosed it."

Glorious. Unh. I wondered if Moon would think it was glorious if I choked him until he was dead.

"I'd like to stay around and toast some marshmallows," Vinnie said, "but I need to get back to the office."

"Yeah, and I'm missing *Hollywood Squares*," Moon said. "We need to conclude our business, dude."

It was close to four when I made the final arrangements for the car to get towed away. I'd been able to salvage a tire iron and that was about it. I was outside in the lot, pawing through my shoulder bag for my cell phone, when the black Lincoln pulled up.

"Tough luck with the car," Mitchell said.

"I'm getting used to it. It happens to me a lot."

"We've been watching from a distance, and we figure you need a ride."

"Actually, I just called a friend, and he's going to come pick me up."

"That's a big fat lie," Mitchell said. "You been standing here for an hour and you haven't called anyone. I bet your mother wouldn't like it if she knew you were telling lies."

"Better than me getting into this car with you," I said. "That'd give her a heart attack."

Mitchell nodded. "You got a point." The tinted window slid shut, and the Lincoln rolled out of the lot. I found my phone and called Lula at the office.

"Boy, if I had a nickel for every car you destroyed I'd be able to retire," Lula said when she picked me up.

"It wasn't my fault."

"Hell, it's *never* your fault. It's one of them karma things. You're a number ten on the Bad-Shit-O-Meter when it comes to cars."

"I don't suppose you've got any news on Ranger?"

"Only that Vinnie gave the file to Joyce."

"Was she happy?"

"Had an orgasm right there in the office. Connie and me had to excuse ourselves so we could go throw up."

Joyce Barnhardt is a fungus. When we were in kindergarten together she used to spit in my milk carton. When we were in high school she started rumors and took secret photos in the girls' locker room. And before the ink had even dried on my marriage certificate I found her bare-assed with my husband (now my ex-husband) on my brand-new dining room table.

Anthrax was too good for Joyce Barnhardt.

"Then a funny thing happened to Joyce's car," Lula said. "While she was in the office talking to Vinnie, someone drove a screwdriver into her tire."

I raised my eyebrows.

"Was an act of God," Lula said, putting her red

46

Firebird in gear and punching on the sound system, which could shake the fillings out of your teeth.

She took North Clinton to Lincoln and then Chambers. When she dropped me in my lot, there was no sign of Mitchell and Habib.

"You looking for someone?" she wanted to know.

"Two guys in a black Lincoln were following me earlier today, hoping I'd find Ranger for them. I don't see them now."

"Lot of people looking for Ranger."

"Do you think he killed Homer Ramos?"

"I could see him killing Ramos, but I can't see him burning down a building. And I can't see him being stupid."

"Like getting caught on a security camera."

"Ranger had to know there were security cameras. That building's owned by Alexander Ramos. And Ramos just don't go around leaving the lid off the cookie jar. He had offices in that building. I know on account of I did a house call there once while I was working at my former profession."

Lula's former profession was being a ho', so I didn't ask for details on the house call.

I left Lula and swung through the double glass doors that led to the small lobby of my apartment building. I live on the second floor, and I had a choice of stairs or elevator. I chose the elevator today, having exhausted myself watching my car burn.

I let myself into my apartment, hung up my shoulder bag and jacket, and peeked in on my hamster, Rex. He was running on his wheel in his glass aquarium, his little feet a pink blur against the red plastic.

"Hey, Rex," I said. "How's things?"

He paused for a moment, whiskers twitching, eyes bright, waiting for food to drop from the sky. I gave him a raisin from the box in the refrigerator and told him about the car. He stuffed the raisin into his cheek and returned to his running. If it was me I'd have eaten the raisin right off and opted for a nap. I don't understand this running-for-fun stuff. The only way I could really get into running would be if I was being chased by a serial mutilator.

I checked my message machine. One message. No words. Just breathing. I hoped it was Ranger's breathing. I listened to it again. The breathing sounded normal. Not pervert breathing. Not head-cold breathing. Could have been telephone-solicitor breathing.

I had a couple hours before the chicken arrived, so I went across the hall and knocked on my neighbor's door.

"What?" Mr. Wolesky yelled, above the roar of his TV.

"I was wondering if I could borrow your paper. I had an unfortunate mishap with my car, and I thought I'd check out the used-car section of the classifieds."

"Again?"

"It wasn't my fault."

He handed me the paper. "If I was you, I'd be looking at army surplus. You should be driving a tank."

I took the paper back to my apartment and read the car ads and the funnies. I was pondering my horoscope when the phone rang.

"Is your grandmother there?" my mother wanted to know.

"No."

"She had some words with your father, and she went stomping up to her room. And then next thing I know she's outside getting into a cab!"

"She probably went to visit one of her friends."

"I tried Betty Szajak and Emma Getz but they haven't seen her."

My doorbell rang and my heart went dead in my chest. I looked out my peephole. It was Grandma Mazur.

"She's here!" I whispered to my mother.

"Thank goodness," my mother said.

"No. Not thank goodness. She has a suitcase!"

"Maybe she needs a vacation from your father."

"She's not living here!"

"Well, of course not . . . but maybe she could just visit with you for a day or two until things calm down."

"No! No, no, no."

The doorbell rang again.

"She's ringing my doorbell," I said to my

mother. "What should I do?"

"For goodness' sakes, let her in."

"If I let her in, I'm doomed. It's like inviting a vampire into your house. Once you invite them in, that's it, you're as good as dead!"

"This isn't a vampire. This is your grandmother."

Grandma pounded on the door. "Hello?" she called.

I hung up and opened the door.

"Surprise," Grandma said. "I've come to live with you while I look for an apartment."

"But you live with Mom."

"Not anymore. Your father's a horse's patoot." She dragged her suitcase in and hung her coat on a wall hook. "I'm getting my own place. I'm tired of watching your father's TV shows. So I'm staying here until I find something. I knew you wouldn't mind if I moved in for a while."

"I only have one bedroom."

"I can sleep on the couch. I'm not fussy when it comes to sleeping. I could sleep standing up in a closet if I had to."

"But what about Mom? She'll be lonely. She's used to having you around." Translation: What about me? I'm used to *not* having anybody around.

"I suppose that's true," Grandma said. "But she's just gonna have to make her own life. I can't keep livening that house up. It's too much of a strain. Don't get me wrong, I love your mother, but she can be a real wet blanket. And I haven't got a lot of time to waste. I've probably only got about thirty more years before I start to slow down."

Thirty years would put Grandma well over a hundred — and me at sixty, if I didn't die on the job.

Someone gave a light rap on my door. Morelli was here early. I opened the door, and he got halfway through the foyer before spotting Grandma.

"Grandma Mazur," he said.

"Yep," she answered. "I'm living here now. Just moved in."

The corners of Morelli's mouth twitched up ever so slightly. Jerk.

"Was this a surprise move?" Morelli asked.

I took the bucket of chicken from him. "Grandma got into it with my father."

"Is that chicken?" Grandma asked. "I can smell it all the way over here."

"Plenty for everyone," Morelli told her. "I always get extra."

Grandma pushed past us, into the kitchen. "I'm starved. All this moving gave me an appetite." She looked into the bag. "Are those biscuits, too? And coleslaw?" She grabbed some plates from the cabinet and ran them out to the dining room table. "Boy, this is gonna be fun. I hope you've got beer. I feel like having a beer."

Morelli was still grinning.

For some time now, Morelli and I had been engaged in an off-again-on-again romance.

Which is a nice way of saying we occasionally shared a bed. And Morelli wasn't going to think this was so funny when the occasional overnighter turned to no overnighters at all.

"This is going to put a crimp in our plans for the evening," I whispered to Morelli.

"We just need to change the address," he said. "We can go to my house after dinner."

"Forget your house. What would I tell Grandma? 'Sorry, I'm not sleeping here tonight, because I have to go do the deed with Joe'?"

"Something wrong with that?"

"I can't say that. It would make me feel icky."

"Icky?"

"My stomach would get squishy."

"That's silly. Your grandma Mazur wouldn't mind."

"Yes, but she'd know."

Morelli looked pained. "This is one of those woman things, isn't it?"

Grandma was back in the kitchen, getting glasses. "Where are your napkins?" she asked.

"I don't have any," I told her.

She stared at me blank-faced for a moment, unable to comprehend a house with no napkins.

"There are napkins in the bag with the biscuits," Morelli said.

Grandma peeked into the bag and beamed. "Isn't he something," she said. "He even brings the napkins."

Morelli rocked back on his heels and gave me

a look that told me I was a lucky duck. "Always prepared," Morelli said.

I rolled my eyes.

"That's a cop for you," Grandma said. "Always prepared."

I sat across from her and grabbed a piece of chicken. "It's the Boy Scouts who are always prepared," I said. "Cops are always hungry."

"Now that I'm going off on my own I've been thinking I should get a job," Grandma said. "And I've been thinking maybe I'd get a job as a cop. What do you think?" she asked Morelli. "You think I'd make a good cop?"

"I think you'd make a great cop, but the department has an age limit."

Grandma pressed her lips together. "Don't that tear it. I hate those darn age limits. Well, I guess that just leaves being a bounty hunter."

I looked to Morelli for help, but he was keeping his eyes glued to his plate.

"You need to be able to drive to be a bounty hunter," I said to Grandma. "You don't have a driver's license."

"I've been planning on getting one of them anyway," she said. "First thing tomorrow I'm signing up for driving school. I've even got a car. Your uncle Sandor left me that Buick and since you aren't using it anymore I guess I'll give it a try. It's a pretty good-looking car."

Shamu with wheels.

When the chicken bucket was empty Grandma pushed back from the table. "Let's get things cleaned up," she said, "and then we can watch a movie. I stopped off at the video store on my way over."

Grandma fell asleep halfway through *The Terminator*, sitting on the couch ramrod straight, head dropped to her chest.

"Probably I should leave," Morelli said. "Let you two girls get things straightened out."

I walked him to the door. "Is there any word on Ranger?"

"Nothing. Not even a rumor."

Sometimes no news was good news. At least he hadn't floated in with the tide.

Morelli pulled me to him and kissed me, and I felt the usual tingle in the usual places. "You know my number," he said. "And I don't give a rat's ass what anyone thinks."

I woke up on my couch with a stiff neck and feeling cranky. Someone was clanking around in my kitchen. Didn't take a rocket scientist to figure out who.

"Isn't this a terrific morning?" Grandma said. "I got pancakes started. And I got the coffee on."

Okay, maybe it wasn't so bad having Grandma here.

She stirred the pancake batter. "I thought we could get going early today, and then maybe you could take me out for a driving lesson."

Thank God my car had burned to a cinder. "I don't have a car right now," I said. "There was an accident."

"Again? What happened this time. Torched? Bombed? Flattened?"

I poured myself a cup of coffee. "Torched. But it wasn't my fault."

"You've got a pip of a life," Grandma said. "Never a dull moment. Fast cars, fast men, fast food. I wouldn't mind having a life like that."

She was right about the fast food.

"You didn't get a paper this morning," Grandma said. "I went and looked in the hall and all your neighbors got papers but you didn't get one."

"I don't have paper delivery," I told her. "If I want a paper I buy one." Or borrow one.

"Breakfast isn't gonna seem right without a paper to read," Grandma said. "I gotta read the funnies and the obits, and this morning I wanted to look for an apartment."

"I'll get you a paper," I said, not wanting to slow down the apartment search.

I was wearing a green plaid flannel nightshirt, which went well with my bloodshot blue eyes. I covered it with a short denim Levi's jacket, stuffed myself into gray sweatpants, shoved my feet into boots, which I left unlaced, clapped a Navy SEALs ball cap onto my rat's nest of shoulder-length curly brown hair, and grabbed my car keys.

"I'll be back in a minute," I yelled from the hall. "I'll just run out to the 7-Eleven."

I punched the button for the elevator. The elevator doors opened and my mind went blank.

Ranger was lounging against the far wall, arms crossed over his chest, his eyes dark and assessing, the corners of his mouth hinting at a smile.

"Get in," he said.

He'd abandoned his usual outfit of black rap clothes or GI Joe cammies. He was wearing a brown leather jacket, a cream-colored Henley, faded jeans, and work boots. His hair, which had always been slicked back in a ponytail, was cut short. He had a two-day beard, making his teeth seem whiter and his Latino complexion seem darker. A wolf in Gap clothing.

"Jeez," I said, feeling a flutter of something I'd rather not admit to in the pit of my stomach. "You look different."

"Just your average guy."

Yeah, right.

He reached forward, grabbed the front of my jacket, and pulled me into the elevator. He pushed the button to close the doors and then hit Stop. "We need to talk."

THREE

Ranger had been Special Forces, and he still had the build and the carriage. He was standing close, forcing me to tip my head back ever so slightly to look into his eyes.

"Just get out of bed?" he asked.

I glanced down. "You mean the nightshirt?"

"The nightshirt, the hair . . . the stupor."

"You're the reason for the stupor."

"Yeah," Ranger said. "I get that a lot. I cause stupor in women."

"What happened?"

"I had a meeting with Homer Ramos, and someone killed him when I left."

"The fire?"

"Not me."

"Do you know who killed Ramos?"

Ranger stared at me for a moment. "I have some ideas."

"The police think you did it. They have you on video."

"The police *hope* I did it. Hard to believe

they'd actually *think* I did it. I don't have a reputation for being stupid."

"No, but you do have a reputation for . . . um, killing people."

Ranger grinned down at me. "Street talk." He looked at the keys in my hand. "Going somewhere?"

"Grandma's moved in with me for a couple days. She wanted a paper, so I was going to run out to the 7-Eleven."

The grin spread to his eyes. "You haven't got a car, babe."

Damn! "I forgot." I narrowed my eyes at him. "How did you know?"

"It's not in the lot."

Well, duh.

"What happened to it?" he asked.

"It's gone to car heaven."

He pressed the button for the third floor. The doors opened, he hit the hold, stepped out and grabbed the paper lying on the floor in front of 3C.

"That's Mr. Kline's paper," I said.

Ranger handed the paper over to me and pushed the button for the second floor. "You owe Mr. Kline a favor."

"Why did you skip on your court date?"

"Bad timing. I need to find someone, and I can't find him if I'm detained."

"Or dead."

"Yeah," Ranger said, "that, too. I didn't think a scheduled public appearance right now was in my best interest."

"I was approached by two Mob-type guys yesterday. Mitchell and Habib. Their plan is to follow me around until I lead them to you."

"They work for Arturo Stolle."

"Arturo Stolle, the carpet king? What's his connection in this?"

"You don't want to know."

"Like if you told me, you'd have to kill me?"

"If I told you, someone else might want to kill you."

"No love lost between Mitchell and Alexander Ramos."

"None at all." Ranger handed me a card with an address on it. "I want you to do some part-time surveillance for me. Hannibal Ramos. He's the firstborn son and the second in command of the Ramos empire. He lists California as his residence, but he's spending more and more time here in Jersey."

"Is he here now?"

"He's been here for three weeks. Has a condo in a complex off Route 29."

"You don't think he killed his brother, do you?"

"He's not at the top of my list," Ranger said. "I'll have one of my men drop off a car for you."

Ranger loosely employed a small army of men to help with his various enterprises. Most were ex-military and most were even crazier than Ranger.

"No! Not necessary." I have bad luck with cars. Their demise frequently results in police intervention, and Ranger's cars have unexplainable origins.

Ranger stepped back into the elevator. "Don't get too close to Ramos," he said. "He's not a nice guy." The doors closed. And he was gone.

I emerged from the bathroom, dressed in my usual uniform of jeans and boots and T-shirt, fresh out of the shower, ready to start the day. Grandma was at the dining room table, reading the paper, and Moon was across from her, eating pancakes. "Hey, dude," he said, "your granny fixed me some pancakes. You're, like, so lucky to have your granny living with you. She's totally the bomb, dude."

Grandma smiled. "Isn't he the one," she said.

"I felt real bad about yesterday," Moon said, "so I brought you a car. It's, like, a loaner. Remember I was telling you about this friend of mine who's the *Dealer?* Well, he was ragged when I told him about the fire, and he said it'd be cool if you used one of his cars until you got new wheels."

"This isn't a stolen car, is it?"

"Hey, dude, what do I look like?"

"You look like a guy who'd steal a car."

"Well, yeah, but not *all* the time. This here's a genuine loaner."

I really did need a car. "It would only be for a couple days," I said. "Just until I get my insurance money."

Moon pushed back from his empty plate and

dropped a set of keys into my hand. "Knock yourself out. It's a cosmic car, dude. I picked it out myself so it'd complement your aura."

"What kind of car is it?"

"It's a Rollswagen. A silver wind machine."

Uh-huh. "Okay, well, thanks. Can I give you a ride home?"

He ambled out into the hall. "Gonna walk. Need to convene."

"I've got my whole day lined up," Grandma said. "Driving lesson this morning. Then this afternoon Melvina is going to take me around to look at some apartments."

"Can you afford your own apartment?"

"I've got some money put aside from when I sold the house. I was saving it to go into one of them nursing homes in my old age but maybe I'll just use my gun instead."

I grimaced.

"Well, it isn't like I'm gonna eat lead tomorrow," Grandma said. "I've got a whole lot of years left. And besides, I've got it figured out. See, if you put the gun in your mouth, then you blow the back of your head off. That way Stiva don't have to work so hard to make you look good when he lays you out on account of no one sees the back of your head anyway. You just got to be careful not to jiggle the gun so you don't botch the job and take your ear off." She put the paper aside. "I'll stop at the store on the way home and get some pork chops for supper. I gotta go get ready for my driving lesson now."

And I had to go to work. Problem was, I didn't want to do any of the things that were sitting in front of me. I didn't want to snoop on Hannibal Ramos. And I definitely didn't want to meet Morris Munson. I could go back to bed, but that wouldn't get the rent money. And besides, I didn't have a bed anymore. Grandma had the bed.

Okay, might as well take a look at the Munson file. I hauled the paperwork out and thumbed through it. Aside from the beating, the rape, and the attempted cremation Munson didn't seem so bad. No priors. No swastikas carved into his forehead. He'd listed his address as Rockwell Street. I knew Rockwell. It was down by the button factory. Not the best part of town. Not the worst. Mostly small single-family bungalows and row houses. Mostly blue-collar or no-collar.

Rex was asleep in his soup can, and Grandma was in the bathroom, so I left without ceremony. When I got to the lot I searched for a silver wind machine. And sure enough, I found one. And it was a Rollswagen, too. The body of the car was an ancient Volkswagen Beetle, and the front end was vintage Rolls-Royce. It was iridescent silver with celestial blue swirls sweeping the length of it, the swirls dotted with stars.

I closed my eyes and hoped that when I opened them the car would be gone. I counted to three and opened my eyes. The car was still there.

I ran back to the apartment, got a hat and dark glasses, and returned to the car. I slid behind the wheel, slouched low in the seat, and chugged out of the lot. This is *not* compatible with my aura, I told myself. My aura was *not* half Volkswagen Beetle.

Twenty minutes later I was on Rockwell Street, reading numbers, looking for Munson's house. When I found it the house seemed normal enough. One block from the factory. Convenient if you wanted to walk to work. Not so good if you liked scenic. It was a two story row house, very much like Mooner's house. Faced in maroon asbestos shingle.

I parked at the curb and walked the short distance to the door. It wasn't likely Munson would be home; this was Wednesday morning and he was probably in Argentina. I rang the bell and was caught off guard when the door opened and Munson stuck his head out.

"Morris Munson?"

"Yeah?"

"I thought you'd be . . . at work."

"I took a couple weeks off. I've been having some problems. Who are you, anyway?"

"I represent Vincent Plum Bail Bonds. You missed your court date, and we'd like to get you rescheduled."

"Oh. Sure. Go ahead and reschedule me."

"I need to take you downtown to do that."

He looked beyond me to the wind machine. "You don't expect me to go with you in that, do you?"

"Well, yeah."

"I'd feel like an idiot. What would people think?"

"Hey listen, pal, if I can ride in it, you can ride in it."

"You women, you're all alike," he said. "Snap your fingers and expect a man to jump through the hoops."

I had my hand in my shoulder bag, scrounging for my pepper spray.

"Stay here," Munson said. "I'm gonna go get my car. It's parked out back. I don't mind rescheduling, but I'm not riding in that dopey-looking car. I'll come around the block and then follow you into town." Slam. He closed and locked the door.

Damn. I got into the car and turned the key in the ignition, waiting at idle for Munson, wondering if I'd ever see him again. I checked my watch. I'd give him five minutes. Then what? Storm the house? Break the door down and go in guns blazing? I looked in my shoulder bag. No gun. I forgot to bring my gun. Gee, guess that means I have to go home and leave Munson for some other day.

I looked straight ahead and saw a car turn the corner. It was Munson. What a nice surprise, I thought. You see, Stephanie, don't be so quick to judge. Sometimes people turn out just fine. I put the wind machine in gear and watched him come closer. Hold on here, he was speeding up instead of slowing down! I could see his face, pinched in concentration. The maniac was going to ram me!

I threw the car into reverse and stomped on the gas pedal. The Rolls jumped back. Not fast enough to avoid the collision, but fast enough to avoid getting totally smashed. My head snapped on impact. No big deal for a woman born and raised in the Burg. We grow up riding bumper cars at the Jersey shore. We know how to take a hit.

Problem was, Munson was banging into me with what looked like a retired cop car, a Crown Victoria. Bigger than the Rollswagen. He came at me again, bouncing me back about fifteen feet, and the wind machine stalled. He scrambled out of his car while I was trying to restart, and ran at me with a tire iron. "You want to see me jump through hoops," he yelled. "I'll show you jump through hoops."

A pattern was emerging here. Ram somebody with your car, beat them with the tire iron. I didn't want to think about what would come after the tire iron. The Rolls engine caught, and I catapulted forward, barely missing him.

He swung the tire iron and caught my back fender. "I hate you!" he yelled. "You women are all alike!"

I went from zero to fifty m.p.h. in half a block and took the corner on two wheels. I didn't look back for a quarter of a mile, and when I did there was no one behind me. I forced myself to ease up on the gas and sucked in some deep breaths. My heart was thumping in my chest, and my hands had the wheel in a white-knuckled death grip. A

McDonald's popped up in front of me, and the car automatically turned into the drive-through lane. I ordered a vanilla milkshake and asked the kid in the window if they were hiring.

"Sure," he said, "we're always hiring. You want an application?"

"Do you get held up a lot here?"

"Not a *lot*," he said, passing the application through with the straw. "We get a few crazies, but usually you can buy them off with extra pickles."

I parked in the far corner of the lot and drank my milkshake while I read the application. It might not be so bad, I thought. You probably get free french fries.

I got out and looked at the car. The Rolls-Royce grill was crumpled, and the left rear fender had a big dent in it, and the back light was smashed.

The black Lincoln cruised into the lot and parked alongside me. The window rolled down, and Mitchell smiled at the Rollswagen. "What the hell is that?"

I gave him my PMS look.

"You need a car? We could get you a car. Any kind of car you want," Mitchell said. "You don't need to drive this . . . embarrassment."

"I'm *not* looking for Ranger."

"Sure," Mitchell said, "but maybe he's looking for you. Maybe he needs to get his oil changed, and he figures you're safe. It happens, you know. A man gets these *needs.*"

"Do you not have oil changed at a garage in

this country?" Habib asked Mitchell.

"Christ," Mitchell said. "Not that kind of oil. I'm talking about the old hide-the-salami thing."

"I do not understand this 'hiding salami,'" Habib said. "What is salami?"

"Fucking vegetarian don't know nothing," Mitchell said. He grabbed himself in the crotch and gave a hike up. "You know — the old salami."

"Ahh," Habib said. "I understand. This man Ranger hides his salami deep in this daughter of a pig."

"Daughter of a pig? Excuse me?" I said.

"Just so," Habib said. "Unclean slut."

I was going to have to start carrying my gun. I really felt like shooting these guys. Nothing serious. Just maybe take out an eye. "I have to go," I said. "I have stuff to do."

"Okay," Mitchell said, "but don't be a stranger. And think about the car offer."

"Hey," I yelled. "How did you find me?" But they were already out of the lot.

I drove around for a while, making sure no one was following me, then headed for Ramos's condo. I caught Route 29 and traveled north toward Ewing Township. Ramos lived in an affluent neighborhood with big old trees and professionally landscaped yards. Tucked away on Fenwood was a small cluster of recently constructed redbrick town houses, with attached two-car garages and brick-walled privacy yards. The houses sat behind well-tended lawns with curving walkways and dormant flower beds. Very tasteful. Very respectable. Just the place for an international black-market arms dealer.

The wind machine was going to make surveillance tough in this neighborhood. For that matter, any surveillance was going to be tough. A strange car parked too long would be noticed. Ditto a strange woman loitering on the sidewalk.

The drapes were drawn on all Ramos's windows, so it was impossible to tell if anyone was at home. Ramos was second from the end in a row of five attached houses. Trees peeked from behind the houses. The developer had left a greenbelt between condo sections.

I drove around the neighborhood, getting a feel for it, then cruised past Ramos's house again. No change. I paged Ranger and got a call back five minutes later.

"Just exactly what is it you want me to do?" I asked. "I'm in front of his house, but there's nothing to see, and I can't hang out here much longer. There's no place to hide."

"Go back tonight when it's dark. See if he gets visitors."

"What does he do all day?"

"Different things," Ranger said. "There's a family compound in Deal. When Alexander is in residence, business is conducted at the shore. Before the fire, Hannibal spent most of his time in the building downtown. He had an office on the fourth floor."

"What kind of car does he drive?"

"Dark green Jag."

"Is he married?"

"When he's in Santa Barbara."

"Anything else to tell me?"

"Yeah," Ranger said. "Be careful."

Ranger disconnected, and the phone rang again.

"Is your grandmother with you?" my mother wanted to know.

"No. I'm working."

"Well, where is she? I've been calling your apartment and there's no answer."

"Grandma had a driving lesson this morning."

"Holy Mary, Mother of God."

"And then she's going out with Melvina."

"You're supposed to be keeping an eye on her. What are you thinking? That woman can't drive! She'll kill hundreds of innocent people."

"It's okay. She's with an instructor."

"An instructor. What good is an instructor with your grandmother? And what about her gun? I looked in every nook and cranny, and I can't find that gun."

Grandma has a .45 long-barrel that she keeps hidden from my mother. She got it from her friend Elsie, who picked it up at a yard sale. Probably it was in Grandma's purse. Grandma says it gives the bag some heft, in case she has to beat off a mugger. This might be true, but I think mostly Grandma likes pretending she is Clint Eastwood.

"I don't want her out on the road with a gun!" my mother said.

"Okay," I said, "I'll talk to her. But you know how she is with that gun."

"Why me?" my mother asked. "Why me?"

I didn't know the answer to that question, so I hung up. I parked the car, walked around to the end of the town houses, and picked up a macadam bike path. The path ran through the greenbelt behind Ramos's town house, and gave me a nice view of the second-story windows. Unfortunately, there was nothing to see because the shades were drawn. The brick privacy fence obscured the first-floor windows. And I'd bet dollars to doughnuts the first-floor windows were wide open. No reason to draw the drapes there. No one could look in. Unless, of course, someone rudely climbed the brick wall and sat there like Humpty Dumpty waiting for disaster to strike.

I decided disaster would be slower in coming if Humpty climbed the wall at night when it was dark and no one could see her, so I continued on down the path to the far end of the town houses, cut back to the road, and returned to my car.

Lula was standing in the doorway when I parked in front of the bail bonds office. "Okay, I give up," she said. "What is it?"

"A Rollswagen."

"It's got a few dents in it."

"Morris Munson was feeling cranky."

"He did that? Did you bring him in?"

"I decided to delay that pleasure."

Lula looked like she was giving herself a hernia trying to keep from laughing out loud. "Well, we gotta go get his ass. He got a lotta nerve denting up a Rollswagen. Hey, Connie," she yelled, "you gotta come see this car Stephanie's driving. It's a genuine Rollswagen."

"It's a loaner," I said. "Until I get my insurance check."

"What are those swirly designs on the side?"

"Wind."

"Oh, yeah," Lula said. "I should have known."

A shiny black Jeep Cherokee pulled to the curb behind the wind machine, and Joyce Barnhardt got out. She was dressed in black leather pants, a black leather bustier, which barely contained her C-cup breasts, a black leather jacket, and high-heeled black boots. Her hair was a brilliant red, teased high and curled. Her eyes were ringed by black liner, and her lashes were thick with mascara. She looked like Dominatrix Barbie.

"I hear they put rat hairs in that lash-lengthening mascara," Lula said to Joyce. "Hope you read the ingredients when you bought it."

Joyce looked at the wind machine. "The circus in town? This is one of those clown cars, right?"

"It's a one-of-a-kind Rollswagen," Lula said. "You got a problem with that?"

Joyce smiled. "The only problem I've got is

trying to decide how I'm going to spend Ranger's capture money."

"Oh, yeah," Lula said. "You want to waste a lot of time on that one."

"You'll see," Joyce said. "I always get my man."

And dog and goat and vegetable . . . and everybody else's man, too.

"Well, we'd love to stand here talking to you, Joyce," Lula said. "But we got better things to do. We got a big important apprehension to make. We were just on our way to go catch a high-bond motherfucker."

"Are you going in the clown car?" Joyce asked.

"We're going in my Firebird," Lula said. "We always take the Firebird when we got serious ass-kicking lined up."

"I have to see Vinnie," Joyce said. "Someone made a mistake on Ranger's bond application. I checked out the address, and it's a vacant lot."

Lula and I looked at each other and smiled.

"Gee, imagine that," Lula said.

No one knows where Ranger lives. The address on his driver's license is for a men's shelter on Post Street. Not likely for a man who owns office buildings in Boston and checks with his stockbroker daily. Every now and then Lula and I make a halfhearted effort to track him down, but we've never had any success.

"So what do you think?" Lula asked when Joyce disappeared inside the office. "You want to go do some damage on Morris Munson?"

"I don't know. He's kind of crazy."

"Hunh," Lula said. "He don't scare me. I guess I could fix his bony ass. He didn't shoot at you, did he?"

"No."

"Then he isn't as crazy as most of the people on my block."

"Are you sure you want to risk going after him in your Firebird, after what he did to the wind machine?"

"First off, assuming I'd even be able to get my full figure into the wind machine, I think you'd need to take a can opener to it to get me out. And then, being that there's two seats in this little bitty car, and we'd be sitting in them, suppose we'd have to strap Munson to the hood to bring him in. Not that it's such a bad idea, but it'd slow us down some."

Lula walked over to the file cabinets and gave the bottom right-hand drawer a kick. The drawer popped open; Lula extracted a forty-caliber Glock and dropped it into her shoulder bag.

"No shooting!" I said.

"Sure, I know that," Lula said. "This here's car insurance."

By the time we got to Rockwell Street my stomach was queasy and my heart was tap-dancing in my chest.

"You don't look too good," Lula said.

"I think I'm carsick."

"You never get carsick."

"I do when I'm after some guy who just came at me with a tire iron."

"Don't worry. He do that again, and I'll pop a cap up his ass."

"No! I told you before — no shooting."

"Well, yeah, but this here's *life* insurance."

I tried to give her a stern look, but I sighed instead.

"Which house is his?" Lula wanted to know.

"The one with the green door."

"Hard to tell if anybody's in there."

We drove by the house twice, and then we took the one-lane service road to the rear and stopped at Munson's garage. I got out and looked in the grimy side window. The Crown Victoria was there. Rats.

"This is the plan," I told Lula. "You go to the front door. He's never seen you. He won't be suspicious. Tell him who you are and tell him you want him to go downtown with you. Then he'll sneak out the back door to his car, and I'll catch him off guard and cuff him."

"Sounds okay to me. And if you got a problem, you just holler, and I'll come around back."

Lula cruised away in the Firebird, and I tippy-toed up to Munson's back door and flattened myself against the house so he couldn't see me. I shook my pepper spray to make sure it was live and listened for Lula's knock on his door.

The knock came after a few minutes; there was some muffled conversation, and then came the sounds of scuffling at the back door and the lock being retracted. The door opened and Morris Munson stepped out.

"Hold it," I said, kicking the door shut. "Stay exactly where you are. Don't move a muscle or I'll hit you with the pepper spray."

"You! You tricked me!"

I had the pepper spray in my left hand and the cuffs in my right. "Turn around," I said. "Hands over your head, palms flat against the house."

"I hate you!" he shrieked. "You're just like my ex-wife. Sneaky, lying, bossy bitch. You even look like her. Same dopey curly brown hair."

"Dopey hair? Excuse me?"

"I had a good life until that bitch screwed it up. I had a big house and a nice car. I had Surround Sound."

"What happened?"

"She left me. Said I was boring. Boring ol' Morris. So one day she got herself a lawyer, backed a truck up to the patio door, and cleaned me out. Took every fucking stick of furniture, every goddamn piece of china, every freaking spoon." He gestured to the row house. "This is what I'm left with. This piece-of-shit row house and a used Crown Victoria with two years of payments. After fifteen years at the button factory, working my fingers to the bone, I'm eating cereal for supper in this rat trap."

"Jeez."

"Wait a minute," he said. "Let me at least lock the door. This place isn't much, but it's all I've got."

"Okay. Just don't make any sudden moves."

He turned his back to me, locked the door, whirled around, and jostled me. "Oops," he said. "Sorry. I lost my balance."

I stepped away. "What have you got in your hand?"

"It's a cigarette lighter. You've seen a cigarette lighter before, right? You know how it works?" He flicked it, and a flame shot out.

"Drop it!"

He waved it around. "Look how pretty it is. Look at the lighter. Do you know what kind of lighter this is? I bet you can't guess."

"I said, Drop it."

He held it in front of his face. "You're gonna burn. You can't stop it now."

"What are you talking about? *Yikes!*" I was wearing jeans and a white T-shirt, tucked in, and a green-and-black flannel shirt jacket-style over the T-shirt. I looked down and saw that my shirt-tail was on fire.

"Burn!" he yelled to me. "Burn in hell!"

I dropped the cuffs and the pepper spray and ripped the shirt open. I fumbled out of it, threw it to the ground, and stomped the fire out. When I was done stomping I looked around and Munson was gone. I tried his back door. Locked. There was the sound of an engine catching. I looked to the service road and saw the Crown Victoria speed away.

I picked my shirt up and put it back on. The bottom half on the right side was missing.

Lula was leaning against her car when I turned the corner.

"Where's Munson?" she asked.

"Gone."

She looked at my shirt and raised an eyebrow. "I could have sworn you started out with a whole shirt."

"I don't want to talk about it."

"Looks to me like your shirt's been barbecued. First your car, now your shirt. This could be turning into a record week for you."

"I don't have to do this, you know," I said to Lula. "There are lots of good jobs I could get."

"Such as?"

"The McDonald's on Market is hiring."

"I hear you get free french fries."

I tried Munson's front door. Locked. I looked in the street-level window. Munson had tacked a faded flowered sheet over it, but there was a gap at the side. The room beyond was shabby. Scarred wood floor. A sagging couch covered by a threadbare yellow chenille bedspread. An old television on a cheap metal TV cart. A beech-wood coffee table in front of the couch, and even from this distance I could see the veneer peeling off.

"Crazy ol' Munson isn't doing too good," Lula said, looking into the room with me. "I always imagined a homicidal rapist would live better than this."

"He's divorced," I said. "His wife cleaned him out."

"See, let this be a lesson. Always make sure you're the one to back the truck up to the door first."

When we got back to the office Joyce's car was still parked in front.

"Would have thought she'd be gone by now," Lula said. "She must be in there giving Vinnie a nooner."

My upper lip involuntarily curled back across my teeth. It was rumored that Vinnie had once been in love with a duck. And Joyce was said to be fond of large dogs. But somehow, the thought of them together was even more horrible.

To my great relief, Joyce was sitting on the outer office couch when Lula and I swung through the door.

"I knew you two losers wouldn't be out long," Joyce said. "Didn't get him, did you?"

"Steph had an accident with her shirt," Lula said. "So we decided not to pursue our man."

Connie was at her desk painting her nails. "Joyce thinks you know where Ranger lives."

"Sure we do," Lula said. "Only we're not telling Joyce on account of we know how she likes a challenge."

"You better tell me," Joyce said, "or I'll tell Vinnie you're holding back."

"Boy," Lula said, "that's got me thinking twice."

"I don't know where he lives," I said. "No one knows where he lives. But I heard him talking on the phone once, and he was talking to his sister in Staten Island."

"What's her name?"

"Marie."

"Marie Manoso?"

"Don't know. She might be married. She shouldn't be too hard to find, though. She works at the coat factory on Macko Street."

"I'm outta here," Joyce said. "If you think of anything else call me on my car phone. Connie's got the number."

There was silence in the office until we saw Joyce's Jeep pull away and roll down the street.

"She comes in here and I swear I can smell sulfur," Connie said. "It's like having the Antichrist sitting on the couch."

Lula cut her eyes at me. "Ranger really got a sister in Staten Island?"

"Anything's possible." But not probable. In fact, now that I thought about it, the coat factory might not even be on Macko Street.

FOUR

"Uh-oh," Lula said, glancing over my shoulder. "Don't look now, but here comes your granny."

My eyebrows shot up to the top of my head. "*My* granny?"

"Shit," Vinnie said from deep in his inner office. There was the sound of scuffling. The door to his office slammed shut, and the lock clicked into place.

Grandma walked in and looked around. "Boy, this place is a dump," she said. "Just what you'd expect from the Plum side of the family."

"Where's Melvina?" I asked.

"She's next door at the deli, getting some lunch meat. I thought as long as we were in the neighborhood I'd talk to Vinnie about a job."

We all swiveled our heads to Vinnie's closed door.

"What kind of job were you thinking about?" Connie asked.

"Bounty hunter," Grandma said. "I want to

80

make the big bucks. I got a gun and everything."

"Hey Vinnie!" Connie yelled. "You've got a visitor."

The door opened, and Vinnie stuck his head out and gave Connie the evil eye. Then he looked at Grandma. "Edna," he said, trying to force a smile, not having much luck at it.

"Vincent," Grandma said, her smile saccharine.

Vinnie shifted his weight from one foot to the other, wanting to bolt, knowing it was futile. "What can I do for you, Edna? Need to bond someone out?"

"Nothing like that," Grandma said. "I've been thinking about getting a job, and I thought I might like to be a bounty hunter."

"Oh, bad idea," Vinnie said. "Very bad idea."

Grandma bristled. "You don't think I'm too old, do you?"

"No! Jeez, nothing like that. It's your daughter — she'd pitch a fit. I mean, not to say anything bad about Ellen, but she wouldn't like this idea."

"Ellen's a wonderful person," Grandma said, "but she has no imagination. She's like her father, rest his soul." She pressed her lips together. "He was a pain in the behind."

"Tell it like it is," Lula said.

"So what about it?" Grandma said to Vinnie. "Do I get the job?"

"No can do, Edna. Not that I wouldn't want to help you out, but being a bounty hunter takes a lot of special skills."

"I have skills," Grandma said. "I can shoot and cuss and I'm real nosy. And besides, I've got some rights. I've got a right to employment." She gave Vinnie the squinty eye. "I don't see where you got any old people working for you. That don't look like equal opportunity to me. You're discriminating against old people. I've got a mind to get the AARP after you."

"The AARP is the American Association of Retired People," Vinnie said. "The 'R' stands for 'Retired.' They don't care about old people working."

"Okay," Grandma said, "how about this? How about, if you don't give me a job I'll sit on that couch over there until I starve to death."

Lula sucked in a breath. "Whoa, hardball."

"I'll think about it," Vinnie said. "I'm not promising anything, but maybe if the right thing comes in . . ." He ducked back into his office and closed and relocked the door.

"Well, that's a start," Grandma said. "I gotta go now and see how Melvina's doing. We have a big afternoon planned. We have some apartments to look at and then we're going to stop in for Stiva's afternoon viewing. Madeline Krutchman just got laid out, and I hear she looks real good. Dolly did her hair, and she said she gave her a tint to add some color around her face. She said if I like it, she could do it for me too."

"Rock on," Lula said.

Grandma and Lula did one of those complicated handshakes, and Grandma left.

"Anything new on Ranger or Homer Ramos?"
I asked Connie.

Connie opened a bottle of top coat for her
nails. "Ramos was popped at close range. Some
people are saying it smells like an execution."

Connie comes from a family that knows a lot
about executions. Jimmy Curtains is her uncle. I
don't know his real last name. All I know is if
Jimmy is looking for you . . . it's curtains. I grew
up hearing stories about Jimmy Curtains like
other kids heard stories about Peter Pan. Jimmy
Curtains is famous in my neighborhood.

"How about the police? What's their angle
today?" I asked.

"They're looking for Ranger, big time."

"As a witness?"

"As far as I can tell, as an anything."

Connie and Lula looked at me.

"Well?" Lula asked.

"Well, what?"

"You know well, what."

"I'm not sure, but I don't think he's dead," I
said. "Just a feeling I've got."

"Hah!" Lula said. "I knew it! Were you naked
when you got this feeling?"

"No!"

"Too bad," Lula said. "I would have been
naked."

"I have to go," I said. "I need to give Mooner
the bad news about the wind machine."

The good thing about the Mooner is that he's

almost always home. The bad thing is that, while his house is occupied, his head is frequently vacant.

"Oh, wow," he said, answering the door. "Did I forget my court date again?"

"Your court date is two weeks from tomorrow."

"Cool."

"I need to talk to you about the wind machine. It's sort of dented. And it's missing a rear light. But I'll fix it."

"Hey, don't worry about it, dude. These things happen."

"Maybe I should talk to the owner."

"The *Dealer.*"

"Yeah, the dealer. Where's he located?"

"He's at the end row house. He's got a garage, dude. Can you dig it? A garage." Since I'd just spent the winter scraping ice off my windshield, I could appreciate Mooner's garage excitement. I thought a garage was a pretty wondrous thing, too.

The end row house was about a quarter-mile away so we drove.

"Do you think he'll be home?" I asked Mooner when we got to the end of the block.

"The Dealer's always home. He's gotta be there to deal."

I rang the bell, and Dougie Kruper opened the door. I went to school with Dougie but hadn't seen him in years. In fact, I'd heard a rumor that he'd moved to Arkansas and died.

84

"Jeez, Dougie," I said, "I thought you were dead."

"Naw, I just *wished* I was dead. My dad got transferred to Arkansas, so I went with them, but I'm telling you, Arkansas was no place for me. No action, you know what I mean? And if you want to go to the ocean it takes days."

"Are you the dealer?"

"Yessiree. I'm the Dealer. I'm the man. You want something. I got it. We make a deal."

"Bad news, Dougie. The wind machine was in an accident."

"Girl, the wind machine *is* an accident. Seemed like a good idea at the time, but I can't unload it on anyone. Soon as you brought it back I was gonna push it off a bridge. Unless, of course, you want to buy it."

"It doesn't actually suit my purposes. It's too memorable. I need a car that disappears."

"A stealth car. The Dealer might have such a vehicle," Dougie said. "Come around back, and we'll take a look-see."

Around back was wall-to-wall cars. There were cars on the road, and cars in his yard, and a car in his garage.

Dougie led me to a black Ford Escort. "Now this here is a genuine disappearing car."

"How old is it?"

"I don't exactly know, but it's got a few miles on it."

"Isn't the year on the title?"

"This particular car doesn't have a title."

Hmm.

"If you need a car with a title, that would adversely effect the price," Dougie said.

"How adversely?"

"I'm sure we can come to terms. After all, I'm the Dealer."

Dougie Kruper was the big geek of my graduating class. He didn't date, and he didn't do sports, and he didn't eat like a human being. His greatest accomplishment in high school was being able to suck Jell-O into his nose through a straw.

Mooner was walking around laying his hands on the cars, divining karma. "This is it," he said, standing by a small khaki-colored Jeep. "This car has protective qualities."

"You mean like a guardian angel?"

"I mean, like, it has seat belts."

"Does this car come with a title?" I asked Dougie. "Does it run?"

"I'm pretty sure it runs," Dougie said.

Thirty minutes later I had two new pairs of jeans and a new watch, but no new car. Dougie was also willing to make a deal on a microwave, but I already had one.

It was early in the afternoon, and the weather wasn't terrible, so I walked to my parents' house and borrowed Uncle Sandor's '53 Buick. It was free, and it ran, and it had a title. I told myself it was a very cool car. A classic. Uncle Sandor had bought it new, and it was still in prime condition, which was more than could be said for Uncle Sandor, who was deep in the ground. Powder blue and white with gleaming chrome portholes and a big V-8 engine. I hoped I'd have my insurance money by the time Grandma got her license and needed the Buick. I hoped the insurance money would come through *fast* because I *hated* the car.

When I finally headed home the sun was low in the sky. The lot to my apartment building was filled and the big black Lincoln was parked next to one of the few open spaces. I pulled the Buick into the open space, and the Lincoln's passenger-side window rolled down.

"What's this?" Mitchell asked. "Another car? You wouldn't be trying to confuse us, would you?"

Ah, if only it was that simple. "I've been having some car problems."

"You don't find that Ranger guy soon and you're gonna have other problems that could be fatal."

Probably Mitchell and Habib were very tough guys, but I was having a hard time working up genuine fear. They just didn't seem to be in the same league as psycho Morris Munson.

"What happened to your shirt?" Mitchell asked.

"Someone tried to set me on fire."

He shook his head. "People are nuts. You gotta have eyes in the back of your head today."

From the guy who just threatened me with death.

I entered the lobby, keeping my eyes peeled for Ranger. The elevator doors opened, and I peeked inside. Empty. I didn't know if I was relieved or disappointed. The hall was also empty. No such luck with my apartment. Grandma popped out of the kitchen the instant I opened my front door.

"Right on time," she said. "I've got the pork chops ready to put on the table. And I made macaroni and cheese, too. Only we don't have any vegetables because I figure your mother isn't here so we can eat what we want."

The table in the dining area was set with real dishes and knives and forks and paper napkins folded into triangles.

"Wow," I said. "It's nice of you to make supper like this."

"I could have done an even better job, but you've only got one pot. What happened to that set of Revere Ware you got at your wedding shower?"

"I threw it away when I found Dickie doing . . . you know, with Joyce."

Grandma brought the macaroni and cheese to the table. "I guess I can understand that." She sat down and helped herself to a pork chop. "I gotta get a move on. Melvina and me didn't have time to go to the viewing this afternoon, so we're going tonight. You're welcome to come along."

Next to sticking myself in the eye with a fork, my favorite thing in the world is to go visit dead people. "Thanks, but I have to work tonight. I'm doing surveillance for a friend."

"Too bad," Grandma said. "It's going to be a good viewing."

After Grandma left I watched a *Simpsons* rerun, a *Nanny* rerun and a half-hour of ESPN, trying to distract myself from thinking about Ranger. There was a nasty little corner of my mind that harbored doubt of his innocence in the Ramos murder. And the rest of my head was filled with anxiety that he'd get shot or arrested before the real killer was found. And to further complicate things, I'd agreed to do surveillance for him. Ranger was Vinnie's primo bounty hunter, but Ranger also engaged in a variety of entrepreneurial activities, some of which were even legal. I'd worked for Ranger in the past, with varying degrees of success. I'd eventually taken my name off his employment roster, deciding it wasn't in *anyone's* best interest for us to partner up. It seemed like now was the time to make an exception. Although I wasn't sure why he wanted *my* help. I wasn't especially competent. On the other hand, I was loyal and lucky, and I guess I was affordable.

When it was almost dark I changed my clothes. Black spandex running shorts, black T-shirt, running shoes, a black hooded sweatshirt, and, to complete the outfit, a pocket-sized pepper spray. If I got caught snooping I could claim to be out jogging. Every pervert peeper in the state used the same lame M.O., and it worked every time.

I gave Rex a piece of cheese and explained that I'd be home in a couple hours. Out in the parking lot, I looked for a Honda Civic, and then I remembered it had been toasted. Then I looked for the wind machine, but that wasn't right either. And finally, with a disheartened sigh, I picked out the Buick.

Fenwood Street was cozy at night. Lights were on in house windows, and walk lights dotted the pathways leading to the town houses. There was no activity on the street.

Hannibal Ramos still had his drapes drawn, but light peeked from behind the drapes. I drove around the block once and parked the Buick just beyond the bike path I'd walked earlier in the day.

I did some stretches and some jogging in place in case someone was watching me, wondering if I was a suspicious character. I took off at a slow jog and quickly reached the path that ran through the common ground behind the houses. Less ambient light filtered through the trees back here. I took a moment to let my eyes adjust. Each privacy fence had a back door, and I cautiously walked along, counting off doors until I figured I was behind Hannibal's house. His upper story windows were dark, but light spilled over the privacy fence from the ground-level windows in the back of the house.

I tried the door to the fence. Locked. The brick fence was seven feet tall. The brick was smooth, impossible to climb. No handholds or footholds. I looked around for something to stand on.

Nothing. I eyeballed the pine growing next to the fence. Slightly mishapen from the fence pressing into some lower branches. The upper branches hanging over the yard. If I could get up in the tree, the branches would give me cover, and I could spy on Hannibal. I grabbed hold of a bottom branch and hoisted myself up. I scrabbled a couple feet higher and was rewarded with a view of Hannibal's backyard. The fence was bordered with flower beds, which were covered with mulch. An irregular stone patio backed up to the patio doors. And the rest of the yard was grass.

Just as I'd suspected, the drapes at the back of the house weren't drawn. A double window looked into the kitchen. The patio doors opened to a dining area. A small piece of another room was visible beyond the dining area. Probably the living room, but it was hard to tell. I didn't see anyone moving around.

I sat there for a while, watching nothing happen. No action in Hannibal's house. No action in either of his neighbors' houses. Very boring. No one on the bike path. No dog walkers. No joggers. Too dark. This is why I love surveillance. Nothing ever happens. Then you have to go to the bathroom and you miss a double homicide.

After an hour my butt was asleep and my legs were feeling twitchy from inactivity. Bag this, I thought. I didn't know what I was supposed to be looking for, anyway.

I turned to climb down, lost my balance, and flopped to the ground. *Wump!* Flat on my back.

In Hannibal's backyard.

The patio light flashed on, and Hannibal looked out at me. "What the hell?" he said.

I wiggled my fingers and moved my legs. Everything seemed to be working.

Hannibal stood over me, hands on hips, looking like he wanted an explanation.

"I fell out of the tree," I said. Pretty obvious, since there were pine needles and twigs scattered around me.

Hannibal didn't move a muscle.

I dragged myself to my feet. "I was trying to get my cat to come down. "He's been up there since this afternoon."

He looked up at the tree. "Is your cat still there?" Not sounding like he believed a word of it.

"I think he jumped when I fell."

Hannibal Ramos was California tan and couch-potato soft. I'd seen photos of him so I wasn't surprised. What I hadn't expected was the exhaustion in his face. But then, he'd just lost a brother, and that had to be taking a toll. His brown hair was thin and receding. His eyes were assessing behind tortoiseshell glasses. He was wearing gray suit slacks that were badly in need of pressing, and a white dress shirt, open at the collar, also rumpled. Mr. Average Businessman after a hard day at the office. I guessed he was in his early forties and a couple years away from a quadruple bypass.

"And I suppose he ran away?" Ramos said.

"God, I hope not. I'm tired of chasing after him." I am the *best* liar. Sometimes I amaze even myself.

Hannibal opened the door to the fence and gave the bike path a cursory glance. "Bad news. I don't see a cat."

I looked over Hannibal's shoulder. "Here, kitty, kitty," I called. I was feeling pretty stupid now, but there was no place to go with this but forward.

"You know what I think?" Hannibal said. "I think there's no cat. I think you were in that tree spying on me."

I gave him a look of total incredulity. Like . . . oh, duh? "Listen," I said, scooting around him to the door. "I've got to go. I need to find my cat."

"What color is it?"

"Black."

"Good luck."

I looked under a couple bushes en route to the bike path. "Here kitty, kitty."

"Maybe you should give me your name and phone number in case I find him," Hannibal said.

Our eyes locked for a couple beats, and my heart stumbled in my chest.

"No," I told him. "I don't think I want to do that." And then I left, walking in the opposite direction I came.

I exited the bike path and circled the block to get to my car. I crossed the street and stood in the shadows for a few minutes, looking at

Hannibal's house, wondering about the man. If I'd seen him on the street I'd have pegged him as an insurance salesman. Or maybe middle management in corporate America. That he was the crown prince of black market arms wouldn't occur to me.

A light blinked on in an upstairs window. The crown prince was probably changing into something more comfortable. Too early for bed, and the lights were still on downstairs. I was about to leave when a car cruised down the street and turned into Hannibal's driveway.

Woman at the wheel. Couldn't see her face. The driver's door opened and a long, stocking-clad leg swung out, followed by a killer body in a dark suit. Short blond hair. Briefcase under her arm.

I copied the license number on the pad I kept in my shoulder bag, got my mini-binoculars out of the glove compartment, and scuttled around to the back of Hannibal's house. Again. Everything was quiet. Hannibal probably felt confident that he'd scared me off. I mean, what idiot would be crazy enough to try to snoop on him twice in one night?

This idiot, that's who.

I went up the tree as quietly as possible. Easier this time. I knew where I was going. I found my perch and got the binoculars out. Unfortunately, there wasn't much to see. Hannibal and his caller were in the front room. I could see a slice of Hannibal's back, but the woman was out of view.

After a few minutes there was the distant sound of Hannibal's front door closing and of a car driving off.

Hannibal walked into the kitchen, got a knife from a drawer, and used it to open an envelope. He took a letter out and read it. Had no reaction. He carefully returned the letter to the envelope and put the envelope on his kitchen counter.

He looked at the kitchen window, seemingly lost in thought. Then he moved to the patio door, slid it open and stared out at the tree. I froze in place, not daring to breathe. He can't see me, I thought. It's dark in the tree. Don't move and he'll go back inside. Wrong, wrong, wrong. His hand came up from his side, a flashlight snapped on, and I was caught.

"Here kitty, kitty," I said, shielding my eyes with my hand to see past the light.

He raised his other arm, and I saw the gun.

"Get down," he said, walking toward me. "Slowly."

Yeah, right. I *flew* from the tree, breaking branches on the way, landing with my feet already running.

Zing. The unmistakable sound of a bullet being fired through a silencer.

I don't ordinarily think of myself as fast, but I moved down that path at the speed of light. I went straight to the car, jumped inside, and roared off.

I checked the mirror several times to make sure I wasn't being followed. Closer to my apartment I drove down Makefield, turned at the corner, cut my lights, and waited. No car in sight. I popped the lights back on and noticed my hands had almost stopped shaking. I decided that was a good sign and headed for home.

When I turned into my parking lot, I caught Morelli in my lights. He was lounging against his 4X4, arms crossed over his chest, feet crossed at the ankles. I locked the Buick and walked over to him. His expression changed from bored calm to grim curiosity.

"Back to driving the Buick?" he asked.

"For a while."

He looked me over head to toe and picked a pine sprig out of my hair. "I'm afraid to ask," he said.

"Surveillance."

"You're all sticky."

"Sap. I was in a pine tree."

He grinned. "I hear they're hiring at the button factory."

"What do you know about Hannibal Ramos?"

"Oh, man, don't tell me you're spying on Ramos. He's a real bad guy."

"He doesn't look bad. He looks ordinary." He had, until he pointed the gun at me.

"Don't underestimate him. He runs the Ramos empire."

"I thought his father did that."

"Hannibal manages the day-to-day business. Rumor has it the old man is sick. He's always been volatile, but a source tells me his behavior is increasingly erratic, and the family has hired baby-sitters to make sure he doesn't just wander away, never to be seen again."

"Alzheimer's?"

Morelli shrugged. "Don't know."

I glanced down and realized my knee was scraped and bleeding.

"You could become an accessory to something ugly by helping Ranger," Morelli said.

"Who, me?"

"Did you tell him to get in touch with me?"

"I didn't get a chance. Besides, if you're leaving messages on his pager, he's getting them. He just doesn't want to answer."

Morelli pulled me flat against him. "You smell like a pine forest."

"Must be the sap."

He put his hands to my waist and kissed me at the base of my neck. "Very sexy."

Morelli thought everything was sexy.

"Why don't you come back to the house with me?" he said. "I'll kiss your skinned knee and make it all better."

Tempting. "What about Grandma?"

"She'll never notice. She's probably sound asleep."

A second-story window opened in the apartment building. My window. And Grandma stuck her head out. "Is that you, Stephanie? And who's that with you? Is that Joe Morelli?"

Joe waved at her. "Hello, Mrs. Mazur."

"What are you standing out there for?"

Grandma wanted to know. "Why don't you come in and have some dessert? We stopped at the supermarket on the way home from the viewing, and I bought a layer cake."

"Thanks," Joe said, "but I have to be getting home. I have an early shift tomorrow."

"Wow," I said, "passing up layer cake!"

"I'm not hungry for cake."

My pelvic muscles contracted.

"Well, I'm cutting a piece for myself," Grandma said. "I'm starved. Viewings always make me hungry." The window closed, and Grandma disappeared.

"You're not coming home with me, are you?" Morelli said.

"Do you have cake?"

"I've got something better."

This was true. I knew it for a fact.

The window opened again, and Grandma stuck her head out. "Stephanie, you've got a phone call. Do you want me to tell him to call back later?"

Morelli raised his eyebrows. "Him?"

Both of us thinking, Ranger.

"Who is it?" I asked.

"Some guy named Brian."

"Must be Brian Simon," I said to Morelli. "I had to whine at him to get a deal for Carol Zabo."

"This is about Carol Zabo?"

"God, I hope so." That, or Brian Simon was calling in his marker. "I'll be right there," I yelled to Grandma. "Get his number, and tell him I'll call him back."

"You're breaking my heart," Morelli said.

"Grandma will only be here for a couple more days, and then we can celebrate."

"In a couple days I'll be gnawing my arm off."

"That's pretty serious."

"Don't ever doubt it," Morelli said. He kissed me, and I didn't doubt anything. He had his hand under my shirt, and his tongue deep in my mouth . . . and I heard someone give a wolf whistle.

Mrs. Fine and Mr. Morgenstern were hanging out their windows, whistling, drawn to the shouting between Grandma and me. They both started clapping and making hooting sounds.

Mrs. Benson opened her window. "What's going on?" she wanted to know.

"Sex in the parking lot," Mr. Morgenstern said.

Morelli looked at me speculatively. "It's possible."

I turned and ran for the door and sprinted up the stairs. I cut myself a piece of cake, and then I called Simon.

"What's up?" I said.

"I need a favor."

"I don't do phone sex," I said.

"It's not phone sex. Cripes, what made you think that?"

"I don't know. It just popped out."

"It's about my dog. I have to go out of town for a couple days, and I don't have anybody to take care of my dog. So since you owe me a favor . . ."

"I live in an apartment! I can't have a dog."

"It's only for a couple days. And he's a real good dog."

"What about a kennel?"

"He hates kennels. He won't eat. He gets all depressed."

"What kind of dog is it?"

"It's a little dog."

Damn. "It's only for a couple days?"

"I'll drop him off tomorrow first thing in the morning and pick him up on Sunday."

"I don't know. This isn't a good time. My grandmother is staying with me."

"He loves old ladies. I swear to God. Your grandma will love him."

I looked over at Rex. I'd hate to see him all depressed and not eating, so I guess I could understand how Simon felt about his dog. "Okay," I said. "What time tomorrow?"

"Around eight?"

I opened my eyes and wondered about the time. I was on the couch, it was pitch black out, and I smelled coffee. There was a moment of panicky disorientation. My eyes settled on the chair across from the couch, and I realized someone was sitting in it. A man. Hard to see in the dark. My breathing stopped altogether.

"How'd it go tonight?" he said. "Learn any-thing worthwhile?"

Ranger. No point asking how he'd gotten in when the windows and doors were closed and locked. Ranger had ways. "What time is it?"

"Three."

"Has it occurred to you that some people sleep at this time of night?"

"It smells like a pine forest in here," Ranger said.

"It's me. I was in the pine tree behind Hannibal's house, and I can't get the sap off. It's all stuck in my hair."

I saw Ranger smile in the darkness. Heard him laugh softly.

I sat up. "Hannibal has a lady friend. She drove up at ten o'clock in a black BMW. She was with Hannibal for about ten minutes, gave him a let-ter, and left."

"What's she look like?"

"Short blond hair. Slim. Nicely dressed."

"Did you get the license plate?"

"Yeah. I wrote it down. Didn't get a chance to check it out yet."

He sipped his coffee. "Anything else?"

"He sort of saw me."

"Sort of?"

"I fell out of the tree into his backyard."

The smile disappeared. "And?"

"And I told him I was looking for my cat, but I'm not sure he bought it."

"If he knew you better . . ." Ranger said.

"Then the second time he caught me in the tree, he pulled a gun, so I jumped down and ran away."

"Quick thinking."

"Hey," I said, tapping my finger to my head, "no grass growing here."

Ranger was smiling again.

FIVE

"I thought you didn't drink coffee," I said to Ranger. "What about your body being a temple?"

He sipped at the coffee. "It's my disguise. It goes with the haircut."

"Will you let your hair grow back?"

"Probably."

"And then will you stop drinking coffee?"

"You ask a lot of questions," Ranger said.

"Just trying to figure this out."

He was slouched in the chair, one long leg extended, his arms on the arms of the chair, his eyes on me. He set his cup on the coffee table, rose from the chair, and stood over the couch. He bent and kissed me lightly on the lips. "Some things are better left a mystery," he said. And then he moved to the door.

"Hey, wait a minute," I said. "Am I supposed to keep watching Hannibal?"

"Can you watch him without getting shot?"

I gave him a pissy look in the dark.

"I see that," he said.

"Morelli wants to talk to you."

"I'll call him tomorrow, maybe."

The front door opened and clicked shut. Ranger was gone. I padded to the door and looked out the peephole. No Ranger anywhere. I slid the security chain in place and went back to the couch. I fluffed up my pillow and crawled under the quilt.

And I thought about the kiss. What was I supposed to make of the kiss? Friendly, I told myself. It had been friendly. No tongue. No groping hands. No gnashing of teeth in uncontrollable passion. A friendly kiss. Only it hadn't felt friendly. It had felt . . . sexy.

Damn!

"What would you like for breakfast?" Grandma asked. "How about some nice warm oatmeal?"

Left to my own devices, I'd have eaten the cake. "Sure," I said, "oatmeal would be okay."

I poured a cup of coffee, and there was a knock on the door. I opened the door, and a big orange thing rushed in.

"Holy cow!" I said. "What is it?"

"Golden retriever," Simon said. "Mostly."

"Isn't he big for a golden retriever?"

Simon dragged a fifty-pound bag of dog food into the foyer. "I got him at the pound, and that's what they told me. Golden retriever."

"You said you had a small dog."

"I lied. So sue me."

The dog ran into the kitchen, stuck his nose in Grandma's crotch, and snuffled.

"Dang," Grandma said. "Guess my new perfume really works. I'm gonna have to try it out at the seniors meeting."

Simon pulled Bob away from Grandma and handed me a brown grocery bag. "Here's his stuff. Two dog bowls, some dog treats, a chew toy, a hairbrush and his pooper-scooper."

"Pooper-scooper? Hey, wait a minute —"

"I gotta run," Simon said. "I got a plane to catch."

"What's his name?" I yelled down the hall.

"Bob."

"Isn't this something," Grandma said. "A dog named Bob."

I filled Bob's water bowl and set it on the floor in the kitchen. "He's only staying for a couple days," I said. "Simon will be back for him on Sunday."

Grandma eyeballed the dog food bag. "Awful big bag of food for a couple days."

"Maybe he eats a lot."

"He eats all that in two days and you're not gonna need a pooper-scooper," Grandma said. "You're gonna need a shovel."

I unhooked Bob's leash and hung it on a hall peg. "Well, Bob," I said, "this won't be so bad. I always wanted a golden retriever."

Bob wagged his tail and looked from Grandma to me.

Grandma ladled out oatmeal for the three of us. She and I took our bowls into the dining area, and Bob ate his in the kitchen. When Grandma and I went back to the kitchen, Bob's bowl was empty. The cardboard box that used to hold the cake was also empty.

"Guess Bob's got a sweet tooth," Grandma said.

I shook my finger at him. "That was rude. And besides, you'll get fat."

Bob wagged his tail.

"He might not be too smart," Grandma said.

Smart enough to eat the cake.

Grandma had a driving lesson scheduled for nine o'clock. "I'm probably gonna be gone all day," she said. "So don't worry if you don't see me. After my driving lesson I'm going to the mall with Louise Greeber. And then we're gonna look at some more apartments. If you want, I can stop and get some ground beef this afternoon. I thought a meatloaf might be nice for supper."

Major guilt trip coming on. Grandma was doing all the cooking. "My turn," I told her. "I'll make the meatloaf."

"I didn't know you could cook meatloaf."

"Sure," I said. "I can cook lots of stuff." A big lie. I can cook nothing.

I gave Bob a dog treat, and Grandma and I left together. Halfway down the hall, Grandma stopped. "What's that sound?" she asked.

We both listened. Bob was howling on the other side of my door.

My next-door neighbor, Mrs. Karwatt, stuck her head out. "What's that sound?"

"It's Bob," Grandma said. "He don't like being at home alone."

Ten minutes later I was on the road with Bob riding shotgun, head out the window, ears flapping in the wind.

"Uh-oh," Lula said when we walked in the office. "Who's this?"

"His name's Bob. I'm dog-sitting him."

"Oh yeah? What kind of dog is he?"

"Golden retriever."

"He looks like he been under the blow-dryer too long."

I smoothed some of his hair down. "He had his head out the window."

"That'll do it," Lula said.

I let Bob off the leash and he ran over to Lula and did the crotch thing again.

"Hey," Lula said, "back off, you're getting nose prints all over my new pants." She gave Bob a pat on the head. "He keep this up, and we're gonna have to pimp him out."

I used Connie's phone to call my friend Marilyn Truro at the DMV. "I need to run a plate through," I said. "Do you have time?"

"Are you kidding me? There are forty people standing in line. They see me talking on the phone, and they'll go postal." She spoke more softly. "Is this for a case? Is this for a murderer or something?"

"It might tie in to the Ramos murder."

"Are you shitting me? That is *so* cool."

I gave her the number.

"Hold on," she said. There was some clicking of computer keys, and Marilyn came back on. "The plate belongs to Terry Gilman. Isn't she working for Vito Grizolli?"

I was momentarily speechless. Next to Joyce Barnhardt, I disliked Terry Gilman most. For lack of a better term, she'd *dated* Joe in high school, and I had a feeling she wouldn't mind resuming the relationship. Terry worked for her Uncle Vito Grizolli now, which put a crimp in her Joe designs, since Joe was in the business of stamping out crime, and Vito was in the business of producing it.

"Uh-oh," Lula said. "Did I hear you right? Are you sticking your big fat nose in the Ramos case?"

"Well, I happened to run across —"

Lula's eyes widened. "You're working for Ranger!"

Vinnie popped out of his inner office. "Is that true? Are you working for Ranger?"

"No. It's not true. There's not a shred of truth to it." Well, what the hell — what's *one more lie?*

The front door crashed open and Joyce Barnhardt stomped in.

Lula, Connie, and I all ran to get Bob on the leash.

"You dumb bitch," Joyce yelled at me. "You sent me on a wild goose chase. Ranger doesn't have a sister working at the Macko Coat Factory."

"Maybe she quit," I said.

"Yeah," Lula said, "people quit all the time."

Joyce looked down at Bob. "What's this?"

"It's a dog," I said, shortening his lead.

"Why's his hair standing up like that?"

From the woman who adds five inches to her height with a rat-tail comb.

"Beside the wild goose chase, how're you doin' on the Ranger hunt?" Lula asked. "You track him down yet?"

"Not yet, but I'm getting close."

"I think you're fibbing," Lula said. "I bet you don't have anything."

"And I bet you don't have a waistline," Joyce said.

Lula leaned forward. "Oh yeah? If I throw a stick, will you go fetch it?"

Bob wagged his tail.

"Maybe later," I told him.

Vinnie popped back out of his office. "What's going on out here? I can't hear myself think."

Lula, Connie, and I all exchanged glances and bit down hard on our lower lips.

"Vinnie!" Joyce cooed, pointing her C cups in his direction. "Looking good, Vinnie."

"Yeah, you're not looking so bad yourself," Vinnie said. He looked at Bob. "What's with the dog with the bad hair day?"

"I'm dog-sitting," I told him.

"I hope you're getting paid a lot of money. He's a train wreck."

I fondled Bob's ear. "I think he's cute." In a prehistoric way.

"So what's going on here?" Joyce asked. "You got anything new for me?"

Vinnie thought about it for a moment, looked from Connie to Lula to me, and retreated into his office.

"Nothing new," Connie said.

Joyce narrowed her eyes at Vinnie's closed door. "Chickenshit."

Vinnie opened the door and glared out at her.

"Yeah, you," Joyce said.

Vinnie pulled his head back inside his office, closed the door, and clicked the dead bolt.

"Fungule," Joyce said, with a gesture. She turned on her stiletto heel and swung her ass out the door.

We all rolled our eyes.

"Now what?" Lula wanted to know. "You and Bob got some big day planned?"

"Well, you know . . . a little of this, a little of that."

Vinnie's office door opened again. "How about a little of Morris Munson?" he yelled. "I'm not running a charity here, you know."

"Morris Munson is a nut!" I yelled back. "He tried to set me on fire!"

Vinnie stood, hands on hips. "So what's your point?"

"Fine. Just fine," I said. "I'll go get Morris Munson. So what if he runs me over. So what if he sets me on fire and bashes my head in with a tire iron. It's my job, right? So here I go to do my job."

"That's the spirit," Vinnie said.

"Hold on," Lula said. "I don't want to miss this one. I'll go with you."

She shoved her arms into a jacket and grabbed a purse that was big enough to hold a sawed-off shotgun. "Okay," I said, eyeballing the purse. "What have you got in there?"

"Tech-9."

The urban assault weapon of choice.

"Do you have a license to carry that?"

"Say what?"

"Call me crazy, but I'd feel a lot better if you left your Tech-9 here."

"Boy, you sure know how to ruin a good time," Lula said.

"Leave it with me," Connie told her. "I'll use it for a paperweight. Give the office some atmosphere."

"Hunh," Lula said.

I opened the office door, and Bob bounded out. He stopped at the Buick and stood there, tail wagging, eyes bright.

"Look at this smart dog," I said to Lula. "He knows my car after only riding in it once."

"What happened to the Rollswagen?"

"I gave it back to the Dealer."

The sun was climbing in the sky, burning off a morning haze, warming Trenton. Bureaucrats and shopkeepers were pouring into center city. School buses were back at the lot, awaiting the end of the school day. Burg housewives were bent over their Hoovers. And my friend Marilyn

Truro at the DMV was on her third double decaf latte, wondering if it would help if she added a second nicotine patch to the one she already had on her arm, thinking it would feel really good to be able to choke the next person in line.

Lula and Bob and I kept to our own thoughts as we rolled along Hamilton en route to the button factory. I was going through a mental inventory of equipment. Stun gun: in my left pocket. Pepper spray: in my right pocket. Cuffs: hooked to the back loop on my Levi's. Gun: at home, in the cookie jar. Courage: at home, with the gun.

"I don't know about you," Lula said when we got to Munson's house, "but I'm not planning on going up in smoke today. I vote we bash this guy's door in and stomp on him before he has a chance to light up."

"Sure," I said. Of course, I knew from past experience that neither of us was actually capable of bashing in a door. Still, it sounded good while we were idling at the curb, locked up in the car.

I cruised around back, got out, and looked in Munson's garage window. No car. Gee, too bad. Probably Munson wasn't home.

"No car here," I said to Lula.

"Hunh," Lula said.

We drove around the block, parked, and knocked on Munson's front door. No answer. We looked in his front windows. Nothing.

"He could be hiding under the bed," Lula said. "Maybe we should still bash his door in."

I stepped back and made a sweeping gesture

with my hand. "After you."

"Unh-unh," Lula said. "After you."

"No, no . . . I insist."

"The hell you do. *I* insist."

"Okay," I said. "Let's face it. Neither of us is going to bash this door down."

"I could do it if I wanted," Lula said. "Only I don't feel like it right now."

"Yeah, right."

"You think I couldn't do serious damage to this door?"

"That's what I'm suggesting."

"Hunh," Lula said.

The door to the adjoining house opened, and an old woman stuck her head out. "What's going on?"

"We're looking for Morris Munson," I said.

"He isn't home."

"Oh, yeah? How do you know?" Lula said. "How can you be sure he isn't hiding under the bed?"

"I was out back when he drove away. I was letting the dog out, and Munson came with a suitcase. Said he was gonna be gone for a while. As far as I'm concerned, he could be gone forever. He's a wacko. He was arrested for killing his wife, and some idiot judge let him out on bail. Can you imagine?"

"Go figure," Lula said.

The woman looked us over. "I guess you're friends of his."

"Not exactly," I said. "We work for Munson's

bail bonds agent." I handed her my business card. "If he returns I'd appreciate a call."

"Sure," the woman said, "but I got a feeling he isn't returning anytime soon."

Bob was waiting patiently in the car, and he got all happy-looking when we opened the doors and slid in.

"Maybe Bob needs breakfast," Lula said.

"Bob already had breakfast."

"Let me put it another way. Maybe Lula needs breakfast."

"You have anything special in mind?"

"I guess I could use one of those Egg McMuffins. And a vanilla shake. And breakfast fries."

I put the Buick in gear and headed for the drive-through.

"How's it going?" the kid at the window said. "You still looking for a job?"

"I'm thinking about it."

We got three of everything and parked on the edge of the lot to eat and regroup. Bob ate his Egg McMuffin and breakfast fries in one chomp. He slurked his milkshake down and looked longingly out the window.

"Think Bob needs to stretch his legs," Lula said.

I opened the door and let him out. "Don't go far."

Bob jumped out and started walking around in circles, occasionally sniffing the pavement.

"What's he doing?" Lula wanted to know.

"Why's he walking in circles? Why's he — Uh-oh, this don't look good. Looks to me like Bob's taking a big poop in the middle of the parking lot. Holy cow, look at that! That's a mountain of poop."

Bob returned to the Buick and sat down, wagging his tail, smiling, waiting to be let back in.

I let him in, and Lula and I slumped down low in our seats.

"Do you think anyone saw?" I asked Lula.

"I think *everyone* saw."

"Damn," I said. "I don't have the pooper-scooper with me."

"Pooper-scooper, hell. I wouldn't go near that with a full contamination suit and a front-loader."

"I can't just leave it there."

"Maybe you could run over it," Lula said. "You know . . . flatten it out."

I cranked the engine over, backed up, and pointed the Buick at the pile of poop.

"Better roll the windows up," Lula said.

"Ready?"

Lula braced herself. "Ready."

I stomped on the gas and took aim.

SQUISH!

We rolled the windows down and looked out.

"So what do you think? You think I should make another pass?"

"Wouldn't hurt," Lula said. "And I'd forget about getting a job here."

I wanted to do a fast check on Hannibal's town house and I didn't want to get Lula involved in my Ranger business, so I told her a fib about spending the day bonding with Bob, and drove her back to the office. I slid to a stop at the curb and the black Town Car eased up behind me.

Mitchell got out of the Town Car and came to peek in my window. "Still driving this old Buick," he said. "Must be some kind of a personal record for you. And what's with the dog and the big babe, here?"

Lula gave Mitchell the once-over.

"It's okay," I told Lula. "I know him."

"I bet," Lula said. "You want me to shoot him, or something?"

"Maybe later."

"Hunh," Lula said. She heaved herself out of the car and ambled into the office.

"Well?" Mitchell asked.

"Well, nothing."

"That's real disappointing."

"So, you don't like Alexander Ramos?"

"Let's just say we're not on the same team."

"Must be hard for him these days, grieving over his son."

"That son was nothing to grieve over," Mitchell said. "He was a fuckin' loser. Fuckin' cokehead."

"How about Hannibal? Does he do drugs, too?"

"Nah, not Hannibal. Hannibal's a goddamn

shark. Alexander should have named that one Jaws."

"Well, I've gotta go now," I said. "Things to do. People to see."

"The raghead and me haven't got a lot to do today, so we thought we'd follow you around."

"You should get a life."

Mitchell smiled.

"And I don't want you following me around," I said.

He smiled some more.

I glanced up at the traffic coming toward us on Hamilton and focused on a blue car. Looked like a Crown Victoria. Looked like Morris Munson behind the wheel!

"Yikes!" I yelled as Munson yanked the car over the white line and aimed it at me.

"Shit!" Mitchell yelped, panicked, dancing in place like a big trained bear.

Munson swerved to avoid Mitchell at the last second, lost control, and crashed into the Town Car. For a moment the cars seemed fused together, and then there was the sound of Munson gunning his engine. The Crown Vic jumped back a couple feet, its front bumper clattered to the ground, and it sped away.

Mitchell and I ran back to the Town Car and looked in at Habib.

"What by everything holy was that?" Habib shouted.

The Town Car's left front quarter panel was crumpled into the wheel, and the hood was buckled. Habib seemed okay, but the Town Car wasn't going anywhere until someone crowbarred the fender away from the wheel. Too bad for them. Lucky break for me. Habib and Mitchell weren't going to be in following mode for a while.

"He was a madman," Habib said. "I saw his eyes. He was a madman. Did you get his license plate number?"

"It happened so fast," Mitchell said. "And cripes, he was coming right at me. I thought he was aiming for me. I thought . . . Jeez, I thought . . ."

"You were frightened like a woman," Habib said.

"Yeah," I said, "like the daughter of a pig."

Now here was a dilemma. I dearly wanted to tell them who was behind the wheel of the car. If they killed Munson, I was off the hook. No more flaming shirttails. No more maniac with a tire iron. Unfortunately, I'd also be sort of responsible for Munson's death, and that didn't feel entirely comfortable. Better to leave him to the court.

"You should report this to the police," I said. "I'd stick around and help out, but you know how it is."

"Yeah," Mitchell said. "Things to do. People to see."

It was almost noon when Bob and I rolled past Hannibal's town house. I parked at the corner and dialed Ranger's number to tell his answering machine I had news. Then I chewed on my lower lip some while I worked up enough nerve to get out of the car and snoop on Hannibal.

Hey, it's no big deal, I told myself. Look at the house. Nice and quiet. He isn't home. Just like yesterday. You go around back, take a peek, and leave. No sweat.

Okay, I can do this. Deep breath. Think positive. I grabbed Bob's leash and headed for the bike path behind the houses. When I got to Hannibal's backyard I stopped and listened. Very quiet. Plus, Bob looked bored. If someone was on the other side of the wall Bob would be excited, right? I studied the wall. Daunting. Especially since I'd gotten shot at the last time I was here.

Hold it, I said to myself. None of that negative thinking. What would Spiderman do in a situation like this? What would Batman do? What would Bruce Willis do? Bruce would get a running start, plant his sneaker, and scale the wall. I tied Bob's leash to a bush and ran at the wall. I got my size eight Skechers halfway up, slapped my palms onto the top of the wall, and dug in and hung there. I took a deep breath, clenched my teeth and attempted a pull-up . . . but nothing pulled up. Damn. Bruce would have made it to the top. But then, Bruce probably goes to the gym.

I dropped to the ground and cut my eyes to the tree. The tree had a bullet lodged in its trunk. I really didn't want to climb the tree. I did some pacing and knuckle cracking. What about Ranger? I asked myself. You're supposed to be helping him. If the situation was reversed Ranger would climb the tree to take a look.

"Yeah, but I'm not Ranger," I said to Bob.

Bob gave me a long look.

"Okay, fine," I said. "I'll climb the stupid tree."

I went up fast, looked around, saw nothing going on in the house or the yard, and scrambled down. I untied Bob and skulked back to the car, where I settled in and waited for the phone to ring. After a couple minutes, Bob moved to the backseat and got into nap position.

At one o'clock, I was still waiting for Ranger's call back, and I was thinking I needed lunch, when Hannibal's garage door slid open and the green Jag backed out.

Holy cow, the house hadn't been empty!

The door closed; the Jag turned away from me and rolled down the street, toward the freeway. Hard to tell who was behind the wheel but I bet it was Hannibal. I cranked the engine over and raced around the block, picking the Jag up just as it was leaving the subdivision. I stayed as far back as possible without losing sight.

We bypassed the center of town, heading south, and then went east on the interstate. The horses weren't running at Monmouth yet, and Great Adventure was still closed for the season. That pretty much narrowed the field to the house in Deal.

Bob was taking the excitement in stride, sound

asleep in the backseat. I wasn't feeling nearly so relaxed. I don't usually tail mobsters. Although technically, Hannibal Ramos wasn't a Mob member. Well, actually I didn't know that for sure, but my understanding was that the Mob was a different fraternal order from the gun cartel.

Hannibal exited Route 195 at the Parkway, drove two exits north, then cut over to Asbury Park, where he left-turned onto Ocean Avenue and followed the road to Deal.

Deal is an oceanside town where gardeners coax grass to grow in the inhospitable salt air, nannies commute in from nearby Long Branch, and property value supersedes all issues of national origin. The houses are large and sometimes behind gated drives. The residents are mostly plastic surgeons and rug merchants. And the only truly memorable event ever to take place in Deal was the gunning down of crime boss Benny "The Roach" Raguchi in the Sea Breeze Motel in 1982.

Hannibal was two cars ahead of me. He slowed and signaled for a right turn into a walled compound with a gated drive. The house sat back on the dune, so the second story and roof were visible from the road and the rest of the property was hidden behind the pink stucco wall. The gate was fancy wrought-iron scrollwork. Alexander Ramos, international arms dealer and all-around macho man, lived in a pink house behind a pink wall. Go figure. Never happen in the Burg.

Living in a pink house in the Burg would be right up there with castration.

Probably the pink stucco was very Mediterranean. And probably in the summer, when the awnings were unrolled and the porch furniture was uncovered, and the sun and the heat washed over the Jersey shore, the pink house felt like life itself. In March it looked like it was waiting for the Prozac to kick in. Pale and cold and stolid.

I caught a glimpse of a man exiting the Jag as I cruised past the house. Same build and hair color as Hannibal, so it must be Hannibal. Unless, of course, Hannibal saw me in the tree again, and then saw me watching from the street and had a look-alike next-door neighbor sneak over through the backyards and drive the Jag to Deal, just to throw me off.

"What do you think?" I asked Bob.

Bob opened an eye, gave me a blank stare, and went back to sleep.

That was what I thought, too.

I drove about a quarter-mile down Ocean Avenue, hung a U-turn, and made another pass by the pink house. I parked out of sight, around the corner. I tucked my hair up, under a Metallica ball cap, put on some dark glasses, grabbed Bob's leash, and set off toward the Ramos compound. Deal was a civilized town with pristine cement sidewalks designed with nannies and baby strollers in mind. Also very nice for snoopers masquerading as dog-walkers.

I was a few feet from the gate when a black Town Car rolled up. The gates opened and the Town Car slid through. Two men in front. The back windows were tinted. I fussed with Bob's leash and let him sniff around some. The Town Car stopped at the porticoed house entrance, and the two men in front got out. One went around to get bags from the trunk. The other man opened the door for the passenger in back. The passenger looked to be in his sixties. Medium height. Slim. Dressed in sports coat and slacks. Wavy gray hair. From the way people were dancing attendance I guessed this was Alexander Ramos. Probably flew in for his son's burial. Hannibal came out to greet the older man. A younger, slimmer version of Hannibal appeared in the doorway to the house but didn't descend the stairs. Ulysses, the middle son, I thought.

No one looked especially happy at the reunion. Understandable, I guess, considering the circumstances. Hannibal said something to the older man. The older man stiffened and smacked him on the side of the head. It wasn't a hard smack. Not something designed to knock a guy out. It was more of a statement. *Fool.*

Still, I reflexively flinched. And even at this distance I could see Hannibal clamp his teeth together.

SIX

Here's the thing that stuck in my brain all the way home. If you were a father grieving over losing a son, would you greet your firstborn with a smack in the head?

"Hey, what do I know," I said to Bob. "Maybe they're going for Dysfunctional Family of the Year."

And to tell the truth, it's always a comfort to discover a family more dysfunctional than my own. Not that my family is all that dysfunctional, by Jersey standards.

When I got to Hamilton Township I stopped at the Shop Rite, hauled out my cell phone, and dialed my mother.

"I'm at the meat counter," I said. "I want to make a meatloaf. What do I need?"

There was silence at the other end, and I could imagine my mother making the sign of the cross, wondering what could possibly have inspired her daughter to want to make a meatloaf, hoping against hope that it was a man.

"A meatloaf," my mother finally said.

"It's for Grandma," I told her. "She needs a meatloaf."

"Of course," my mother said. "What was I thinking?"

I called my mother again when I got home. "Okay, I'm home," I said. "Now what do I do with this stuff?"

"You mix it together and put it in a loaf pan and bake it at three hundred and fifty degrees for an hour."

"You didn't say anything about a loaf pan when I was at the store!" I wailed.

"You don't have a loaf pan?"

"Well, of course I have a loaf pan. I just meant . . . Never mind."

"Good luck," my mother said.

Bob was sitting in the middle of the kitchen, taking it all in.

"I don't have a loaf pan," I told Bob. "But hey, we're not gonna let a little thing like that stop us, are we?"

I dumped the ground beef into a bowl along with the other essential meatloaf ingredients. I added an egg and watched it slime across the surface. I poked it with a spoon.

"Eeeeyeu," I said to Bob.

Bob wagged his tail. Bob looked like he loved gross stuff.

I mashed at the mess with the spoon, but the egg wouldn't mix in. I took a deep breath and plunged in with both hands. After a couple of minutes of hand squishing, everything was nice and mushy. I shaped it into a snowman. And then I shaped it into Humpty Dumpty. And then I smashed it flat. Smashed flat, it looked a lot like what I'd left in the McDonald's parking lot. Finally I rolled it into two big meatballs.

I'd bought a frozen banana cream pie for dessert, so I slid the pie out of its aluminum plate onto a dinner plate and used the pie plate for the giant meatballs.

"Necessity is the mother of invention," I told Bob.

I put the meatballs in the oven, cut up some potatoes and set them to cooking, and opened a can of creamed corn and dumped it in a bowl so I could heat it up in the microwave at the last minute. Cooking wasn't so bad, I thought. In fact, it was a lot like sex. Sometimes it didn't seem like such a good idea in the beginning, but then after you got into it . . .

I set the table for two, and the phone rang just as I was finishing.

"Yo, babe," Ranger said.

"Yo yourself. I have some news. The car that came to visit Hannibal last night belongs to Terry Gilman. I should have recognized her when she got out of the car, but I only saw her from the back, and I wasn't expecting her."

"Probably carrying condolences from Vito."

"I didn't realize Vito and Ramos were friends."

"Vito and Alexander co-exist."

"Another thing," I said. "This morning I followed Hannibal to the house in Deal." Then I told Ranger about the older man in the Town Car, and the smack in the head, and the appearance of a younger man who I thought was Ulysses Ramos.

"How do you know it was Ulysses?"

"Just a guess. He looked like Hannibal, but slimmer."

There was a moment of silence.

"Do you want me to keep watching the town house?" I asked.

"Do a spot check once in a while. I want to know if anyone's living there."

"Don't you think it's strange that Ramos would smack his son?" I asked.

"I don't know," Ranger said. "In my family we smack each other all the time."

Ranger disconnected, and I stood without moving for several minutes, wondering what I was missing. Ranger never gave much away, but there'd been a moment's pause and a small change of inflection that had me thinking I'd told him something interesting. I reviewed our conversation and everything seemed ordinary. A father and two brothers gathered together at a time of family tragedy. Alexander's reaction to Hannibal's greeting had seemed odd to me, but I got the impression that wasn't what had caught Ranger's attention.

Grandma staggered through the front door. "Boy, have I had a day," she said. "I'm all done in."

"How'd the driving lesson go?"

"Pretty good, I guess. I didn't run anybody over. And I didn't wreck the car. How was your day?"

"About the same."

"Louise and me went to the mall to do some senior citizen power walking but we kept getting sidetracked into the stores. And then after lunch we went looking at apartments. I saw a couple I might settle for, but nothing that really floated my boat. Tomorrow we're gonna look at some condos." Grandma snooped into the potato pot. "Isn't this something. I come home from a hard day of running around and here's dinner all waiting for me. Just like being a man."

"I got a banana cream pie for dessert," I said, "but I had to use the pie plate for the meatloaf."

Grandma peeked at the pie in the refrigerator. "Maybe we should eat it now before it defrosts and loses its shape."

That sounded like a good idea to me, so we all had some pie while the meatloaf was baking.

When I was a little girl I'd never thought of my grandmother as the sort of person to eat her pie first. Her house had always been neat and clean. The furniture was dark wood and the upholstered pieces were comfortable but unmemorable. Meals were traditional Burg meals, ready at noon and at six o'clock. Stuffed cabbage, pot roast, roast chicken, an occasional ham or pork roast. My grandfather wouldn't have had it any other way. He'd worked in a steel mill all his life.

He had strong opinions, and he dwarfed the rooms of their row house. Truth is, the top of my grandmother's head comes to the tip of my chin, and my grandfather wasn't much taller. But then I guess stature doesn't have much to do with inches.

Lately I've been wondering who my grandmother would have been if she hadn't married my grandfather. I wonder if she would have eaten her dessert first a lot sooner.

I took the meatballs out of the oven and set them side by side on a plate. Sitting there together they looked like troll gonads.

"Well, will you look at these big boys," Grandma said. "Reminds me of your grandfather, rest his soul."

When we were done eating I took Bob for a walk. Street lights were on, and light poured from the front windows of the houses behind my apartment building. We walked several blocks in comfortable silence. It turns out that's one of the good things about a dog. They don't talk a lot, so you can go along, thinking your own thoughts, making lists.

My list consisted of Catch Morris Munson, Worry about Ranger, and Wonder about Morelli. I didn't exactly know what to do about Morelli. My heart felt like it was in love. My head wasn't so sure. Not that it mattered, because Morelli didn't want to get married. So here I was with my biological clock ticking and nothing around me but indecision.

"I hate this!" I said to Bob.

Bob stopped and looked over his shoulder at me, like, What's the big deal back there? Well, what did Bob know. Someone had whacked off his doodles when he was a puppy. Bob was just left with some extra skin and a distant memory. Bob didn't have a mother waiting for grandchildren. Bob didn't have all this *pressure!*

When I got back to the apartment Grandma was asleep in front of the television. I wrote a note saying I had to go out for a while, pinned the note to Grandma's sweater, and told Bob to behave himself and not eat any of the furniture. Rex was buried under a mound of shavings, sleeping off his piece of pie. All was well in the Stephanie Plum household.

I drove directly to Hannibal's town house. It was eight o'clock, and the place looked like no one was home, but then it always looked like no one was home. I parked two streets over, got out of the car, and walked to the back of the house. No light shining from any of the windows. I climbed the tree and looked down into Hannibal's yard. Totally dark. I dropped out of the tree and retraced my steps on the bike path, thinking this was very spooky. Black trees and bushes. No moon overhead to light the way. Only the occasional streak of light spilling from a window.

Wouldn't want to meet a bad guy out here. Not Munson. Not Hannibal Ramos. Maybe not even Ranger . . . although he was bad in a very intriguing way.

I moved the car to the end of Hannibal's block, where I had better visibility. I pushed the seat back, locked the doors, and watched and waited.

It didn't take long for waiting to get old. To pass the time, I dialed Morelli on my cell phone. "Guess who?" I said.

"Is Grandma gone?"

"No. I'm working, and she's home with Bob."

"Bob?"

"Brian Simon's dog. I'm baby-sitting him while Simon's on vacation."

"Simon's not on vacation. I saw him today."

"What?"

"I can't believe you fell for that vacation scam," Morelli said. "Simon's been trying to pawn that dog off ever since he got him."

"Why didn't you tell me?"

"I didn't know he was gonna give you the dog."

I narrowed my eyes at the phone. "Are you laughing? Is that laughter I hear?"

"No. I swear."

But it *was* laughter. The rat was laughing.

"This is no laughing matter," I said. "What am I going to do with a dog?"

"I thought you always wanted a dog."

"Well, yeah . . . someday. But not *now!* And the dog howls. He doesn't like being left alone."

"Where are you?" Morelli asked.

"It's a secret."

"Christ, you aren't staking out Hannibal's house again, are you?"

"Nope. I'm not doing that."

"I have a cake," he said. "Do you want to come over and have some cake?"

"You're lying. You don't have a cake."

"I could get one."

"I'm not saying I'm staking out Hannibal's house, but if I was, do you think there'd be any value to it?"

"As far as I can tell, Ranger has a handful of people he trusts, and he has those people watching the Ramos family. I've spotted someone at Homer's house in Hunterdon County, and I know there's someone in place in Deal. He's got you sitting over there on Fenwood. I don't know what he expects to find, but my guess is, he knows where he's going. He has information about this crime that we don't have."

"Doesn't look like there's anyone home, here," I said.

"Alexander's in town, so Hannibal has probably moved into the south wing of the Deal house." Morelli let a beat go by. "Probably Ranger's got you sitting there because it's safe. Make you feel like you're doing something, so you don't stumble into a more important surveillance situation. Probably you should give up on it and come over to my house."

"Nice try, but I don't think so."

"It was worth a shot," Morelli said.

We disconnected, and I hunkered in to do my surveillance thing. Probably Morelli was right, and Hannibal was living at the shore. There was only one way to find out: watch and wait. By twelve o'clock Hannibal still hadn't appeared. My feet were cold, and I was sick of sitting in the car. I got out and stretched. A final check of the back, and then I was going home.

I walked the bike path with my pepper spray held in my hand. It was stygian. No lights anywhere. Everyone was in bed. I got to Hannibal's back door and looked up at his windows. Cold, dark glass. I was about to leave when I heard the muffled sound of a toilet flushing. No question which house the sound emanated from. Hannibal's. A chill raced the length of my spine. Someone was living in the dark, in Hannibal's house. I stood dead still, barely breathing, listening with every molecule of my body. There were no more sounds, and no further sign of life in the house. I didn't know what this meant, but I was totally creeped out. I scurried down the path, crossed the grass to the car, and took off.

Rex was running on the wheel when I walked in the door, and Bob ran up to me, eyes bright, panting in anticipation of a pat on the head and possible food. I said hello to Rex and gave him a raisin. Then I gave a couple raisins to Bob, making him wag his tail so hard the whole back half of his body whipped side to side.

I set the box of raisins on the counter and went to the bathroom, and when I returned the raisins were gone. Only a slobbery, mangled corner of the box remained.

"You have an eating disorder," I said to Bob. "And take it from someone who knows, compulsive eating isn't the way to go. Before you know it your skin won't fit."

Grandma had set a pillow and blanket out for me in the living room. I kicked my shoes off, crawled under the blanket, and was asleep in seconds.

I woke up feeling tired and disoriented. I looked at my watch. Two o'clock. I squinted into the darkness. "Ranger?"

"What's with the dog?"

"I'm baby-sitting. Guess he's not much of a watchdog."

"He would have opened the door if he could have found the key."

"I know it's not that hard to pick a lock, but how do you get past the security chain?"

"Trade secret."

"I'm in the trade."

Ranger handed me a large envelope. "Check out these pictures and tell me who you recognize."

I sat up, switched the table lamp on, and opened the envelope. I identified Alexander Ramos and Hannibal. There were also photos of Ulysses and Homer Ramos and two first cousins. All four were very much alike; each could have been the man I saw standing in the doorway of the Deal house. Except, of course, Homer, who was dead. There was another woman, photographed with Homer Ramos. She was small and blond and smiling. Homer had his arm around her, and he was smiling back.

"Who's this?" I asked.

"Homer's latest girlfriend. Her name's Cynthia Lotte. She works downtown. Receptionist for someone you know."

"Omigod! Now I recognize her. She works for my ex-husband."

"Yeah," Ranger said. "Small world."

I told Ranger about the town house being dark, with no sign of life, and then the toilet flushing.

"What does that mean?" I asked Ranger.

"It means someone's in the house."

"Hannibal?"

"Hannibal's in Deal."

Ranger snapped the table lamp off and stood. He was wearing a black T-shirt, black Gore-Tex windbreaker, and black cargo pants tucked into black boots, army style. The well-dressed urban commando. I could guarantee that any man facing him in a blind alley would have an empty scrotum, his most prized possessions gone north. And any woman would be licking dry lips and checking to make sure all her buttons were buttoned. He looked down at me, hands in pockets, his face barely visible in the dark room.

"Would you be willing to visit your ex and check out Cynthia Lotte?"

"Sure. Anything else?"

He smiled, and when he answered his voice was soft. "Not with your grandmother in the next room."

Eek.

When Ranger left I slid the security chain in place and flopped back onto the couch, thrashing around, thinking erotic thoughts. No doubt about it. I was a hopeless slut. I looked heavenward, only the ceiling got in the way. "It's all hormones," I said to Whoever might be listening. "It's not my fault. I have too many hormones."

I got up and drank a glass of orange juice. After the orange juice I returned to the couch and thrashed around some more because Grandma was snoring so loud I was afraid she'd suck her tongue down her throat and choke to death.

"Isn't this a pip of a morning!" Grandma said, on her way to the kitchen. "I feel like having some pie!"

I checked my watch. Six-thirty. I dragged myself off the couch and into the bathroom where I stood under the shower for a long time, sullen and bitchy. When I got out of the shower I looked at myself in the mirror over the sink. I had a big zit on my chin. Well, isn't this just great. I have to go see my ex-husband with a zit on my chin. Probably God's punishment for last night's mental lusting.

I thought about the .38 in the cookie jar. I made a fist, thumb up, index finger extended. I put the index finger to my temple and said, "Bang."

I dressed myself up in an outfit like Ranger's. Black T-shirt, black cargo pants, black boots. Big zit on my face. I looked like an idiot. I took the black T-shirt and pants and boots off and stuffed myself into a white T-shirt, topped with a plaid flannel shirt and a pair of Levi's with a small hole in the crotch which I convinced myself no one could see. This was an outfit for someone with a zit.

Grandma was reading the paper when I came out of the bedroom.

"Where'd you get the paper?" I asked.

"Borrowed it from that nice man across the hall. Only he don't know it yet."

Grandma was a fast learner.

"I don't have another driving lesson until to-morrow, so Louise and me are going to look at some condos today. I've been checking out the job situation too, and it looks to me like there's lots of good stuff. There's jobs for cooks and cleaning people and makeup ladies and car sales-men."

"If you could have any job in the world, what would you choose?"

"That's easy. I'd be a movie star."

"You'd make a good one," I said.

"Of course, I'd want to be a leading lady. Some of my parts have started to sag, but my legs are still pretty good."

I looked at Grandma's legs sticking out from under her dress. I guess everything is relative.

Bob was standing at the door with his knees to-gether, so I clipped his leash on him and we headed out. Look at this, I thought, I'm getting exercise first thing in the morning. Probably after two weeks of Bob I'll be so skinny I'll have to buy all new clothes. And the fresh air is good for my pimple, too. Hell, it might even cure it. Maybe the pimple will be *gone* by the time I get back to the apartment.

Bob and I were walking along at a pretty good rate. We rounded the corner and swung into the lot, and there were Habib and Mitchell, waiting for me in a ten-year-old Dodge totally upholstered in chartreuse broadloom. A neon sign on the top of the car advertised Art's Carpet's. It made the wind machine look tasteful.

"Holy cow," I said. "What *is* this?"

"It was all that was available on short notice," Mitchell said. "And I wouldn't make a big deal out of it if I was you, because it's a sensitive topic. And not to change the subject, or anything, but we're getting impatient. We don't want to freak you out, but we're gonna have to do something real mean if you don't deliver your boyfriend pretty soon."

"Is that a threat?"

"Well, yeah, sure," Mitchell said. "It's a threat."

Habib was behind the wheel, wearing a large foam whiplash collar. He gave a small nod of acknowledgment.

"We're professionals," Mitchell said. "You don't want to be fooled by our pleasant demeanor."

"Just so," Habib said.

138

"Are you going to follow me around today?" I asked.

"That's the plan," Mitchell said. "I hope you're gonna do something interesting. I don't feel like spending the day at the mall lookin' at ladies' shoes. Like we said, our boss is getting antsy."

"Why does your boss want Ranger?"

"Ranger has something that belongs to him, and he'd like to discuss the matter. You could tell him that."

I suspected that discussing the matter might involve a fatal accident. "I'll pass it along if I happen to hear from him."

"You tell him he just gives back what he's got and everyone's gonna be happy. Bygones will be bygones. No hard feelings."

"Uh-huh. Well, I've got to be running along now. I'll see you guys later."

"When you come back to the parking lot I would appreciate your bringing me an aspirin," Habib said. "I am suffering with this neck whiplashing."

"I don't know about you," I said to Bob when we got in the elevator, "but I'm sort of freaked out."

Grandma was reading the comics to Rex when I came in. Bob sidled up to join in the fun, and I took the phone into the living room to call Brian Simon.

Simon answered on the third ring. "'Lo."

"That was a short trip," I said.

"Who's this?"

"It's Stephanie."

"How'd you get my number? I have an unlisted number."

"It's printed on your dog's collar."

"Oh."

"So I imagine now that you're home, you're going to be around to get Bob."

"I'm kind of busy today —"

"No problem. I'll drop him off. Where do you live?"

A moment of silence. "Okay, here's the thing," Simon said. "I don't actually want Bob back."

"He's *your* dog!"

"Not anymore. Possession is nine-tenths of the law. You have the food. You have the pooper-scooper. You have the dog. Listen, he's a nice dog, but I don't have time for him. And he makes my nose run. I think I'm allergic."

"I think you're a *jerk*."

Simon sighed. "You're not the first woman to tell me that."

"I can't keep him here. He howls when I leave."

"Don't I know it. And if you leave him alone he eats the furniture."

"What? What do you mean, he eats the furniture?"

"Forget I said that. I didn't mean to say that. He doesn't actually *eat* the furniture. I mean, chewing isn't really eating. And not that he even chews. Oh, shit," Simon said. "Good luck." And he hung up. I redialed, but he wouldn't answer.

I returned the phone to the kitchen and gave

Bob his breakfast bowl of dog crunchies. I poured a cup of coffee and ate a chunk of pie. There was one piece of pie left so I gave it to Bob. "You don't eat furniture, do you?" I asked.

Grandma was hunkered down in front of the television, watching the Weather Channel. "Don't worry about supper tonight," she said. "We can have leftover balls."

I gave her a thumbs-up, but she was concentrating on the weather in Cleveland and didn't see me.

"Well, I guess I'll go out now," I said.

Grandma nodded.

Grandma looked all rested. And I felt all done in. I wasn't getting enough sleep. The late-night visits and the snoring were taking a toll on me. I dragged myself out of the apartment and down the hall. My eyes drooped closed while I waited for the elevator.

"I'm exhausted," I said to Bob. "I need more sleep."

I drove to my parents' house and Bob and I trooped in. My mother was in the kitchen, humming as she put together an apple pie.

"This must be Bob," she said. "Your grandmother told me you had a dog."

Bob ran over to my mother.

"No!" I yelled. "Don't you dare!"

Bob stopped two feet from my mother and looked back at me.

"You know what I'm talking about," I said to Bob.

"What a well-mannered dog," my mother said.

I stole a chunk of apple from the pie. "Did Grandma also tell you she snores, and she's up at the crack of dawn, and she watches the Weather Channel for hours on end?" I poured myself a cup of coffee. "Help," I said to the coffee.

"She's probably taking a couple nips before bed," my mother said. "She always snores after she's belted back a few."

"That can't be it. I don't have any liquor in the house."

"Look in the closet. That's where she usually keeps it. I clean bottles out of her closet all the time."

"You mean she buys it herself and hides it in the closet?"

"It's not *hidden* in the closet. That's just where she keeps it."

"Are you telling me Grandma's an alcoholic?"

"No, of course not. She just tipples a little. She says it helps get her to sleep."

Maybe that was my problem. Maybe I should be tippling. Trouble is, I throw up when I tipple too much. And once I start tippling it's hard to tell when it's too much until it's too late. One tipple always seems to lead to another.

The kitchen heat washed over me and soaked into the flannel shirt, and I felt like the pie, sitting in the oven, steaming. I struggled out of the flannel shirt, put my head down on the table, and fell asleep. I had a dream that it was summer, and I was baking on the beach in Point Pleasant. Hot sand under me, and hot sun above me. And my skin all brown and crispy like pie crust. When I woke up the pie was out of the oven, and the house smelled like heaven. And my mother had ironed my shirt.

"Do you ever eat the dessert first?" I asked my mother.

She looked at me dumbfounded. As if I'd asked whether she ritually sacrificed cats every Wednesday at the stroke of midnight.

"Suppose you were home alone," I said, "and there was a strawberry shortcake in the refrigerator and a meatloaf in the oven. Which would you eat first?"

My mother thought about it for a minute, her eyes wide. "I can't remember ever eating dinner alone. I can't even imagine it."

I buttoned myself into the shirt and slipped into my denim jacket. "I have to go. I have work to do."

"You could come to dinner tomorrow night," my mother said. "You could bring your grandmother and Joseph. I'm making a pork roast and mashed potatoes."

"Okay, but I don't know about Joe."

I got to the front door and saw that the carpet car was parked behind the Buick.

"Now what?" my mother asked. "Who are those men in that weird car?"

"Habib and Mitchell."

"Why are they parked here?"

"They're following me, but don't worry about it. They're okay."

"What do you mean, 'Don't worry about it'? What kind of thing is that to say to a mother. Of course, I'll worry about it. They look like thugs." My mother pushed past me, walked up to the car, and rapped on the window.

The window slid down and Mitchell looked out at my mother. "How ya doin?" he asked.

"Why are you following my daughter?"

"Did she tell you we're following her? She shouldn't have done that. We don't like to worry mothers."

"I have a gun in the house, and I'll use it if I have to," my mother said.

"Jeez, lady, you don't have to get your panties all in a bunch," Mitchell said. "What is it with this family? Everybody's always so hostile. We're just following your kid around a little."

"I have your license plate number," my mother said. "If anything happens to my daughter I'll tell the police all about you."

Mitchell pressed the window button and his window slid closed.

"You don't really have a gun, do you?" I asked my mother.

"I just said that to throw a scare into them."

"Hmm. Well, thanks. I'm sure I'll be okay now."

"Your father could pull some strings and get you a good job at the Personal Products plant," my mother said. "Evelyn Nagy's girl is working there, and she gets three weeks' paid vacation."

I tried to visualize Wonder Woman working the

line at the Personal Products plant, but the picture wouldn't fine-tune. "I don't know," I said. "I don't think I have a future in Personal Products." I got into Big Blue and waved good-bye to my mother.

She gave Mitchell one last warning glare and returned to her house.

"She's going through the change," I said to Bob. "She gets excited. Nothing to worry about."

SEVEN

I drove over to the office with Mitchell and Habib tagging along behind.

Lula looked out the storefront window when Bob and I swung through the door. "Looks like those two idiots got a carpet car."

"Yeah. They've been with me since the crack of dawn. They tell me their employer's losing patience with the Ranger hunt."

"He's not the only one," Vinnie said from his inner office. "Joyce is turning up a big fat nothing on Ranger, and I'm feeling an ulcer coming on. Not to mention, I'm in for big bucks with Morris Munson. You better get your ass out there and find that creep."

With any luck Munson was in Tibet by now and I'd *never* find him. "Anything new?" I asked Connie.

"Nothing you want to know about."

"Tell her anyway. This is a good one," Lula said.

"Last night Vinnie bonded out a guy named

Douglas Kruper. Kruper sold a car to the fifteen-year-old daughter of one of our illustrious state senators. On the way home from buying the car the kid got picked up for running a light and driving without a license, and the car turned out to be stolen. Now this is the good part. The car is described as a Rollswagen. You happen to know anyone named Douglas Kruper?"

"Also known as the Dealer," I said. "I went to school with him."

"Well, he isn't gonna be doin' any dealing for a while."

"How'd he take to getting arrested?" I asked Vinnie.

"Cried like a baby," Vinnie said. "It was disgusting. He was a disgrace to criminals everywhere."

Just for the heck of it I went to the file cabinet and looked to see if we had anything on Cynthia Lotte. I wasn't too surprised when she didn't show up.

"I have an errand to run downtown," I said. "Is it okay if I leave Bob here? I should be back in about an hour."

"As long as he doesn't come into my private office," Vinnie said.

"Yeah, you wouldn't be talkin' like that if Bob was a female goat," Lula said.

Vinnie slammed his door shut and threw the dead bolt.

I told Bob I'd be back in time for lunch and hustled out to the car. At the nearest ATM I withdrew fifty dollars from my checking; then I drove over to Grant Street. Dougie had two cases of Dolce Vita perfume that had seemed like too much of a luxury when I returned the wind machine but might be marked down now that he had legal problems. Not that I was one to take advantage of someone else's misfortune . . . but, hell, we're talking about Dolce Vita here.

There were three cars parked in front of Dougie's house when I got there. I recognized one as belonging to my friend Eddie Gazzara. Eddie and I grew up together. He's a cop now, and he's married to my cousin Shirley the Whiner. There was a PBA shield on the second car, and the third car was a fifteen-year-old Cadillac that still had its original paint and not a speck of rust anywhere. I didn't want to consider the implications, but it looked a lot like Louise Greeber's car. What was one of Grandma's friends doing here?

Inside, the tiny row house was cluttered with people and merchandise. Dougie shuffled from person to person, looking dazed.

"Everything has to go," he said to me. "I'm shutting down."

The Mooner was there, too. "Hey, it's not fair, dude," he said. "This individual had a business going on. He's entitled to run a business, right? I mean, where are his rights? Okay, so he sold a stolen car to a kid. Hey, we all make mistakes. Am I right, here?"

"You do the crime, you pay the time," Gazzara

said, holding a stack of Levi's. "How much do you want for these, Dougie?"

I pulled Gazzara aside. "I need to talk to you about Ranger."

"Allen Barnes is looking for him big time," Gazzara said.

"Does Barnes have anything on Ranger besides the videotape?"

"I don't know. I'm not in the loop. There's not a lot leaking out on this one. No one wants to make any mistakes with Ranger."

"Is Barnes looking at other suspects?"

"Not that I know of. But then, like I said, I'm not in the loop."

A squad car double-parked on the street and two uniforms came in. "I hear there's a fire sale going on," one of the uniforms said. "Are there any toasters left?"

I picked two bottles of perfume out of the case and gave Dougie a ten. "What are you going to do now?"

"I don't know. I feel real defeated," Dougie said. "Nothing ever works out for me. Some guys just don't have any luck."

"You gotta keep your chin up, dude," Mooner said. "Something else will come along. You gotta be like me. You gotta go with the flow."

"I'm going to jail!" Dougie said. "They're gonna send me to jail!"

"You see what I'm saying?" Mooner said. "Something else always comes along. You go to jail, you don't have to worry about anything. No rent to pay. No food bill to sweat. Free dental plan. And that's worth something, dude. You don't want to stick your nose up at free dental."

We all looked at Mooner for a minute, debating the wisdom of a response.

I walked through the house and peeked out back, but I didn't see Grandma or Louise Greeber. I said good-bye to Gazzara and threaded my way through the crowd to the door.

"Real nice of you to support the Dougster," Moon said as I was leaving. "Damn mellow of you, duder."

"I just wanted some Dolce Vita," I said.

The Cadillac was no longer parked on the street. The carpet car idled at the corner. I sat in the Buick and gave myself a splash of perfume to compensate for the chin zit and the crappy, holey jeans. I decided I needed more than perfume, so I swiped on some extra mascara and teased up my hair. Better to look like a slut with a zit than a dork with a zit.

I drove downtown to my ex-husband's office in the Shuman Building. Richard Orr, attorney-at-law and womanizing asshole. He was a junior partner in a multiname law firm — Rabinowitz, Rabinowitz, Zeller and Asshole. I took the elevator to the second floor and looked for the door with his gold-lettered name. I wasn't a frequent visitor here. It hadn't been a friendly divorce, and Dickie and I don't exchange Christmas cards. Once in a while our professional paths cross.

Cynthia Lotte was sitting at the front desk,

looking like an Ann Taylor advertisement in her simple gray suit and white shirt. She looked up in alarm when I pushed through the door, obviously recognizing me from my last visit, when Dickie and I had a small disagreement.

"He isn't in his office," she said.

There *is* a God. "When do you expect him in?"

"Hard to say. He's in court today."

She didn't have a ring on her finger. And she didn't seem grief-stricken. In fact, she seemed downright happy, aside from the fact that Dickie's crazy ex-wife was in her office.

I faked some goggle-eyed interest in the reception area. "This is pretty nice. It must be great to work here."

"Usually."

I took this to mean "almost always, except for now." "I guess this is a good place to work if you're single. Probably you have a chance to meet lots of men."

"Is this going somewhere?"

"Well, I was just thinking about Homer Ramos. You know, wondering if you met him at the office here."

There was a dead silence for several seconds, and I could swear I heard her heart beating. She didn't say anything. And I didn't say anything. I couldn't tell what was going on inside *her* head, but *I* was doing some interior knuckle-cracking. The question about Homer Ramos had actually come out a little more abrupt than I'd planned, and I was feeling sort of uncomfortable. I'm usually only *mentally* rude to people.

Cynthia Lotte gathered herself together and looked me straight in the eye. Her manner was demure and her voice was solicitous. "I don't mean to change the subject, or anything," she said, "but have you tried concealer on that zit?"

I sucked in some air. "Uh, no. I didn't think —"

"You should be careful, because when they get that big and all red and filled with pus they can leave scars."

My fingers flew to my chin before I could stop them. God, she was right. The zit felt *huge*. It was *growing*. Damn! My emergency reaction mode kicked in, and the message it sent to my brain was *Flee! Hide!*

"I should be moving along, anyway," I said, backing away. "Tell Dickie I didn't want anything special. I was in the neighborhood and I thought I'd say hello."

I let myself out, took the stairs, and rushed through the lobby and out the door. I crammed myself into the Buick and yanked at the rearview mirror so I could see my zit.

Gross!

I leaned back in the seat and closed my eyes. Bad enough I had the zit from hell, but Cynthia Lotte had out-ruded me. I'd found out nothing for Ranger. The only thing I knew about Lotte was that she looked good in gray and had pushed my button. One mention of my pimple, and I was out the door.

I looked back at the Shuman Building and

wondered if Ramos had done business with Dickie's firm. And what sort of business? It would have made sense for Lotte to have met Ramos that way. Of course, she could also have met him on the street. The Ramos office building was only a block away.

I put the Buick into gear and slowly cruised past the Ramos building. The crime scene tape had been removed, and I could see workmen in the lobby. The service road that ran past the rear door was clogged with repair trucks.

I doubled back through town, stopping at the Radio Shack on Third.

"I need some kind of an alarm," I told the kid at the register. "Nothing fancy. Just something that tells me when my front door gets opened. And stop staring at my chin!"

"I wasn't staring at your chin. Honest! I didn't even notice that big zit."

A half-hour later I was on my way to the office to get Bob. Sitting in a little bag, on the seat beside me, was a small motion detector gizmo for my front door. I told myself it was necessary for general security, but truth is, I knew it had one purpose: to alert me whenever Ranger broke in to my apartment. And why did I feel the need for the gizmo? Did it have anything to do with fear? No. Although there were times when Ranger *could* be scary. Did it have to do with distrust? Nope. I trusted Ranger. The fact is, I got the gizmo because just once I wanted to have the advantage. It was driving me nuts that Ranger could get into my apartment without even waking me.

I stopped at Cluck-in-a-Bucket and got a barrel of chicken nuggets for lunch. I figured that was best for Bob. No bones to hork up.

Everyone's eyes got bright when I walked through the door with my barrel of nuggets.

"Bob and me were just thinking about chicken," Lula said. "You must have read our minds."

I took the lid off the barrel, set the lid on the floor, and dumped a bunch of nuggets onto it for Bob. I took a nugget for myself and handed the rest off to Lula and Connie. Then I called my cousin Bunny at the credit bureau.

"What have you got on Cynthia Lotte?" I asked Bunny.

A minute later she was back with the answer. "Not much here," she said. "A recent car loan. Pays her bills on time. No derogatory information. Lives in Ewing." The phone went silent for a couple beats. "What are you looking for?"

"I don't know. She works for Dickie."

"Oh." As if that explained it all.

I got Lotte's address and phone and said adios to Bunny.

The next person I called was Morelli. None of his numbers picked up so I left a message on his pager.

"That's funny," Lula said. "Didn't you put those nuggets on the bucket lid? I can't find that bucket lid anywhere."

We all looked at Bob. He had a small piece of cardboard stuck to his lip.

"Dang," Lula said. "He makes me look like an amateur."

"So, do you notice anything unusual about me?" I asked.

"Only that you got a big zit on your chin. Must be that time of the month, huh?"

"It's stress!" I stuck my head in my shoulder bag and looked for concealer. Flashlight, hairbrush, lipstick, Juicy Fruit gum, stun gun, tissues, hand lotion, pepper spray. No concealer.

"I've got a Band-Aid," Connie said. "You could try to cover it with a Band-Aid."

I stuck the Band-Aid over the pimple.

"That's better," Lula said. "Now it looks like you cut yourself shaving."

Great.

"Before I forget," Connie said, "a call came in about Ranger while you were on the phone with the credit bureau. There's a warrant written for his arrest in connection with the Ramos murder."

"How does the warrant read?" I asked.

"Wanted for questioning."

"That's how it started with O.J.," Lula said. "They just wanted him for questioning. And look how that turned out."

I wanted to check on Hannibal's town house, but I didn't want to drag Mitchell and Habib over with me.

"I need a diversion," I said to Lula. "I need to

get rid of those guys in the carpet car."

"Do you mean you want to get *rid* of them? Or do you mean you don't want them following you?"

"I don't want them following me."

"Well, that's easy." She took a .45 out of her desk drawer. "I'll just shoot out a couple tires."

"No! No shooting!"

"You always got all these rules," Lula said.

Vinnie stuck his head out of his office. "How about the burning bag thing?"

We swiveled our heads in his direction.

"Usually you do it as a gag on somebody's front porch," Vinnie said. "You put some dog shit in a bag. Then you put the bag on the sucker's front porch and ring the bell. Then you set the bag on fire and run like hell. When the mark opens the door he sees the bag burning and stomps on it to put it out."

"And?"

"And then he gets dog shit all over his shoe," Vinnie said. "If you did it to these guys and they got dog shit all over their shoes they'd be distracted, and you could drive away."

"Only we haven't got a front porch," Lula said.

"Use your imagination!" Vinnie said. "You put it just behind the car. Then you sneak away and someone from the office here yells out at them that something's burning under their car."

"I kinda like the sound of that," Lula said. "Only thing is, we need some dog poop."

We all turned our attention to Bob.

Connie took a brown paper lunch bag from her bottom drawer. "I've got a bag and you can use the empty chicken bucket as a pooper-scooper."

I snapped the leash on Bob, and Lula and Bob and I went out the back door and walked around some. Bob tinkled about forty times, but he didn't have any contributions for the bag.

"He don't look motivated," Lula said. "Maybe we should take him over to the park."

The park was only two blocks away, so we walked Bob to the park and stood around waiting for him to answer nature's call. Only nature wasn't calling Bob's name.

"You ever notice how when you don't want dog poop it just seems to be everywhere?" Lula said. "And now when we *want* some. . ." Her eyes opened wide. "Hold the phone. Dog at twelve o'clock. And it's a *big* one."

Sure enough, someone else was walking their dog in the park. The dog was big and black. The old woman at the other end of the leash was small and white. She was wearing low-heeled shoes and a bulky brown tweed coat, and she had her gray hair stuffed into a knit hat. She was holding a plastic bag and a paper towel in her hand. The bag was empty.

"I don't mean to blaspheme or anything," Lula said. "But God sent us this dog."

The dog suddenly stopped walking and hunched over, and Lula and Bob and I took off across the grass. I had Bob on the leash, and Lula was waving the chicken bucket and paper bag, and we were running full tilt when the woman looked up and saw us. The color drained from her face, and she staggered backward.

"I'm old," she said. "I haven't got any money. Go away. Don't hurt me."

"We don't want your money," Lula said. "We want your poop."

The woman choked up on the dog's leash. "You can't have the poop. I have to take the poop home. It's the law."

"The law don't say *you* gotta take it home," Lula said. "It's just *somebody* gotta do it. And we're volunteering."

The big black dog stopped what he was doing and gave Bob an inquisitive sniff. Bob sniffed back, and then he looked at the old woman's crotch.

"Don't even think about it," I said to Bob.

"I don't know if that's right," the woman said. "I never heard of that. I think I'm supposed to take the poop home."

"Okay," Lula said, "we'll pay you for the poop." Lula looked over at me. "Give her a couple bucks for her poop."

I searched my pockets. "I don't have any money on me. I didn't bring my purse."

"I won't take any less than five dollars," the woman said.

"Turns out we don't have any money on us," Lula said.

"Then it's my poop," the woman said.

"The heck it is," Lula said, muscling the old woman out of the way and scooping the poop up in the chicken bucket. "We need this poop."

"Help!" the woman yelled. "They're taking my poop! Stop! Thief!"

"I got it," Lula said. "I got it all." And Lula and Bob and I ran like the wind back to the office with our bucket of poop.

We collected ourselves at the back door to the office. Bob was all happy, dancing around. But Lula and I were gasping for breath.

"Boy, for a while there I was afraid she was gonna catch us," Lula said. "She could run pretty fast for an old lady."

"She wasn't running," I said. "The dog was *dragging* her, trying to get at Bob."

I held the paper bag open, and Lula dumped the poop into it.

"This here's gonna be fun," Lula said. "I can't wait to see those two guys stomping on this bag of shit."

Lula went around front with the bag and a Bic. And Bob and I went into the office through the back door. Habib and Mitchell were parked curbside, in front of the office, directly behind my Buick.

Connie and Vinnie and I peeked out the front window while Lula crept up behind the carpet car. She put the bag on the ground just past the rear bumper. We saw the lighter flame, and Lula jumped away and scuttled off around the corner.

Connie stuck her head out the door. "Hey!"

she yelled. "Hey, you guys in the car . . . there's something burning behind you!"

Mitchell rolled the window down. "What?"

"There's something on fire behind your car!"

Mitchell and Habib got out to take a look and we all hustled through the door to join them.

"It's just some trash," Mitchell said to Habib. "Kick it out of the way so it don't damage the car."

"It is flaming," Habib said. "I do not want to touch a flaming bag with my shoe."

"This is what happens when you hire a fucking camel jockey," Mitchell said. "You people have no work ethic."

"This is not true. I work very hard in Pakistan. In my village in Pakistan we have a rug factory, and my job is to beat the unruly children who work there. It is a very good job."

"Wow," Mitchell said. "You beat the little kids who work in the factory?"

"Yes. With a stick. It is a highly skilled position. You must be careful when beating the children not to crush their little fingers or they will not be able to tie the very fine knots."

"That's disgusting," I said.

"Oh no," Habib said. "The children like it, and they make much money for their families." He turned to Mitchell and shook his finger at him. "And I work very hard beating the little children, so you should not say such things about me."

"Sorry," Mitchell said. "Guess I was wrong about you." He gave the bag a kick. The bag broke and some of the debris stuck to his shoe.

"What the hell?" Mitchell shook his foot, and flaming dog shit flew everywhere. A big glob landed on the carpet on the car; there was the hiss of ignition, and flames spread everywhere.

"Holy crap," Mitchell said, grabbing Habib, falling backward over the curb.

The fire popped and crackled, and the interior went conflagration. There was a small explosion when the gas tank caught and the car was engulfed in black smoke and flame.

"Guess they didn't use one of them flame-retardant carpets," Lula said.

Habib and Mitchell were pressed flat to the building, mouths open.

"You could probably go now," Lula said. "I don't think they're gonna follow you."

By the time the fire trucks arrived, the carpet car was mostly carcass, and the fire had settled down to wienie-roast size. My Buick was about ten feet in front of the carpet car, but Big Blue was untouched. The Buick's paint wasn't even blistered. The only noticeable difference was a slightly warmer than usual door handle.

"I've got to go now," I said to Mitchell. "Too bad about your car. And I wouldn't worry about your eyebrows. They're a little singed right now, but they'll probably grow back. I had this happen to me once and everything turned out okay."

"What . . . How . . . ?" Mitchell said.

I loaded Bob into the Buick and eased away from the curb, winding my way around the police cars and fire trucks.

Carl Costanza was in uniform, directing traffic. "Looks like you're on a roll," he said. "This is the second car you've toasted this week."

"It wasn't my fault! It wasn't even my car!"

"I heard someone pulled the old bag-full-of-crapola gag on Arturo Stolle's two stooges."

"No kidding? I don't suppose you know who did it?"

"Funny thing, I was just going to ask if *you* knew who did it."

"I asked you first."

Costanza did a small grimace. "No. I don't know who did it."

"Me either," I said.

"You're a pip," Constanza said. "I can't believe you got suckered into taking Simon's dog."

"I kind of like him."

"Just don't leave him alone in your car."

"You mean because it's against the law?"

"No. Because he ate Simon's front seat. Only thing left was some scraps of foam rubber and a few springs."

"Thanks for sharing that with me."

Costanza grinned. "I thought you'd want to know."

I cruised off, thinking that if Bob ate Big Blue's seat it would probably regenerate. At the risk of sounding like Grandma, I was beginning to wonder about Big Blue. It was as if the darn thing was impervious to damage. It was almost fifty years old and the original paint was in perfect condition. All around it cars got dented and torched and smushed flat as a pancake, but nothing ever happened to Big Blue.

"It's downright creepy," I said to Bob.

Bob had his nose pressed to the window and didn't look like he cared a whole lot.

I was still on Hamilton when my cell phone rang.

"Hey, babe," Ranger said. "What have you got for me?"

"Only basic facts on Lotte. Do you want to know where she lives?"

"Pass."

"She looks good in gray."

"That's going to keep me alive."

"Hmm. Feeling cranky today?"

"Cranky doesn't come close. I have a favor to ask. I need you to take a look at the back of the house in Deal. Everyone else on the team would be suspect, but a woman walking her dog down the beach won't feel threatening to Ramos's security. I want you to catalogue the house. Count off windows and doors."

There was a public-access beach about a quarter-mile from the Ramos compound. I parked on the road, and Bob and I crossed a short stretch of low dunes. The sky was overcast and the air was cooler than it had been in Trenton. Bob tipped his nose into the wind and looked all perky, and I buttoned my jacket up to my neck and wished I'd brought something warmer to wear. Most of the big, expensive houses that sat on the dunes were shuttered and unoccupied. Frothy gray waves came whooshing in at us. A few seagulls ran around at the water's edge, but that was it. Just me and Bob and the seagulls.

The big pink house came into view, more exposed on the beach side than to the street. Most of the first floor and all of the second story were clearly visible. A porch ran the length of the main structure. Attached to this main structure were two wings. The north wing consisted of first-floor garages and possibly bedrooms over the garages. The south wing was two stories and seemed to be entirely residential.

I continued to plow through the sand, not wanting to seem overly curious as I counted off the windows and doors. Just a woman walking her dog, freezing her ass off. I had binoculars with me but I was afraid to use them. I didn't want to arouse suspicion. It was impossible to tell if I was being observed from a window. Bob raced around me, oblivious to everything but the joy of being outdoors. I walked several houses farther, drew myself a diagram on a piece of paper, turned, and walked back to the public-access ramp where Blue was parked. Mission accomplished.

Bob and I piled into Blue and rumbled down the street, past the Ramos house, one last time. When I paused at the corner, a man in his sixties jumped off the curb at me. He was wearing a running suit and running shoes. And he was waving his hands.

"Stop," he said. "Stop a minute."

I could have sworn it was Alexander Ramos. No, that was ridiculous.

He trotted to the driver's side and rapped on my window. "Have you got any cigarettes?" he asked.

"Gee . . . uh, no."

He shoved a twenty at me. "Drive me to the store for some cigarettes. It'll only take a minute."

Thick accent. Same hawklike features. Same height and build. *Really* looked like Alexander Ramos.

"Do you live around here?" I asked him.

"Yeah, I live in that piece-of-shit pink monstrosity. What's it to you? Are you gonna drive me to the store, or not?"

My god! It *was* Ramos. "I don't usually let strange men in my car."

"Give me a break. I need some cigarettes. Anyway, you got a big dog in the backseat, and you look like you drive strange men around all the time. What'd ya think, I was born yesterday?"

"Not yesterday."

He wrenched the passenger door open and got in the car. "Very funny. I have to flag down a comedian."

"I don't know my way around here. Where do you go for cigarettes?"

"Turn the corner here. There's a store about a half-mile down."

"If it's just a half-mile away why don't you walk?"

"I have my reasons."

"Not supposed to be smoking, huh? Don't want anyone to catch you going to the store?"

"Goddamn doctors. I have to sneak out of my own house just to get a cigarette." He made a dismissive gesture. "I can't stand being in that house, anyway. It's like a mausoleum filled with a bunch of stiffs. Goddamn pink piece of shit."

"If you don't like the house, why do you live in it?"

"Good question. I should sell it. I never liked it, right from the beginning, but I just got married and my wife had to have this house. Everything with her was pink." He reflected for a minute. "What was her name? Trixie? Trudie? Christ, I can't even remember."

"You can't remember your wife's name?"

"I've had a lot of wives. A *lot*. Four. No, wait a minute . . . five."

"Are you married now?"

He shook his head. "I'm done with marriage. Had a prostate operation last year. Used to be, women married me for my balls and my money. Now they'd just marry me for my money." He shook his head. "It's not enough. You've gotta have standards, you know?"

I stopped at the store, and he jumped out of the car. "Don't go away. I'll be right back."

Part of me wanted to flee the scene. That was the cowardly part. And part of me wanted to go *Yippee!* That was the stupid part.

In two minutes he was back in the car, lighting up.

"Hey," I said, "no smoking in the car."

"I'll give you another twenty."

"I don't want the first twenty. And the answer is no. No smoking in the car."

"I hate this country. Nobody knows how to live. Everybody drinks fucking skim milk." He pointed to the cross street. "Turn up there and take Shoreline Avenue."

"Where are we going?"

"I know this bar."

Just what I need, to have Hannibal come out looking for his father and find me buddy-buddy with him in a bar. "I don't think this is such a good idea."

"You gonna let me smoke in the car?"

"No."

"Then we're going to Sal's."

"Okay, I'll drive you to Sal's, but I'm not going in."

"Sure, you're going in."

"But my dog . . ."

"The dog can come, too. I'll buy him a beer and a sandwich."

Sal's was small and dark. The bar stretched the length of the room. Two old men sat at the end of the bar, silently drinking, watching the television. Three empty tables were clustered to the right of the door. Ramos sat at one of the tables.

Without asking, the bartender brought Ramos a bottle of ouzo and two shot glasses. Nothing was said. Ramos drank a shot; then he lit up and dragged the smoke deep into his lungs. "Ahh," he said on the exhale.

Sometimes I envy people who smoke. They always look so happy when they suck in that first lungful of tar. I can't think of many things that make me that happy. Maybe birthday cake.

Ramos poured himself a second shot and tipped the bottle in my direction.

"No thanks," I said. "I'm driving."

He shook his head. "Sissy country." He knocked the second shot back. "Don't get me wrong. I like some things okay. I like big American cars. And I like American football. And I like American women with big tits."

Oh, boy.

"Do you flag people down a lot?" I asked him.

"Every chance I get."

"Don't you think that's dangerous? Suppose you get picked up by a nut?"

He pulled a .22 out of his pocket. "I'd shoot him." He laid the gun on the table, closed his eyes, and sucked in more smoke. "You live around here?"

"No. I just come down once in a while to walk my dog. He likes to walk on the beach."

"What's with the Band-Aid on your chin?"

"I cut myself shaving."

He dropped a twenty on the table and stood. "Cut yourself shaving. I like that. You're okay. You can take me home now."

I dropped him off a block from his house.

"Come back tomorrow," he said. "Same time. Maybe I'll hire you on as my personal chauffeur."

Grandma was setting the dinner table when Bob and I got home. The Mooner was slouched on the couch, watching TV.

"Hey," he said, "how's it going?"

"Can't complain," I said. "How's it going with you?"

"I don't know, dude. It's just hard to believe there's no more Dealer. I thought the Dealer'd be around forever. I mean, he was doing a service. He was the Dealer." He shook his head. "It rocks my world, dude."

"He needs to have another brewski and chill some more," Grandma said. "And then we'll all have a nice dinner. I always like when there's company for dinner. Especially when it's a man."

I wasn't sure Mooner counted as a man. Mooner was sort of like Peter Pan on pot. Mooner spent a lot of time in never-never land.

Bob ambled out of the kitchen over to Mooner and gave his crotch a big sniff.

"Hey dude," Mooner said, "not on the first date, man."

"I bought myself a car today," Grandma said. "And the Mooner drove it over here for me."

I felt my mouth drop open. "But you already have a car. You have Uncle Sandor's Buick."

"That's true. And don't get me wrong, I think it's a pip of a car. I just decided it didn't fit my new image. I thought I should get something sportier. It was the darnedest thing how it happened. Louise came over to take me driving and she said she heard about how the Dealer was going out of business. And so, of course, we had to hurry over to stock up on Metamucil. And then while we were there I bought a car."

"You bought a car from Dougie?"

"You bet. And it's a beaut."

I cut Mooner the death look, but it was lost on him. Mooner's emotional range didn't go that far beyond mellow.

"Wait'll you see your granny's car," Mooner said. "It's an *ex*cellent car."

"It's a babe car," Grandma said. "I look just like Christie Brinkley in it."

David Brinkley, I could believe. Christie was a stretch. But hey, if it made Grandma happy then it was fine by me. "What kind of car is it?"

"It's a 'vette," Grandma said. "And it's red."

EIGHT

So my grandmother has a red Corvette, and I have a blue '53 Buick and a big zit on my chin. Hell, it could be worse, I told myself. The zit could be on my nose.

"Besides," Grandma said, "I know how you like the Buick. I didn't want to take the Buick away from you."

I nodded and tried to smile. "Excuse me," I said. "I'm going to wash my hands for dinner."

I calmly walked to the bathroom, closed and locked the door, looked at myself in the mirror over the sink, and sniffled. A tear leaked out of my left eye. Get a grip, I told myself. It's just a pimple. It'll go away. Yes, but what about the Buick? I asked. The Buick was worrisome. The Buick showed no signs of going away. Another tear leaked out. You're too emotional, I said to the person in the mirror. You're making a big deal over nothing. Probably this is just a temporary hormone imbalance resulting from lack of sleep.

I splashed some water on my face and blew my

nose. At least I could sleep easier tonight knowing I had an alarm on the door. I didn't so much mind Ranger visiting at two in the morning . . . it was that I hated him sneaking up on me. What if I was drooling in my sleep, and he was sitting there watching me? What if he was sitting there staring at my pimple?

Mooner left after dinner and Grandma went to bed early after showing me her new car.

Morelli called at five after nine. "Sorry I couldn't get back to you sooner," he said. "It's been one of those days. How about you?"

"I have a pimple."

"I can't compete with that."

"Do you know a woman named Cynthia Lotte? Rumor has it she was Homer Ramos's girlfriend."

"From what I know about Homer, he changed girlfriends like other men change socks."

"Have you ever met his father?"

"I've spoken to him a couple times."

"And your opinion?"

"Typical good ol' boy Greek gun-runner. Haven't seen him lately." There was a pause. "Grandma Mazur still with you?"

"Yep."

Morelli did a big sigh.

"My mom wants to know if you'd like to come to dinner tomorrow. She's making a pork roast."

"Sure," Morelli said. "You're going to be there, right?"

"Me and Grandma and Bob."

"Oh boy," Morelli said.

I hung up, took Bob for a walk around the block, gave Rex a grape, and then watched television for a while. I fell asleep somewhere in the middle of the hockey game and woke up in time to catch the last half of a show on serial killers and forensics. When the show was over I triple-checked the locks on the front door and hung the motion detector from the doorknob. If someone opened the door, the alarm would go off. I sure hoped that didn't happen, because after the show on forensics I felt a little freaked. Ranger staring at my pimple didn't seem like much of a concern compared to someone cutting my tongue out and taking it home for his frozen-tongue collection. Just to play it safe I went into the kitchen and hid all the knives. No sense in making it easy for a madman to sneak in and carve me up with my own steak knife. Then I took my gun out of the cookie jar and tucked it under a couch cushion in case I needed to get at it quickly.

I turned the lights out and crawled under the quilt on my makeshift bed on the couch. Grandma was snoring in the bedroom. The freezer whirred into the defrost cycle in the kitchen. There was the distant sound of a car door slamming shut in the parking lot. All normal sounds, I told myself. Then why was my heart beating with this sickening thud? Because I watched that stupid serial killer show on television, that's why.

Okay, forget the show. Go to sleep. Think about something else.

I closed my eyes. And I thought about Alexander Ramos, who probably wasn't too far down the road from the insane killers who were giving me heart palpitations. What was the deal with Ramos? Here was a man who controlled the flow of clandestine arms worldwide, and he had to flag down a stranger to buy him some cigarettes. The word on the street was that Ramos was sick, but he hadn't seemed senile or crazy when he was with me. A little aggressive, maybe. Not a lot of patience. I guess there are some places where his behavior would have seemed erratic, but this was Jersey, and it looked to me like Ramos fit right in.

I'd been so flustered I'd hardly spoken to him. Now that some time had passed I had a million questions. Not only did I want to talk to him some more, I had a bizarre curiosity to see the inside of his house. When I was a kid my parents took me to Washington to see the White House. We stood in line for an hour, and then we got led through the public rooms. Major rip-off. Who cares about the State Dining Room? I wanted to see the kitchen. I wanted to see the President's bathroom. And now I wanted to see Alexander Ramos's living room rug. I wanted to browse through Hannibal's suite and take a look in the fridge. I mean, they'd all been on the cover of *Newsweek*. So they must be interesting, right?

This led me to thinking about Hannibal, who

hadn't looked interesting at all. And about Cynthia Lotte, who didn't look all that interesting either. How about Cynthia Lotte naked with Homer Ramos? Still not interesting. Okay, how about Cynthia Lotte and Batman? That was better. Wait a minute, how about Hannibal Ramos and Batman? *Sick!* I ran into the bathroom and brushed my teeth. I don't think I'm especially homophobic, but I draw the line at Batman.

When I came out of the bathroom someone was fumbling at my front door, making scraping sounds at the lock. The door popped open and the alarm went off. The door caught on the security chain, and when I got to the foyer I could see Mooner looking in at me between door and jamb.

"Hey dude," he said when I shut the alarm off. "How's it going?"

"What are you doing here?"

"I forgot to give your granny the second key to the car. Had it in my pocket. So I brought it over." He dropped the key in my hand. "Boy, that's a cool alarm you've got. I know someone's who got one that plays the theme song to *Bonanza*. Remember *Bonanza*? Man, that was a great show."

"How did you get my door open?"

"I used a pick. I didn't want to bother you so late at night."

"That was thoughtful of you."

"The Mooner always tries to be thoughtful." He gave me the peace sign and ambled off, down the hall.

I closed the door and reset the alarm. Grandma was still snoring in my bedroom, and Bob hadn't budged from his place by the couch. If the serial murderer showed up in this apartment, I was on my own.

I looked in on Rex and explained to him about the alarm. "Nothing to worry about," I said. "I know it's loud but at least you were already up and running." Rex was balanced on his little hamster butt, front legs dangling in front of him, whiskers twitching, parchment thin ears vibrating, black ball-bearing eyes wide open. I dropped a chunk of cracker into his food cup, and he rushed over, shoved it into his cheek pouch, and disappeared into his soup can. Rex knows how to handle a crisis.

I returned to the couch and pulled the quilt up to my chin. No more thoughts about Batman, I told myself. No more peeking under his big rubber codpiece. And no serial killers. And no Joe Morelli since it might be tempting to call him up and beg him to marry me . . . or something.

Then what should I think about? How about Grandma's snoring? It was loud enough to make me hearing-impaired for the rest of my life. I'd put the pillow over my head, but then I might not hear the alarm and the serial killer would come in and cut out my tongue. Oh shit, now I was thinking about the serial killer again!

There was another sound at my door. I tried to see my watch in the dark. It had to be around one A.M. The door clicked open and the alarm sounded. Undoubtedly Ranger. I ran a hand through my hair and checked to be sure the Band-Aid was still in place. I was wearing flannel boxers and a white T-shirt and had a last-minute panic attack that my nipples might be showing through the T-shirt. Rats! I should have thought of this sooner. I hurried to the foyer to silence the alarm but before I reached the door a pair of shears was shoved between the door and the jamb, the shears snipped through the security chain, and the door flew open.

"Hey," I said to Ranger, "that's cheating!"

But it wasn't Ranger who stepped through the open door. It was Morris Munson. He ripped the alarm off the doorknob and stabbed it with the shears. The alarm gave one last squeak and died. Grandma was still snoring. Bob was still sprawled next to the couch. And Rex was standing at attention, doing his grizzly bear impersonation.

"Surprise," Munson said, closing the door, stepping further into the foyer.

My stun gun, pepper spray, bludgeoning flashlight, and nail file were all in my shoulder bag, which was hanging on a hook, out of reach, behind Munson. My gun was somewhere in the couch, but I really didn't want to use my gun. Guns scare the hell out of me . . . and they kill people. Killing people isn't high on my favorite-things-to-do list.

Probably I should have been happy to see Munson. I mean, I'm supposed to be looking for

177

him, right? And here he is, doing a B & E in my apartment.

"Stop right where you are," I said. "You're in violation of your bond, and you're under arrest."

"You ruined my life," he said. "I did everything for you, and you ruined my life. You took everything. The house, the car, the furniture —"

"That's your ex-wife, you dope! Do I look like your ex-wife?"

"Sort of."

"Not at all!" Especially since his ex-wife was dead, with tire tracks up her back. "How did you find me?"

"I followed you home one day. You're hard to miss in that Buick."

"You don't actually think I'm your wife, do you?"

His mouth pulled back into a loopy grin. "No, but if they think I'm really flipped out I can plead insanity. Poor distraught husband goes berserk. I've laid all the groundwork with you. Now all I have to do is carve you up and set you on fire, and I'm home free."

"You're crazy!"

"See, it's working already."

"Well, you won't have any luck, because I'm a professional trained in self-defense."

"Get real. I asked around about you. You're trained in nothing. You used to sell ladies' underpants until you got fired."

"I wasn't fired. I was laid off."

"Whatever." He opened his hand, palm up, to

show me he held a switchblade. He pressed the button, and the blade flicked out. "Now, if you just cooperate it won't be so bad. It isn't as if I want to kill you. I thought I'd just stab you a couple times to make it look good. Maybe cut off a nipple."

"No way!"

"Listen, lady, give me a break, okay? I'm facing a murder charge here."

"This is stupid. This will never work! Have you talked to a lawyer about this?"

"I can't afford a lawyer! My wife freaking cleaned me out."

I was inching my way back toward the couch as we talked. Now that I knew about his plan to cut off a nipple, using the gun didn't seem like such a bad idea.

"Hold still," he said. "You're not going to make me chase you all around the apartment, are you?"

"I just want to sit down. I don't feel so good." And this wasn't so far from the truth. My heart was flopping around in my chest, and the roots of my hair had started to sweat. I plopped down on the couch and dipped my fingers into the space between the cushions. No gun. I ran my hand under the cushion next to me. Still no gun."

"What are you doing?" he wanted to know.

"I'm looking for a cigarette," I said. "I need one last cigarette to steady my nerves."

"Forget it. Time's up." He lunged at me with the knife, I rolled away, and he plunged the knife into the couch cushion.

I let out a shriek and scrambled on my hands and knees, looking for the gun, finding it deep under the middle cushion. Munson came at me again, and I shot him in the foot.

Bob opened one eye.

"Son of a bitch!" Munson yelled, dropping the knife, grabbing his foot. "Son of a bitch!"

I backed away and held him at gunpoint. "You're under arrest."

"I'm shot. I'm shot. I'm gonna die. I'm gonna bleed to death."

We both looked down at his foot. The blood wasn't exactly pouring out. A small spot by the little toe.

"I must have just nicked you," I said.

"Jesus," he said, "what a lousy shot. You were right on top of me. How could you have missed my foot?"

"Want me to try again?"

"It's all ruined now. You ruined it just like always. Every time I have a plan you have to go ruin it. I had it all worked out. I was going to come over here, cut off a nipple and set you on fire. And now it's ruined." He threw his hands into the air in disgust. "Women!" He turned and started limping toward the door.

"Hey," I yelled, "where are you going?"

"I'm leaving. My toe is killing me. And look at my shoe. It has a big rip in it. You think shoes grow on trees? See, this is what I'm talking about. You have no regard for anybody but yourself. You women are all alike. Just take, take, take. Gimme, gimme, gimme."

"Don't worry about the shoe. The state will see to it that you get a new one." Along with a nice orange jumpsuit and ankle chains.

"Forget it. I'm not going back to jail until everyone's convinced I'm insane."

"You've made a believer out of me. And besides, I've got a gun, and I'll shoot you again if I have to."

He held his hands in the air. "Go ahead and shoot."

Not only couldn't I bring myself to shoot an unarmed man, but I was out of bullets. They'd been on my shopping list. Milk, bread, bullets.

I raced past him, snatched my shoulder bag off the wall hook and dumped everything onto the floor, since that was the fastest route to finding my cuffs and pepper spray. Munson and I both dived at the scattered junk, and he won. He snatched the pepper spray off the floor and hopped to the door. "If you come after me I'll spray you," he said.

I watched him do a sort of gallop down the hall, favoring the injured foot. He stopped at the elevator doors and shook the pepper canister at me. "I'll be back," he said. Then he stepped into the elevator and disappeared.

I closed and locked the door. Terrific . . . for what that was worth. I went to the kitchen and searched for something comforting. The cake was gone. The pie was gone. No Mounds bars hid forgotten in the dark recesses of a cupboard. No booze. No Cheez Doodles. The peanut butter jar was empty.

Bob and I tried a couple of olives, but they weren't totally what the situation called for. "They need frosting," I said to Bob.

I scooped up the mess on the foyer floor and dumped it back into my shoulder bag. I put the broken alarm on the counter, turned the lights off, and returned to the couch. I lay there in the dark, and Munson's parting threat kept replaying in my mind. It really didn't matter if he was crazy by design or for real; the bottom line was that I'd come close to being nippleless. Probably I shouldn't go to sleep until I got a bolt put on the door. He'd said he'd be back, and I didn't know if he meant in an hour or a day.

Trouble was, I could hardly keep my eyes open. I tried singing, but I drifted off somewhere in the middle of "Ninety-nine Bottles of Beer on the Wall." Last I remember I was at fifty-seven bottles of beer, and then I was jolted awake with the feeling that I wasn't alone in the room. I lay perfectly still, my heart skipping beats, my lungs in suspended animation. There had been no sound of shoes treading across carpet. No deranged-madman body odor disturbed the air around me. There was just the irrational knowledge that someone was in my space.

And then, without warning, fingertips settled on my wrist, and I was galvanized into action. Adrenaline spiked into my system, and I catapulted myself off the couch into the intruder.

We were both caught by surprise, the two of us crashing into the coffee table, going down to the floor in a tangle of arms and legs. And in an instant I was pinned beneath him, which was not an entirely unpleasant experience once I realized it was Ranger. We were groin to groin, chest to chest, with his hands locked around my wrists. A moment passed while we did nothing but breathe.

"Nice tackle, babe," he said. And then he kissed me. No doubt about the intention this time. Not the sort of kiss you'd give your cousin, for instance. More like the sort of kiss a man would give a woman when he wanted to rip her clothes off and give her a reason to sing the Hallelujah Chorus.

He deepened the kiss and ran his hands under my T-shirt, splaying them flat on my abdomen. Thank God I still had both of them! A rush of electric heat contracted my nipples.

My bedroom door cracked open and Grandma stuck her head out. "Is everything okay out here?"

Great. *Now* she wakes up!

"Yep. Everything's just fine," I said.

"Is that Ranger on top of you?"

"He was showing me a self-defense move."

"I wouldn't mind knowing some self-defense," Grandma said.

"Well, we were sort of finishing up here."

Ranger rolled off me, onto his back. "If she

wasn't your grandmother I'd shoot her."

"Darn," Grandma said, "I always miss the good stuff."

I popped up onto my feet and adjusted my T-shirt. "You didn't miss much. I was just going to make some hot chocolate. Do you want some?"

"Sure," Grandma said. "I'll go get my bathrobe on."

Ranger looked up at me. It was dark in the room, with only a shaft of light coming from the open bedroom door. Still, it was light enough for me to see that his mouth was smiling but his eyes were serious. "Saved by the grandma."

"Do you want hot chocolate?"

He followed me out to the kitchen. "Pass."

I gave him the piece of paper with the house design on it. "Here's the diagram you wanted."

"Anything else you want to tell me?"

He knew about Alexander Ramos. "How do you know?"

"I've been watching the beach house. I saw you pick Ramos up."

I poured milk into two mugs and put them in the microwave. "What's the deal with him? He flagged me down to mooch a cigarette."

Ranger smiled. "You ever try to quit smoking?"

I shook my head.

"Then you wouldn't understand."

"Did you used to smoke?"

"I used to everything." He picked the motion

detector off the counter and turned it over in his hand. "I noticed the broken security chain."

"You weren't my only visitor tonight."

"What happened?"

"A failure to appear broke into my apartment. I shot him in the foot, and he left."

"You must not have read the *Bounty Hunter Handbook*. We're supposed to catch the bad guys and drag their ass back to jail."

I mixed the cocoa into the hot milk. "Ramos wants me to return today. He offered me a job as his cigarette smuggler."

"That's not a job you want to accept. Alexander can be impulsive and erratic and paranoid. He's on medication, but he doesn't always take it. Hannibal's hired bodyguards to keep an eye on the old man, but he makes them look like amateurs. Sneaks out on them every chance he gets. There's a power struggle going on between him and Hannibal, and you don't want to get caught in the crossfire."

"Isn't this nice," Grandma said, shuffling into the kitchen, taking her mug of chocolate. "It's much more fun living with you. We never had men visiting in the middle of the night when I lived with your mother."

Ranger returned the alarm to the counter. "I have to go. Enjoy your hot chocolate."

I walked him to the door. "Is there anything else you want me to do? Check your mail? Water your plants?"

"My mail is being forwarded to my lawyer.

And I'm watering my own plants."

"So, you feel safe in the Batcave?"

The corners of his mouth curved into the hint of a smile. He leaned forward and kissed me at the base of my neck, just above my T-shirt collar. "Sweet dreams."

Before he left, he said good-night to Grandma, who was still in the kitchen.

"What a nice, polite young man," Grandma said. "And he's got an excellent package."

I went straight to her closet, found the bottle of booze, and dumped some into my cocoa.

The next morning, Grandma and I were both hung over.

"I've gotta stop drinking cocoa so late at night," Grandma said. "I feel like my eyes are going to explode. Maybe I should go get checked for glaucoma."

"Better yet, how about getting checked for the level of hooch in your bloodstream?"

I took a couple aspirin and dragged myself out to the parking lot. Habib and Mitchell were there, sitting waiting in a green minivan with two kiddie seats in the back but no kiddies.

"Nice stakeout car," I said. "Fits right in."

"Don't start," Mitchell said. "I'm not in a good mood."

"It's your wife's car, right?"

He gave me a black look.

"Just to make life easier for you, so you don't

get lost, you might as well know I'm going to the office first thing."

"I *hate* that place," Habib said. "It is cursed! It is evil!"

I drove to the office and parked in front. Habib stayed half a block back and kept the motor running.

"Hey, girlfriend," Lula said. "Where's Bob?"

"He's with Grandma. They're sleeping in today."

"Looks like you should have slept in, too. You look awful. If the rest of your face was as black as the circles under your eyes you could move into my neighborhood. 'Course, the good news is what with the dark circles and bloodshot eyes you don't hardly notice that big nasty pimple."

And the *really* good news was that I didn't give a fig about the pimple today. Funny how a little thing like a life-threatening experience can put a pimple into perspective. What I cared about today was nailing Munson. I didn't want to put in another sleepless night, worrying about going up in flames.

"I have a hunch Morris Munson is back at his row house this morning," I told Lula. "I'm going over there, and I'm going to stomp on him."

"I'll go with you," Lula said. "I wouldn't mind stompin' on someone today. In fact, I'm in a real stompin' *mood.*"

I took my gun out of my shoulder bag. "I'm sort of out of bullets," I said to Connie. "You have any extras lying around?"

187

Vinnie stuck his head out of his office. "You're putting bullets in your gun? Did I hear right? What's the occasion?"

"I have bullets in my gun a lot," I said, eyes narrowed, feeling testy. "In fact, just last night I shot someone."

There was a collective gasp.

"Who'd you shoot?" Lula asked.

"Morris Munson. He broke into my apartment."

Vinnie rushed over. "Where is he? Is he dead? You didn't get him in the back, did you? I keep telling everyone — *not in the back!*"

"I didn't shoot him in the back. I shot him in the foot."

"So? Where is he?"

"Omigod," Lula said. "You shot him in the foot with your last bullet, didn't you? You blew off a little piggy and ran out of bullets." She shook her head. "Don't you just hate when that happens?"

Connie returned from the back room with a box of bullets. "You sure you want these?" she asked me. "You don't look too good. I don't know if it's a good idea to give a woman a box of bullets when she's got a pimple."

I put four rounds in my gun, and dropped the box into my shoulder bag. "I'll be fine."

"This here's a woman with a plan," Lula said.

This here was a woman with a hangover who just wanted to get through the day.

Halfway to Munson's house on Rockwell

Street I pulled to the curb and threw up. Habib and Mitchell grimaced behind me.

"Must have been some night," Lula said.

"I don't want to think about it." And that was more than just an expression. I *really* didn't want to think about it. I mean, what the hell was this thing going on between me and Ranger? I must be crazy! And I couldn't believe I'd actually sat drinking bourbon and hot chocolate with Grandma. I'm no good at drinking. I get drunk on two bottles of beer. I felt like my brain had been beamed into outer space and my body had been left behind.

I drove another quarter-mile and pulled into the McDonald's drive-through for my never-fail hangover remedy: french fries and a Coke.

"As long as we're here I might as well get a little something, too," Lula said. "Egg McMuffin, breakfast fries, chocolate shake, and a Big Mac," she yelled across me.

I felt myself go green. "That's a snack?"

"Yeah, you're right," she said. "Hold the breakfast fries."

The guy in the drive-through window handed me the bag of food and looked into the Buick's backseat. "Where's your dog?"

"Home."

"Too bad. That was pretty cool last time. Lady, that was a mountain of —"

I stepped on the gas and took off. By the time we got to Munson's house the food was gone, and I felt much better.

189

"What makes you think this dude's come back here?" Lula asked.

"Just a feeling I have. He needed to bandage his foot and get a new pair of shoes. If it was me, I'd go home to do those things. And it was late at night. Since I was already in my house I'd want to sleep in my own bed."

We couldn't tell anything from the outside of his house. The windows were dark. No sign of life inside. I drove around the block and took the alley to the garage. Lula jumped out and looked in the garage window.

"He's here, all right," she said, climbing back into Big Blue. "At least, his wreck of a car is here."

"Do you have your stun gun and pepper spray?"

"Does a chicken have a pecker? I could invade Bulgaria with the shit I've got in my handbag."

I drove back to the front of the house and dropped Lula off to guard the front door. Then I parked the car two houses down, out of Munson's line of sight, in the alley. Habib and Mitchell parked behind me in the kiddie car, locked their doors, and opened their McDonald's breakfast bags.

I cut through two yards, came up to the back of Munson's house, and carefully looked in his kitchen window. Nothing happening. A box of Band-Aids and a roll of paper towels on the kitchen table. Am I a genius, or what? I stepped back and looked up to the second floor. There was the very faint sound of running water. Munson was taking a shower. Boy, life didn't get much better than this.

I tried the door. Locked. I tried the windows. Locked. I was about to break one when Lula opened the back door.

"Not much of a lock on the front door," she said.

I had to be the only person in the entire world who couldn't pick a lock.

We stood listening in the kitchen. The water was still running overhead. Lula had pepper spray in one hand and her stun gun in the other. I had one hand free and one hand holding cuffs. We crept up the stairs and paused at the top. The row house was small. Two bedrooms and a bath on the second floor. The doors to the bedrooms were open, and the bedrooms were empty. The bathroom door was closed. Lula stood to one side, poised with the spray. I stood to the other side. We both knew exactly how to do this, because we watched the cop shows on television. Munson wasn't known to carry a gun, and it was unlikely he'd be armed in the shower, but it didn't hurt to be careful.

"On the count of three," I mouthed to Lula, my hand on the doorknob. "One, two, three!"

NINE

"Wait a minute," Lula said, "he's gonna be naked. Maybe we don't want to see this. I've seen a lot of ugly men in my day. I'm not so anxious to see any more."

"I don't care about the naked part," I said. "I care about the part that he won't have a knife or a propane torch."

"Good point."

"Okay, I'm counting again. Get ready. One, two, three!"

I opened the bathroom door, and we both jumped in.

Munson ripped the shower curtain aside. "What the hell?"

"You're under arrest," Lula said. "And we'd appreciate it if you'd get a towel on account of I don't feel like looking at your sad, shriveled privates."

He had his hair full of shampoo, and he had a big bandage on his foot, which he was protecting with a plastic bag held tight at the ankle with an elastic band.

"I'm crazy!" he shrieked. "I'm freaking crazy, and you'll never take me alive!"

"Yeah, whatever," Lula said, handing him a towel. "You want to shut that water off now?"

Munson took the towel and snapped it back at Lula.

"Hey!" Lula said, "hold on here. You snap that towel at me again, and you're gonna get a snootful of pepper spray."

Munson snapped it again. "Fat, fat, fatty," he sang.

Lula forgot about the pepper spray and lunged for his neck. Munson reached up and turned the shower spray on her and jumped out of the shower. I tried to grab him, but he was wet and slippery with soap, and Lula was flailing around, trying to get away from the water.

"Spray him!" I yelled to Lula. "Electrocute him! Shoot him! Do something!"

Munson knocked the two of us aside and streaked down the stairs. He ran the length of the house and out the back door. I was close behind, and Lula was about ten feet behind me. His foot had to be killing him, but he ran flat out through two yards and then cut off to the alley. I took a flying leap and caught him square in the small of his back. The two of us went down to the ground and rolled around, locked together, swearing and clawing. Munson was trying to scramble away, and I was trying to hang on and cuff him. It would have been easier if he'd had clothes to grab hold of. As it was, I didn't really want to grab what was available.

"Hit him where it hurts!" Lula was yelling. "Hit him where it hurts!"

So I did. A person reaches a point where she just doesn't want to roll around anymore. I hauled back and gave Munson a knee in the gonads.

"Ulk," Munson said, and assumed the fetal position.

Lula and I pried his hands away from Mr. Sad Sack and cuffed him behind his back.

"Wish I had a movie of you wrestlin' with this guy," Lula said. "It reminded me of that joke about the midget at the nudist colony who kept sticking his nose in everyone's business."

Mitchell and Habib had gotten out of their car and were standing a few feet away looking pained.

"I could feel that all the way over here," Mitchell said. "If we get the word that we have to rough you up, I'm wearing a cup."

Lula ran back to the house to get a blanket and lock up. And Habib and Mitchell and I dragged Munson over to the Buick. When Lula got back we wrapped Munson up, tossed him into the backseat and drove him to the police station on North Clinton. We took him to the back entrance, which had a drive-in.

"Just like McDonald's," Lula said. "Except we're dropping off instead of picking up."

I rang the buzzer and identified myself. A

moment later Carl Costanza opened the back door and looked over at the Buick. "Now what?" he said.

"I have a body in the backseat. Morris Munson. FTA."

Carl stared into the car window and grinned. "He's naked."

I blew out a sigh. "You aren't going to give me a hard time with this, are you?"

"Hey, Juniak," Costanza yelled, "come take a look at this naked guy. Guess who he belongs to!"

"Okay," Lula said to Munson, "end of the line. You can get out now."

"No," Munson said, "I'm not getting out."

"The hell you aren't," Lula said.

Juniak and two other cops joined Costanza at the door. Everyone was grinning dopey cop grins.

"Sometimes I think this is a really crappy job," one of the cops said. "But then there are other times when you get to see stuff like this, and it makes it all worthwhile. Why's the naked guy got a plastic bag on his foot?"

"I shot him," I said.

Costanza and Juniak exchanged glances. "I don't want to know about it," Costanza said. "I didn't hear anything."

Lula gave Munson her junkyard-dog look. "You don't haul your bony white carcass out of this car, I'm coming back there."

"Fuck you," Munson said. "Fuck your fat ass."

The cops all sucked in a breath and took a step backward.

"That does it," Lula said. "You put me in a bad mood now. You went and wrecked my good disposition. I'm gonna come back there and root you out like the little pencil-dick rodent you are." She heaved herself out of the car and wrenched the back door open.

And Munson jumped out of the car.

I wrapped the blanket around him, and we all shuffled into the police station, except for Lula, who has a phobia about police stations. She backed out of the drive-in, found a space in the lot, and parked.

I cuffed Munson to the bench by the docket lieutenant, handed my paperwork in, and got my body receipt. Next on my list of things to do was visit Brian Simon.

I was on my way to the third floor when Costanza stopped me. "If you're looking for Simon, don't bother. He took off the instant he heard you were here." He gave me the once-over. "I don't want to be insulting, or anything, but you look like hell."

I was dusty from head to foot, the knee was torn out of my Levi's, my hair was in the throes of a *very* bad day, and then there was the pimple.

"You look like you haven't slept in days," Costanza said.

"That's because I haven't."

"I could talk to Morelli."

"It's not Morelli. It's my grandmother. She's

moved in with me, and she snores." Not to mention I had the Mooner in my life. And madmen. And Ranger.

"So let me get this straight. You're living with your granny and with Simon's dog?"

"Yeah."

Costanza grinned. "Hey, Juniak," he yelled, "wait'll you hear this." He looked back to me. "No wonder Morelli's been in such a foul mood."

"Tell Simon I was looking for him."

"You can count on it," Costanza said.

I left the police station and drove to the office and went in with Lula so I could bask in my bounty-hunter excellence. Lula and I had captured our man. It was a big capture, too. A homicidal maniac. Well okay, maybe it hadn't been an entirely flawless operation, but hey, we *got* him.

I slapped the body receipt down on Connie's desk. "Are we good, or what?" I said.

Vinnie popped his head out of his office. "Did I just hear news of an apprehension?"

"Morris Munson," Connie said. "Signed, sealed, and delivered."

Vinnie rocked back on his heels, hands in pants pockets, smile stretching the width of his face. "Lovely."

"He didn't even set either of us on fire this time," Lula said. "We were good. We hauled his ass off to the clink."

Connie eyeballed Lula. "Do you know you're all wet?"

"Yeah. Well, we rousted the jerk out of the shower."

Vinnie's eyebrows shot up into his forehead. "Are you telling me you arrested him naked?"

"It wouldn't have been so bad if it wasn't for him running out of the house and down the street," Lula said.

Vinnie shook his head, the smile broader than ever. "I *love* this job."

Connie gave me my fee; I gave Lula her share and went home to change.

Grandma was still there, getting ready for her driving lesson. She was dressed in her purple warm-up suit, platform sneakers, and a long-sleeved T-shirt that had "Eat My Shorts" written across the chest. "I met a man in the elevator today," she said. "And I'm taking him to dinner with us tonight."

"What's his name?"

"Myron Landowsky. He's an old fart, but I figure I have to start somewhere." She took her purse off the counter, tucked it into the crook of her arm, and gave Bob a pat on the head. "Bob's been a good boy today, except for eating that roll of toilet paper. Oh yeah, and I was hoping we could ride over with you and Joseph. Myron don't drive after dark, on account of his night vision is shot."

"No problem."

I made myself a fried-egg sandwich for lunch, changed my jeans, brushed my hair into a half-assed ponytail, and plastered a ton of concealer over my pimple. I gunked up my lashes with mascara and stared at myself in the mirror. Stephanie, Stephanie, Stephanie, I said. What are you doing?

I was working myself up to going back to the shore, that's what I was doing. I was having brain pain that I'd screwed up my opportunity to talk to Alexander Ramos. I'd sat across the table from him like a big doofus yesterday. We were doing surveillance on the Ramos family, and when I got unexpectedly let into the chicken coop I didn't ask the rooster a single question. I was sure Ranger's advice was sound, that I should stay away from Alexander Ramos, but it felt wimpy not to go back and try to take better advantage of the situation.

I grabbed my jacket and clipped the leash onto Bob's collar. I stopped in the kitchen to say good-bye to Rex and to put my gun back into the cookie jar. I didn't think it'd be a good idea to be packing while I chauffeured Alexander Ramos around. It'd be hard to explain the gun if I got patted down by Ramos or his babysitters.

Joyce Barnhardt was parked in my lot when I came down. "Nice pizza face," she said.

I guessed the concealer wasn't totally effective. "You want something?"

"You know what I want."

Joyce wasn't the only idiot loitering in my lot. Mitchell and Habib were parked at the rear. I walked back to them, and Mitchell rolled the driver's-side window down.

"Do you see that woman I was just talking to?" I asked. "That's Joyce Barnhardt. She's the bond enforcement agent Vinnie hired to bring Ranger in. If you want to get Ranger, you need to follow Joyce around."

Both men looked over at Joyce.

"If a woman dressed like that in my village we would throw stones at her until she was dead," Habib said.

"Nice hooters, though," Mitchell said. "Are they real?"

"As far as I know."

"What do you think her chances are of catching Ranger?"

"None."

"What are your chances?"

"None."

"We were told to watch you," Mitchell said. "That's what we're going to do."

"Too bad," Habib said. "I do like to look at the whore, Joyce Barnhardt."

"Are you going to follow me around all afternoon?"

Color crept up Mitchell's neck into his cheeks. "We got some other things to do."

I smiled. "Have to get the car home?"

"Fuckin' car pool," Mitchell said. "My kid's got a soccer game."

I went back to the Buick and loaded Bob into the backseat. At least I didn't have to worry about being followed, thanks to the soccer game. I looked in the rearview mirror just to make sure.

No Habib and Mitchell — but Joyce was tailing me. I pulled to the side of the road and stopped, and Joyce stopped a few feet behind me. I got out of the car and walked back to her.

"Knock it off," I said.

"It's a free country."

"Are you going to follow me all day?"

"Probably."

"Suppose I ask you nicely."

"Get real."

I looked at her car. A new black SUV. Then I looked at my car. Big Blue. I walked back to Blue and got in. "Hang on," I said to Bob. Then I threw the car into reverse.

CRASH.

I changed gears and moved forward a few feet. I got out and surveyed the damage. The SUV bumper was Crumple City and Joyce was fighting with the deployed airbag. The back of the Buick was perfect. Not a scratch. I returned to the Buick and drove away. It's not a good idea to mess with a woman who has a pimple.

It was overcast in Deal, with a mist coming off the ocean. Gray sky, gray ocean, gray sidewalks, big pink house belonging to Alexander Ramos. I rolled past the house, made a U-turn, passed the house a second time, turned, and parked at the corner. I wondered if Ranger was watching. My guess was yes. No vans or trucks were parked on the street. That meant he'd have to be in a house. And the house would have to be unoccupied.

Easy to tell the unoccupied beachfront houses. Much more difficult to tell the unoccupied houses on the road. None of those were shuttered.

I checked my watch. Same time, same place. No Ramos. After ten minutes my phone rang.

"Yo," Ranger said.

"Yo, yourself."

"You're not very good at following directions."

"You mean about not taking the cigarette smuggler job? Seemed too good to pass up."

"You're going to be careful, right?"

"Right."

"Our man's having problems getting out of the house. Hang in there."

"How do you know this? Where are you?"

"Get ready. It's show time," Ranger said. And he disconnected.

Alexander Ramos was through the gate and running across the road to my car. He wrenched the passenger door open and dove in. "Go!" he shouted. "Go!"

I took off from the curb and saw two men in suits round the gate and sprint toward us. I floored the Buick, and we roared away.

Ramos didn't look good at all. He was pale and sweating and gasping for air. "Christ," he said, "I didn't think I was going to make it. It's a goddamn freak show in that house. Good thing I looked out the window when I did and saw your car. I was going nuts in there."

"Do you want to go to the store?"

"No. That's the first place they'll look. I can't go to Sal's, either."

I was getting a real bad feeling here. Like, this was one of the days Alexander didn't take his medicine.

"Take me to Asbury Park," he said. "I know a place in Asbury Park."

"Why were those men chasing you?"

"No one was chasing me."

"But I saw them."

"You didn't see anything."

Ten minutes later he pointed with his finger. "Over there. Stop at that bar."

The three of us went into the bar, sat at a table, and went through the same ritual as the last time. The bartender brought a bottle of ouzo to the table without being asked. Ramos slugged two back and then lit up.

"Everyone knows you," I said.

He looked around at the scarred booths that lined one wall and the dark mahogany bar that ran the length of the other. Behind the bar was the usual array of bottles. Behind the bottles was the standard bar mirror. One stool was occupied, at the far end of the room. The man stared down, into his drink. "I've been coming here for a few years," Ramos said. "I come here when I need to get away from the freaks."

"The freaks?"

"My family. I raised three worthless sons who spend money faster than I can make it."

"You're Alexander Ramos, right? I saw your

picture in *Newsweek* a while back. I'm sorry about Homer. I read about the fire in the paper."

He poured out another shot. "One less freak to deal with."

I felt the blood drain from my face. It was a chilling statement for a father to make.

He took a long pull on his cigarette, closed his eyes, and savored the moment. "They think the old man don't know what's going on. Well, they're wrong. The old man knows everything. I didn't build this business by being stupid. And I didn't build it by being nice, either, so they better watch their step."

I glanced back at the door. "Are you sure we're safe here?"

"Any time you're with Alexander Ramos, you're safe. Nobody touches Alexander Ramos."

Yeah, right. That's why we're hiding out in a bar in Asbury Park. This was feeling like Bizarro Land.

"I just don't like to be bothered when I smoke," he said. "I don't want to have to look at all the leeches."

"Why don't you get rid of them. Tell them to leave your house?"

He squinted at me through a haze of smoke. "How would it look? They're family." He dropped his cigarette on the floor and stepped on it. "There's only one way to get rid of family."

Oh boy.

"We're done here," he said. "I have to get back before my son runs me into the ground."

"Hannibal?"

"Mr. Big Shot. I should never have sent him to college." He stood and dropped a wad of money onto the table. "How about you? Did you go to college?"

"Yep."

"What are you doing now?"

I was afraid if I told him I was a bounty hunter he'd shoot me. "A little of this and a little of that," I said.

"Big fancy education and you're doing a little of this?"

"You sound like my mother."

"You probably give your mother angina."

That made me smile. He was scary crazy, but I sort of liked him. He reminded me of my uncle Punky. "Do you know who killed Homer?"

"Homer killed himself."

"I read in the paper that they didn't find a gun, so they ruled out suicide."

"More than one way to kill yourself. My son was stupid and greedy."

"Uh . . . you didn't kill him, did you?"

"I was in Greece when he was shot."

We locked eyes. We both knew that didn't answer the question. Ramos could have ordered his son's execution.

I drove him back to Deal and parked on a side street, a block from the pink house.

"Any time you want to make twenty bucks you just show up on the corner," Ramos said.

I smiled. I hadn't taken any money from him,

and probably I wouldn't be back. "Okay," I said, "keep your eyes open for me."

I took off the second he left the car. I didn't want to risk the guys in the suits spotting me. Ten minutes later, my phone rang.

"Short visit," Ranger said.

"He drinks, he smokes, he goes home."

"Did you learn anything?"

"I think he might be crazy."

"That's the consensus."

Sometimes Ranger sounded like he was straight off the street, and sometimes he sounded like a stockbroker. Ricardo Carlos Manoso, Man of Mystery.

"Do you think Ramos might have killed his own son?"

"He's capable of it."

"He said Homer was killed because he was greedy and stupid. You knew Homer. Was he greedy and stupid?"

"Homer was the weakest of the three sons. He'd always take the easy road. But sometimes the easy road got to be a problem."

"How?"

"Homer would drop a hundred thousand gambling and then look for an easy way to get the money, like hijacking a truck or dealing some drugs. In the process he'd step on Mob toes or have a run-in with the police, and Hannibal would have to bail him out."

Which led me to wonder what Ranger was doing with Homer Ramos the night Ramos was shot. No point in asking.

"Later, babe," Ranger said. And he was gone.

I got home in time to walk Bob and take a shower. I spent an extra half-hour styling my hair so it was deceptively casual, as if I really didn't care enough to put in a lot of effort but I was so naturally gorgeous I looked outstanding anyway. It seemed like sacrilege to have such sexy hair and such a big ugly pimple, so I squeezed the pimple until it popped. Then what was left was a big bloody hole in my chin. Crap. I stuck a piece of toilet paper over the hole to stop the bleeding while I did my makeup. I put on black stretch pants and a red sweater with a scoop neck. I peeled the toilet paper off my chin and stood back to take a look. The bags under my eyes were considerably reduced and the hole in my chin was already starting to scab over. Not cover model material, but I'd look okay in dim light.

I heard the front door open and close, and Grandma breezed past the bathroom on her way to the bedroom.

"Boy, this driving is something," Grandma said. "I don't know what I was thinking about, going all those years with no license. I had my lesson this afternoon, and then Melvina came over and took me to the mall and let me drive around in circles. I did real good, too. Except for when I stopped too short once, and Melvina got a sprained back."

The doorbell rang and I opened it to find

Myron Landowsky wheezing in the hall. Landowsky always reminded me of a box turtle, with his bald liver-spotted head thrust forward, his shoulders hunched, his trousers hiked up to his armpits.

"I'm telling you, if they don't do something about that elevator I'm moving," he said. "I've lived here for twenty-two years but I'll go if I have to. That old lady Bestler gets in there with her walker and then pushes the hold button when she leaves. I've seen her do it a million times. Takes her fifteen minutes just to get out of the elevator, and then she goes off and the hold button's still on hold. And meantime what are we supposed to do on the third floor? I just had to walk all the way down here."

"Would you like a glass of water?"

"You got any liquor?"

"No."

"Never mind, then." He looked around. "I'm here to see your grandmother. We're going out to dinner."

"She's getting ready. She'll be out in a minute."

There was a rap on the door and Morelli walked in. He looked at me. And then he looked at Myron.

"We're double-dating," I said. "This is Grandma's friend, Myron Landowsky."

"Would you excuse us, please?" Morelli said, pulling me into the hall.

"I gotta go sit down, anyway," Landowsky said.

"I had to walk all the way down here."

Morelli closed the door, pinned me against the wall, and kissed me. When he was done I looked myself over to make sure I was still dressed.

"Wow," I said.

His lips brushed against my ear. "If you don't get those old people out of your apartment I'm going to self-combust."

I knew just how he felt. I'd self-combusted in the shower that morning, but it didn't help much.

Grandma opened the door and stuck her head out. "For a minute there I thought you left without us."

We took the Buick because we couldn't all fit in Morelli's truck. Morelli drove, Bob sat next to him, and I sat by the window. Grandma and Myron sat in the back, discussing antacids.

"Any news on the Ramos murder?" I asked Morelli.

"Nothing new. Barnes is still convinced it's Ranger."

"No other suspects?"

"Enough suspects to fill Shea Stadium. No evidence against any of them."

"What about the family?"

Morelli cut his eyes at me. "What about them?"

"Are they suspects?"

"Along with everyone else in three countries."

My mother was standing at the door when we

parked. It seemed strange to see her standing alone. For the past couple years Grandma had always stood beside her. The mother and daughter whose roles had reversed — Grandma gladly relinquishing parental responsibility, my mother grimly accepting the task, struggling to find a place for an old woman who'd suddenly become a strange hybrid of tolerant mother and rebellious daughter. My father, in the living room, not wanting any part of it.

"Isn't that something," Grandma said. "It looks different from this side of the door."

Bob bolted out of the car and charged my mother, driven by the scent of pork roast wafting from the kitchen.

Myron moved slower. "That's some car you've got," he said. "It's a real beaut. They don't make cars like that anymore. Everything's a piece of junk today. Plastic crap. Made by a bunch of foreigners."

My father drifted into the foyer. This was his kind of talk. My father was a second-generation American, and he loved bashing foreigners, relatives excluded. He dropped back a step when he saw Turtle Man was doing the talking.

"This here's Myron," Grandma said by way of introduction. "He's my date tonight."

"Nice house you got here," Myron said. "You can't beat aluminum siding. That's aluminum siding on it, right?"

Bob was running through the house like a crazy dog, high on food smells. He stopped in the foyer and gave my father's butt a good sniffing.

"Get this dog outta here," my father said. "Where'd this dog come from?"

"This here's Bob," my grandmother said. "He's just saying hello. I saw a show on the television about dogs and they said sniffing butts was like shaking hands. I know all about dogs now. And we're real lucky that they whacked off Bob's doodles before he got too old and got into the habit of humping your leg. They said it's real hard to break a dog of that habit."

"I had a rabbit once when I was a kid that was a leg humper," Myron said. "Boy, once he got a hold of you it was the devil to get him off. And that rabbit didn't care who he went to town on. Got the cat in a stranglehold one time and almost killed it."

I could feel Morelli shaking with silent laughter behind me.

"I'm starved," Grandma said. "Let's eat."

We all took our places at the table, except for Bob, who was eating in the kitchen. My father helped himself to a couple slabs of pork and passed the rest to Morelli. We started the mashed potatoes going around. And the green beans, applesauce, pickle jar, basket of dinner rolls, and pickled beets.

"No pickled beets for me," Myron said. "They give me the runs. I don't know what it is, you get old and everything gives you the runs."

Something to look forward to.

"You're lucky you can go," Grandma said.

"You're lucky you don't need Metamucil. Now that the Dealer's out of business, drug prices are gonna go sky high. Other stuff's gonna be outta reach too. I bought my car just in time."

My mother and father both looked up from their plates.

"You bought a car?" my mother asked. "Nobody told me."

"It's a pip, too," Grandma said. "It's a red Corvette."

My mother made the sign of the cross. "Dear God," she said.

TEN

"How could you afford a Corvette?" my father asked. "All you get is Social Security."

"I have money from when I sold the house," Grandma said. "And anyway, I made a good deal. Even the Mooner said I got a good deal."

My mother made another cross. "The Mooner," she said with just a touch of hysteria. "You bought a car from the Mooner?"

"Not from the Mooner," Grandma said. "The Mooner don't sell cars. I bought my car from the Dealer."

"Thank goodness," my mother said, hand to her heart. "For a minute there . . . Well, I'm just glad you went to a car dealer."

"Not a *car* dealer," Grandma told her. "I bought my car from the Metamucil dealer. I paid four hundred and fifty bucks for it. That's good, right?"

"Depends," my father said. "Does it have a motor?"

"I didn't look," Grandma said. "Don't all cars have motors?"

Joe looked pained. He didn't want to be the one to rat on my grandmother for possession of stolen property.

"While Louise and I were looking at the cars, there were a couple men in the Dealer's backyard, and they were going on about Homer Ramos," Grandma said. "They said he was a big car distributor. I didn't know the Ramos family sold cars. I thought they just sold guns."

"Homer Ramos sold *stolen* cars," my father said, head bent over his plate. "Everybody knows that."

I turned to Joe. "Is that true?"

Joe shrugged. Noncommittal. Cop face in place. If you knew how to read the signs, this one said "Ongoing Investigation."

"And that's not all," Grandma said. "He cheated on his wife. He was a real skunk. They said his brother is just as bad. He lives out in California, but he keeps a house here so he can see women on the sly. The whole family is rotten, if you ask me."

"He must be pretty rich if he has two houses," Myron said. "I should be so rich. I'd keep a girlfriend, too."

There was a collective pause while we all wondered what Landowsky would do with a girlfriend.

He reached for the potato bowl, but it was empty.

"Here, let me fill that for you," Grandma said. "Ellen always has more keeping warm on the stove."

Grandma took the bowl and trotted off. "Uh-oh," she said, when she stepped into the kitchen.

My mother and I got up simultaneously and went to investigate. Grandma was standing in the middle of the floor, looking at the cake on the table. "The good news is Bob didn't eat the whole cake," Grandma said. "The bad news is he licked the icing off one side."

Without missing a beat, my mother took a butter knife out of the silverware drawer, scooped some icing off the top of the cake, smeared the icing on the side Bob had licked clean, and sprinkled coconut all around the cake.

"Been a long time since we had a coconut cake," Grandma said. "It looks real pretty."

My mother put the cake on top of the refrigerator, out of Bob's reach. "When you were little you used to lick the icing off all the time," she said to me. "We had a lot of coconut cakes."

Morelli gave me raised eyebrows when I got back.

"Don't ask," I said. "And don't eat the outside part of the cake."

The parking lot was almost full when we got back to my apartment building. The seniors were home, settled down in front of their televisions.

Myron dangled his house keys at Grandma. "How about coming over for a nightcap, sweetie."

"You men are all alike," my grandmother said. "Only thinking about one thing."

"What's that?" Myron asked.

Grandma scrinched her mouth up. "If I have to tell you, then there's no sense going in for a nightcap."

Morelli walked Grandma and me to my apartment. He let Grandma in, then pulled me aside. "You could come home with me," he said.

It was very tempting. And not for any of the reasons Morelli would hope for. I was dead on my feet. And Morelli didn't snore. I might actually be able to *sleep* at his house. I hadn't slept through the night in so long, I couldn't remember what it was like.

He brushed a kiss across my lips. "Grandma wouldn't mind. She's got Bob."

Eight hours, I thought. All I wanted was eight hours of sleep, and I'd be good as new.

His hands slid under my sweater. "It would be a night to remember."

It would be a night without a drooling, knife-wielding pyromaniac. "It would be heaven," I said, not even realizing I was talking out loud.

He was so close I could feel every part of him, pressed against me. And one of those parts was growing. Ordinarily this would have triggered a corresponding reaction in *my* body. But tonight my thoughts were that this was something I could do without. Still, if it was the price I had to pay for a decent night's sleep, then let's get to it.

"Let me just scoot inside and grab a few things," I told Morelli, imagining myself all cozy in his bed, in a toasty flannel nightshirt. "And I have to tell Grandma."

"You aren't going to go inside and close and lock the door and leave me out here, are you?"

"Why would I do that?"

"I don't know. I just have this feeling . . ."

"You should come in here," Grandma called out. "There's a show on the television, and it's all about alligators." She cocked her head. "What's that strange sound? It sounds like a cricket."

"Shit," Morelli said.

Morelli and I knew what the sound was. It was his pager. Morelli was trying hard to ignore it.

I was the one to cave first. "You have to look at it sooner or later," I said.

"I don't have to look at it," he said. "I know what it is, and it isn't going to be good." He checked the readout, grimaced, and headed for the phone in the kitchen. When he came back, holding a paper towel with an address scribbled, I gave him an expectant look.

"I have to go," he said. "But I'll be back."

"When? When will you be back?"

"Wednesday at the latest."

I rolled my eyes. Cop humor.

He gave me a fast kiss, and he was gone.

I pressed the redial button on my phone. A woman answered, and I recognized the voice. Terry Gilman.

"Look at this," Grandma said. "The alligator ate a cow. You don't see that every day."

I took a seat beside her. Fortunately, there wasn't any more cow eating. Although now that I knew Joe was on his way to meet Terry Gilman, death and destruction held some appeal. The fact that this was undoubtedly a business meeting took some of the fun out of getting nuts over it. Still, I could probably have worked myself up into a pretty good frenzy if I just hadn't been so darn tired.

When the alligator show was done, we watched the Shopping Network for a while.

"I'm going to turn in," Grandma finally said. "Gotta get my beauty rest."

The second she left the room I hauled out my pillow and quilt, killed the lights, and flopped onto the couch. I was asleep in an instant, my sleep deep and dreamless. And short-lived. I was dragged awake by Grandma's snoring. I got up to close her door, but it was already closed. I sighed, half in self-pity and half in amazement that she could sleep with all that noise. You'd think she'd wake herself up. Bob didn't seem to notice. He was asleep on the floor at one end of the couch, sprawled on his side.

I crawled under the quilt and willed myself to go back to sleep. I thrashed around some. I put my hands over my ears. I thrashed around some more. The couch was uncomfortable. The quilt was tangled. And Grandma kept snoring. "Arrrrgh," I said. Bob didn't stir.

Grandma was going to have to go, one way or another. I got up and padded out to the kitchen. I looked through the cupboards and refrigerator. Nothing interesting. It was a little after twelve.

Not all that late, really. Maybe I should go out and get a candy bar to settle my nerves. Chocolate was calming, right?

I pulled on my jeans and shoes and covered my pajama top with a coat. I snagged my bag from its hook in the foyer and let myself out. It would only take ten minutes to make a candy bar run, and then I'd be home and no doubt I'd clonk right off to sleep.

I stepped into the elevator half-expecting to see Ranger, but Ranger didn't appear. No Ranger in the parking lot, either. I fired up the Buick, drove to the store, and bought a Milky Way and a Snickers. I ate the Snickers immediately, intending to save the Milky Way for bed. But then somehow the Milky Way got eaten right away, too.

I thought about Grandma and the snoring and couldn't get excited about going home, so I drove over to Joe's house. Joe lives just outside the Burg in a row house he'd inherited from his aunt. In the beginning it had felt weird to think of him as a homeowner. But somehow the house had conformed to Joe, and the union had proved comfortable. It was a nice little place on a quiet street. A shotgun-style row house with the kitchen in the rear and bedrooms and bath on the second floor.

The house was dark. No lights shining behind the curtained windows. No truck parked at the curb. No sign of Terry Gilman. Okay, so maybe I was a teensy bit nuts. And maybe the candy bars were just an excuse to come over here. I dialed Joe's number on my cell phone. No answer.

Too bad I didn't have lock-picking skills. I could have let myself in and gone to sleep in Joe's bed. Just like Goldilocks.

I put the Buick in gear and slowly drove the length of the block, not feeling all that tired anymore. What the hell, I thought, as long as I'm out here with nothing to do, why not check up on Hannibal?

I wound my way out of Joe's neighborhood, hit Hamilton, and drove toward the river. I got on Route 29 and in minutes I was cruising past Hannibal's town house. Dark, dark, dark. No lights on here, either. I parked one block up, just around the corner, and walked back to the house. I stood directly in front and looked up at the windows. Did I see the tiniest hint of light in the front room? I crept closer, over the lawn, right into the bushes that hugged the house, and pressed my nose to his window. There was definitely light coming from somewhere in the house. Could have been a night light. Hard to tell where it originated.

I scuttled back to the sidewalk and speedwalked around to the bike path, where I took a moment to let my eyes adjust to the dark. Then I carefully picked my way to Hannibal's yard. I climbed the tree and stared into Hannibal's windows. All the drapes were drawn. But again, there was the hint of a light coming from somewhere downstairs. I was thinking the light wasn't significant when it suddenly blinked out.

This got my heart thumping just a little, since I wasn't keen on getting shot at again. In fact, probably it wasn't a good idea to stay in the tree. Probably it would be better to watch from a safer distance . . . like Georgia. I quietly inched down to the ground and was about to tippy-toe away when I heard a lock tumble. Either someone was closing up for the night, or someone was coming out to shoot me. This got me moving.

I was about to turn for the street when I heard a gate creak open. I scrunched myself flat against the fence, deep in shadow. I held my breath and watched the bike path. A lone figure came into view. He closed the gate. He paused for a moment and looked directly at me. I was pretty sure he had come out of Hannibal's yard. And I was pretty sure he couldn't see me. There was a good chunk of distance between us, and he was almost lost in the dark; the ambient light revealed only an outline. He turned on his heel and walked away from me. He passed under a shaft of window light and was briefly illuminated. My breath caught in my throat. It was Ranger. I opened my mouth to call out his name, but he was gone, dissolved into the night. Like an apparition.

I ran to the street and listened for footsteps. I didn't hear them, but there was the sound of an engine catching not far off. A black SUV crossed the intersection, and quiet returned to the neighborhood. I was half afraid that I was losing my mind, that it had all been a hallucination from lack of sleep. I walked back to the car feeling pretty well creeped out and took off for home.

Grandma was still snoring like a lumberjack when I dropped my shoulder bag on the kitchen counter. I said hello to Rex and shuffled to the couch. I didn't bother taking my shoes off. I just crashed onto the couch and pulled the quilt over myself.

The next time I opened my eyes, the Mooner and Dougie were sitting on the coffee table, staring down at me.

"Yow!" I yelled. "What the hell?"

"Hey duder," the Mooner said, "hope we didn't, like, startle you."

"What are you doing here?" I shrieked.

"The dude formerly known as the Dealer needs someone to talk to. He's, like, confused. You know, one minute he's a successful businessman, and then — *wham* — his whole future is ripped out from under him. It just isn't fair, man."

Dougie shook his head. "It isn't fair," he said.

"So we thought you might have some ideas for future employment," Mooner said. "Since you're so successfully employed. You and the Dougster, you're like . . . an entrepreneurial dude and dudette."

"It isn't like I haven't had offers," Dougie said.

"That's right," Mooner said. "The Dougster is in large demand in the pharmaceutical trade. There's always openings for enterprising young men in pharmaceuticals."

"You mean like Metamucil?"

"That too," Mooner said.

As if Dougie wasn't in enough trouble. Selling hijacked Metamucil was one thing. Selling crack was a whole other ball game.

"Probably pharmaceutical sales isn't a good idea," I told them. "It could have an adverse effect on your life expectancy."

Dougie did another nod. "Exactly what I thought. And now that Homer's out of the picture, things are going to get tight."

"Damn shame about Homer," Mooner said. "He was a fine human being. Now *there* was a businessman."

"Homer?" I asked.

"Homer Ramos. Homer and me were like this," Moon said, holding up two fingers side by side. "We were close, dude."

"Are you telling me Homer Ramos was involved in drugs?"

"Well, sure," Mooner said. "Isn't everybody?"

"How did you know Homer Ramos?"

"I didn't actually know him in the physical sense. It was more of a mutual cosmic connection. Like, he was the big drug kahuna, and I'm, you know, like a consumer. It sure was bummer luck that he got his head ventilated. Just when he got that expensive rug, too."

"Rug?"

"I was at Art's Carpets last week, contemplating a rug purchase. And you know how in the beginning you're thinking all the rugs are totally excellent, and then the more you look at them, the more they all start looking the same. And before you know it you're, like, rug hypnotized? And next thing you know, you're taking a break, laying on the floor, chilling? And while I was laying there behind the rugs, I heard Homer come in. He went into the back room, got a rug, and left. And the rug dude, you know, the owner guy, and Homer were talking about how the rug was worth a million dollars, and Homer should be real careful with it. Far out, huh?"

A million-dollar rug! Arturo Stolle had handed a million-dollar rug over to Homer Ramos just before Ramos was killed. And now Stolle was looking for Ranger, the last person to see Ramos alive . . . with the exception of the guy who killed him. And Stolle was thinking Ranger had something that belonged to him. Could this Stolle business be over a rug? Hard to believe. Must be a hell of a rug.

"I'm pretty sure I wasn't, like, hallucinating," Mooner said.

"That would be a strange hallucination," I said.

"Not as strange as the time I thought I'd turned into a giant blob of bubble gum. That was scary, dude. I had these little hands and feet, and everything else was bubble gum. I didn't even have a face. And I was like, all chewed, you know." Mooner gave an involuntary shiver. "It was a bad trip, dude."

The front door opened, and Morelli walked in.

He looked at Mooner and Dougie, and then he looked at his watch and raised his eyebrows.

"Hey, man," Mooner said. "Long time no see. How's it going, dude?"

"Can't complain," Morelli said.

Dougie, not being nearly as mellow as Mooner, jumped to his feet at the sight of Morelli and accidentally stepped on Bob. Bob yelped in surprise, sank his teeth into Dougie's pants leg and ripped off a chunk of material.

Grandma Mazur opened the bedroom door and looked out. "What's going on?" she asked. "Am I missing something?"

The Dougster was fidgeting on the balls of his feet, ready to sprint for the door at the earliest opportunity. The Dougster didn't feel comfortable being in the presence of a vice cop. The Dougster was lacking many of the talents necessary for success as a criminal.

Morelli raised his hands in a symbol of surrender. "I give up," he said. He gave me a perfunctory kiss on the lips and turned to leave.

"Hey, wait," I said. "I need to talk to you." I looked at Mooner. "Alone."

"Sure," Mooner said. "No problemo. We appreciate the sage advice on the pharmaceutical issue. Me and the Dougster will have to research other avenues of employment for him."

"I'm going back to bed," Grandma said when Mooner and Dougie left. "This doesn't look too interesting. I liked it better the other night when you were on the floor with the bounty hunter."

Morelli gave me the same kind of look Desi always gave Lucy when she'd just done something incredibly stupid.

"It's a long story," I said.

"I bet."

"You probably don't want to hear the whole, boring story right now," I said.

"I think it sounds like it might be entertaining. Is that how your security chain got destroyed?"

"No, Morris Munson did that."

"Busy night."

I gave a sigh and sank back down onto the couch.

Morelli slouched into a chair across from me. "Well?"

"You know anything about rugs?"

"I know they go on the floor."

I told him Mooner's story about the million-dollar rug.

"Maybe it wasn't the rug that was worth a million dollars," Morelli said. "Maybe there was something inside the rug."

"Such as?"

Morelli just looked at me.

I did some out-loud questioning. "What's small enough to fit in a rug? Drugs?"

"I saw a segment of the security tape from the Ramos fire," Morelli said. "Homer Ramos was carrying a gym bag when he walked past the hidden camera the night he met Ranger. And Ranger was carrying the bag when he left. Word on the street is that Arturo Stolle is missing a load of money and wants to talk to Ranger. What do you think?"

"I think maybe Stolle gives Ramos drugs. Ramos passes the drugs on to be cut and distributed and ends up with a gym bag filled with money, some or all of which might belong to Stolle. Something happens between Ranger and Homer Ramos, and Ranger gets the bag."

"And if that's the way it went down, then probably this was an extracurricular activity for Homer Ramos," Morelli said. "Drugs, extortion, and numbers go to organized crime. Guns go to the Ramos family. Alexander Ramos has always respected that."

Except, in Trenton, it was more like *dis*organized crime. Trenton fell right in the middle of New York and Philadelphia. No one cared a whole lot about Trenton. Mostly Trenton had a bunch of middle-management guys who spent their days running numbers through social clubs. The numbers money helped give stability to the drug trade. And the drugs were distributed by black street gangs that had names like the Corleones. If it wasn't for the *Godfather* movies and PBS specials on crime, probably no one in Trenton would know how to act or what to call themselves.

So now I was getting a better picture of why Alexander Ramos might be disenchanted with his son. The question still being, Was he disenchanted enough to have him killed? And maybe I had a reason for Arturo Stolle to be looking for Ranger.

"All this is speculation," Morelli said. "Just conversation."

"You never share police information with me. Why are you telling me this?"

"This isn't exactly police information. This is loose change rattling around in my head. I've been watching Stolle for a long time without much luck. Maybe this is the break I've been waiting for. I need to talk to Ranger, but I can't get him to call me back. So I'm passing this on to you, and you can feed it to Ranger."

I nodded. "I'll give him the message."

"No details on the phone."

"Understood."

"How'd it go with Gilman?"

Morelli grinned. "Let me guess. Your finger accidentally hit the redial button on the phone."

"All right, I admit it, I'm nosy."

"Crimes R Us is having some organizational problems. I noticed an increase in traffic going in and out of the social clubs, so I expressed some concern to Vito. So Vito sent Terry to assure me the boys weren't stockpiling nuclear arms for World War III."

"I saw Terry on Wednesday. She delivered a letter to Hannibal Ramos."

"Crimes R Us and Guns R Us are attempting to reestablish boundaries. Homer Ramos tore down some fences, and now that he's out of the picture, the fences need to be repaired." Morelli nudged my foot with his. "Well?"

"Well, what?"

"How about it?"

I was so tired my lips were numb, and Morelli wanted to fool around. "Sure," I said. "Just let me rest my eyes for a minute."

I closed my eyes, and when I woke up it was morning. Morelli was nowhere to be seen.

"I'm late," Grandma said, trotting from the bedroom to the kitchen. "I overslept. It's all those interruptions every night. This place is like Grand Central Station. I got my last driving lesson in a half-hour. And then tomorrow I take my test. I was hoping you could take me for it. First thing in the morning."

"Sure. I could do that."

"And then I'm moving out. Nothin' personal, but you live in a loony bin."

"Where will you go?"

"I'm going back with your mother. Your father deserves to have to put up with me, anyway."

It was Sunday, and Grandma always went to church on Sunday morning. "What about church today?"

"No time for church. God's just gonna have to make do without me today. Anyway, your mother will be there representing the family."

My mother always represented the family, because my father never went to church. My father stayed home and waited for the white bakery bag to arrive. For as long as I can remember, every Sunday morning, my mother went to church and stopped at the bakery on the way home. Every Sunday morning my mother bought jelly doughnuts. Nothing but jelly doughnuts. Cookies, coffee cakes, and cannoli were bought on weekdays. Sunday was jelly doughnut day. It was like taking communion. I'm a Catholic by birth, but in my own personal religion, the Trinity will forever be the Father, the Son, and the Holy Jelly Doughnut.

I clipped the leash onto Bob's collar and took him out for a walk. The air was cool, and the sky was blue. Spring felt like it wasn't too far away. I didn't see Habib and Mitchell in the parking lot. Guess they didn't work on Sunday. I didn't see Joyce Barnhardt, either. That was a relief.

Grandma was gone when I got back, and the apartment was blissfully quiet. I fed Bob. I drank a glass of orange juice. And I crawled under the quilt. I woke up at one o'clock, and I thought about my conversation with Morelli the night before. I'd held out on Morelli. I hadn't told him I'd seen Ranger leaving Hannibal's town house. I wondered if Morelli had kept information from me, too. Chances were good that he had. Our professional relationship had a whole other set of rules from our personal relationship. Morelli had set the tone from the very beginning. There were cop things he just didn't share. The personal rules were still evolving. He had his. And I had mine. Once in a while we agreed. A while ago we'd had a short fling at living together, but Morelli wasn't comfortable with commitment, and I wasn't comfortable with confinement. So we separated.

I heated up a can of chicken noodle soup and called Morelli. "Sorry about last night," I said.

"At first I was afraid you'd died."

"I was tired."

"I figured that out."

"Grandma's gone for the day, and I have some work to do. I was wondering if you'd baby-sit Bob for me."

"For how long?' Morelli asked. "A day? A year?"

"A couple hours."

I called Lula next. "I need to do some breaking and entering. Want to come along?"

"Hell, yes. Nothing I like better than illegal entry."

I dropped Bob off and gave Morelli instructions. "Keep your eye on him. He eats everything."

"Maybe we should make him a cop," Morelli said. "What's his liquor capacity?"

Lula was waiting on her stoop when I drove up. She was discreetly dressed in poison green spandex pants and a shocking pink faux-fur jacket. You could stand her on a corner, in a fog, at midnight, and she'd be visible for three miles.

"Nice outfit," I said.

"I wanted to look hot in case I got arrested. You know how they take your picture, and all." She buckled herself in and looked over at me. "You're gonna be sorry you wore that drab-ass shirt. It's not gonna show up. And for that matter, you didn't even mousse your hair. What kind of Jersey hair is that?"

"I'm not planning on getting arrested."

"You never know. Doesn't hurt to take some precaution and add a little extra eyeliner. Who we breaking in on, anyway?"

"Hannibal Ramos."

"Say what? You mean like the brother of the dead Homer Ramos? And the number one son of the Gun King, Alexander Ramos? Are you freakin' nuts?"

"He's probably not home."

"How are you gonna find out?"

"I'm going to ring his doorbell."

"And if he answers?"

"I'll ask him if he's seen my cat."

"Uh-oh," Lula said. "You don't have a cat."

All right, so it was a little lame. It was the best I could come up with. I was betting Hannibal wasn't home. I didn't hear Ranger yodel good-bye to anyone last night. I didn't notice lights on after he left.

"What are you looking for?" Lula asked. "Or do you just want to die young?"

"I'll know it when I see it," I said. At least I hoped so.

The truth is, I didn't want to think too hard about what I was looking for. I was half afraid it'd incriminate Ranger. He'd asked me to watch Hannibal's house, and then he'd gone snooping without me. Made me feel just a tad left out. And it had me a little worried. What had he been looking for in Hannibal's house? For that matter, what was he looking for at the Deal house? I suspected my window- and door-counting expedition had given him information he needed to break in to the building. What on earth could be in there to warrant taking such a risk?

Ranger, the Man of Mystery, was okay when everything was going just fine. But I was involved in something serious here, and I was thinking that the constant mystery surrounding Ranger was getting old. I wanted to know what was going on. And I wanted some assurance that Ranger was on the right side of the law on this one. I mean, who *was* this guy?

Lula and I stood on the sidewalk and studied Hannibal's house. Drapes still drawn. Very quiet. The houses on either side of Hannibal were quiet, too. Sunday afternoon. Everyone was out at the mall.

"You sure this is the right address?" Lula asked. "This don't look like no big-ass arms-dealer house. I was expecting something like the Taj Mahal. Like where the Donald lives."

"Donald Trump doesn't live in the Taj Mahal."

"He does when he's in Atlantic City. This turkey don't even have no gun turrets. What kind of arms dealer is he, anyway?"

"Low profile."

"Fuckin' A."

I approached the door and rang the bell.

"Low profile or not," Lula said, "if he answers

I'm gonna mess my pants."

I tried the handle, but the door was locked.

I looked to Lula. "You can pick a lock, right?"

"Hell, yes. They don't make the lock I can't pick. Only I didn't bring my whatchamacallit."

"Your lock-picking thing?"

"That's it. And anyway, what about the alarm system?"

"I have a feeling the alarm system isn't working." And if it is, we run like hell when we set it off.

We walked back to the sidewalk, around the block, and got on the bike path from one street over, just in case someone was watching. We walked to Hannibal's privacy fence and let ourselves in through the gate, which was now unlocked.

"You been here before?" Lula asked.

"Yep."

"What happened?"

"He shot at me."

"Hunh," Lula said.

I put my hand to the patio door and shoved. The door was unlocked.

"You may as well go first," Lula said. "I know how you like to do that."

I pulled the curtain aside and stepped into Hannibal's house.

"It's dark in here," Lula said. "This guy must be a vampire."

I turned and looked at her.

"Uh-oh," she said. "I just scared myself."

"He's not a vampire. He keeps his drapes drawn so no one can look in. I'll do a preliminary check to make sure the house is empty. And then I'll go room by room and see if anything interesting turns up. I want you down here doing lookout."

ELEVEN

The first floor was clear. The basement rooms were clear, too. Hannibal had a small utility room down there, and a larger game room with a large-screen television, a billiard table, and a wet bar. It occurred to me that someone could be in the basement, watching television, and the house would appear dark and unlived-in. There were three bedrooms on the second floor. Also empty of human beings. One bedroom was obviously the master bedroom. Another had been converted into an office, with built-in bookshelves and a large leather-topped desk. And the third bedroom was a guest room. It was the guest room that caught my interest. It looked as if someone was living in it. Bed linens rumpled. Men's clothes draped over a chair. Shoes kicked off in a corner of the room.

I rifled the drawers and closet, checking pockets for something that might identify the guest. Nothing to be found. The clothes were expensive. I guessed their owner to be average height and build, under six feet and probably around 180 pounds. I checked the trousers against the trousers in the master bedroom. Hannibal had a larger waist size and his taste was more conservative. Hannibal's bath was attached to the master bedroom. The guest bathroom was off the hall. Neither held any surprises, with the possible exception of condoms in the guest bathroom. The guest had expected to see some action.

I moved to the office, scanning the bookshelves first. Biographies, an atlas, some fiction. I sat at his desk. No Rolodex or address book. There was a notepad and pen. No messages. A laptop computer. I turned it on. Nothing on the desktop. Everything on the hard drive was benign. Hannibal was *very* careful. I turned the computer off and went through his drawers. Again, nothing. Hannibal was neat. His clutter was minimal. I wondered if his suite at the shore was like this, too.

The guy in the guest room wasn't nearly so neat. His desk, wherever it was, would be a mess.

I hadn't found any weapons in the upstairs rooms. Since I knew, firsthand, that Hannibal had at least one gun, this probably meant he had the gun with him. Hannibal didn't seem like the kind of guy to leave his armaments in the cookie jar.

I went to the basement next. Not much to investigate down there.

"This is disappointing," I said to Lula, closing the basement door behind me. "There's nothing here."

"I couldn't find anything on this floor, either," Lula said. "No matchbooks from bars, no guns stuck under the couch cushions. There's some food in the refrigerator. Beer, juice, loaf of bread, and some cold cuts. There's some cans of soda, too. That's about it."

I went to the refrigerator and looked at the wrapper on the cold cuts. They'd been bought at the Shop Rite two days earlier. "This is really creepy," I said to Lula. "Someone's living in this house." And my unspoken thought was that they could be home any minute.

"Yeah, and he don't know much about cold cuts," Lula said. "He got turkey breast and Swiss cheese when he could have got salami and provolone."

We were in the kitchen, looking in the refrigerator and not paying a lot of attention to what was happening in front of the house. There was the sound of a lock clicking open, and Lula and I both stood up straight.

"Uh-oh," Lula said.

The door opened. Cynthia Lotte stepped into the room and squinted at us in the dim light. "What the hell are you doing here?" she asked.

Lula and I were speechless.

"Tell her," Lula said, giving me an elbow. "Tell her what we're doing here."

"Never mind what we're doing here," I said. "What are *you* doing here?"

"None of your business. And anyway, I have a key, so obviously I belong here."

Lula hauled out a Glock. "Well, I got a gun, so I guess that one-ups you."

Cynthia whipped a .45 out of her purse. "I've got a gun, too. We're even."

They both turned to me.

"I've got a gun at home," I said. "I forgot to bring it."

"That doesn't count," Cynthia said.

"It counts for something," Lula said. "It isn't like she don't have a gun at all. And besides, she's wicked when she got the gun. She killed a man, once."

"I remember reading about it. Dickie almost went into cardiac arrest. He thought it reflected badly."

"Dickie's a hemorrhoid," I said.

Cynthia smiled without humor. "All men are hemorrhoids." She looked around the apartment. "I used to come here with Homer when Hannibal was out of town."

That explained the key. And maybe the condoms in the bathroom. "Did Homer keep clothes in the guest room?"

"A couple shirts. Some underwear."

"There are clothes, upstairs, in the guest room. Maybe you could take a look and tell me if they're Homer's."

"First, I want to know what you're doing here."

"A friend of mine is a possible suspect for the fire and shooting. I'm trying to get a fix on what actually happened."

"And you're thinking, what? That Hannibal killed his brother?"

"I don't know. I'm fishing."

Cynthia headed for the stairs. "Let me tell you about Homer. Everyone wanted to kill Homer. Including me. Homer was a lying, cheating worm. His family was always bailing him out. If I was Hannibal, I'd have shot Homer a long time ago, but the Ramos family ties are strong."

We followed her up the stairs to the guest room and waited at the door while she went in and looked around.

"Some of these are definitely Homer's," she said, going through the drawers. "And some I've never seen before now." She kicked at a pair of red silk paisley boxers lying on the floor. "You see these boxers?" She took aim and fired five rounds into the shorts. "These were Homer's."

"Dang," Lula said. "Don't hold back."

"He could be very charming," Cynthia said. "But he had a short attention span when it came to women. I thought he was in love with me. I thought I could change him."

"What happened to make you think otherwise?"

"Two days before he was shot he told me the relationship was over. He said some very unflattering things to me, told me if I gave him any trouble he'd kill me, and then he cleaned out my jewelry box and took my car. He said he needed money."

"Did you report him to the police?"

"No. I believed him when he said he'd kill me."
She shoved her gun into her jacket pocket.
"Anyway, I got to thinking that Homer might not
have had a chance to fence my jewelry . . . that he
might have stashed it here."

"I've been through the whole house," I said,
"and I didn't see any women's jewelry, but you're
welcome to look for yourself."

She shrugged. "It was a long shot. I should
have checked sooner."

"Weren't you afraid you'd run into Hannibal?"
Lula asked.

"I was counting on Alexander being here for
the funeral, and Hannibal being in residence at
the shore house."

We all trooped downstairs.

"What about the garage?" Cynthia asked. "Did
you look in there? I don't suppose you found my
silver Porsche."

"Damn," Lula said, all impressed. "You drive a
Porsche?"

"I used to. Homer gave it to me for our six-
month anniversary." She sighed. "Like I said,
Homer could be very charming."

"Charming" being synonymous with "generous."

Hannibal had a two-car garage that attached to
the house. The door to the garage was off the
foyer and was locked with a slide bolt. Cynthia
opened the door and flicked the light on in the
garage. And there it was . . . the silver Porsche.

"My Porsche! My Porsche!" Cynthia yelped.

"I never thought I'd see it again." She stopped yelping and wrinkled her nose. "What's that smell?"

Lula and I looked at each other. We knew the smell.

"Uh-oh," Lula said.

Cynthia ran to the car. "I hope he left me the keys. I hope —" She stopped short and looked in the car window. "Someone's sleeping in my car."

Lula and I grimaced.

And Cynthia started screaming. "He's dead! He's dead! He's dead in my Porsche!"

Lula and I approached the car and looked inside.

"Yep. He's dead all right," Lula said. "The giveaway is those three holes in his forehead. You're lucky," she told Cynthia. "Looks like this guy bought it with a twenty-two. If he'd been shot with a forty-five there'd be brains all over the place. A twenty-two goes in and rattles around like PacMan."

It was hard to tell with him slumped over on the seat, but he looked about five ten and maybe fifty pounds overweight. Dark hair, cut short. Mid-forties. Dressed in a knit shirt and sports coat. Diamond pinky ring. Three holes in his head.

"Do you recognize him?" I asked Cynthia.

"No. I never saw him before. This is terrible. How could this happen? There's blood on my upholstery."

"It's not so bad, considering he took three to the head," Lula said. "Just don't use hot water on it. Hot water sets blood."

Cynthia had the door open and was trying to wrestle the dead guy out of the car, but the dead guy wasn't cooperating. "I could use some help, here," Cynthia said. "Someone go around to the other side and push."

"Hey, wait a minute," I said. "This is a crime scene. You should leave everything alone."

"The hell I will," Cynthia said. "This is my car, and I'm driving away with it. I work for a lawyer. I know what happens. They'll impound this car until the world comes to an end. And then his wife'll probably get it." She had the body halfway out, but the legs were stiff and wouldn't unbend.

"We need Siegfried and Roy here," Lula said. "I saw them on television, and they sliced someone in half, and they didn't even make a mess."

Cynthia had the guy by the head, hoping for some leverage. "His foot is stuck around the gear shift," she said. "Someone give his foot a kick."

"Don't look at me," Lula said. "Dead people give me the creeps. I'm not touching no dead person."

Cynthia grabbed his jacket and pulled. "This is impossible. I'm never going to get this idiot out of my car."

"Maybe if you greased him up," Lula said.

"Maybe if you *helped*," Cynthia said. "Go around to the other side and put your foot to his ass while Stephanie helps me pull."

"Long as it's only my foot," Lula said. "Guess I could do that."

Cynthia got the guy's head in a hammerlock, and I grabbed hold of his shirtfront, and Lula pushed him out with one good shove.

We instantly dropped him and stepped back.

"Who do you think killed him?" I asked. Not actually expecting an answer.

"Homer, of course," Cynthia said.

I shook my head. "He hasn't been dead long enough for it to have been Homer."

"Hannibal?"

"Don't think Hannibal would leave a body in his own garage."

"Well, I don't care who killed him," Cynthia said. "I got the Porsche, and I'm going home."

The dead guy was lying in a heap on the floor, legs bent at odd angles, hair mussed, shirt out.

"What about him?" I asked. "We can't just leave him like this. He looks so . . . uncomfortable."

"It's his legs," Lula said. "They froze up in a seated position." She pulled a lawn chair off a stack at the back of the garage and set the chair next to the dead guy. "If we put him in a chair he'll look more natural, like he was waiting for a ride or something."

So we picked him up, set him into the chair, and backed away to take a look. Only, when we backed away, he fell out of the chair. *Smash*, right on his face.

"Good thing he's dead," Lula said, "or that would have hurt like the devil."

We heaved him back into the chair and this time we wrapped a bungee cord around him. His nose was a little smashed and one eye had been jarred closed from the impact when he fell, so one was open and one was closed, but aside from that he looked okay. We backed away again, and he stayed in place.

"I'm outta here," Cynthia said. She rolled all the windows down in the car, hit the garage-door opener, backed out, and took off down the street.

The garage door slid closed, and Lula and I were left with the dead guy.

Lula shifted foot to foot. "Think we should say something over the deceased? I don't like to disrespect the dead."

"I think we should get the hell out of here."

"Amen," Lula said, and she made the sign of the cross.

"I thought you were Baptist."

"Yeah, but we don't got any hand signals for an occasion like this."

We vacated the garage, peeked out the back window to make sure no one was around, and scurried out the patio door. We closed the gate behind us and walked the bike path to the car.

"I don't know about you," Lula said, "but I'm gonna go home and stand in the shower for a couple hours, and then I'm gonna rinse myself off with Clorox."

That sounded like a good plan. Especially since a shower would give me a chance to put off seeing Morelli. I mean, what would I say to him?

"Guess what, Joe, I broke into Hannibal Ramos's house today and found a dead guy. Then I destroyed the crime scene, helped a woman remove evidence, and left. So, if you still find me attractive after ten years in jail . . ." Not to mention, this was the second time Ranger had been seen walking away from a homicide.

By the time I got home I had all the makings of a bad mood. I'd gone to Hannibal's town house looking for information. Now I had more information than I really wanted to have, and I didn't know what any of it meant. I paged Ranger and made lunch, which in my distracted state consisted of olives. Again.

I took the phone into the bathroom with me while I showered. I changed clothes, dried my hair, and gave my lashes a couple swipes of mascara. I was contemplating eyeliner when Ranger called.

"I want to know what's going on," I said. "I just found a dead guy in Hannibal's garage."

"And?"

"And I want to know who he is. And I want to know who killed him. And I want to know what you were doing sneaking out of Hannibal's town house last night."

I could feel the force of Ranger's personality at the other end of the line. "You don't need to know any of those things."

"The hell I don't. I just involved myself in a murder."

"You happened on a crime scene. That's different from being involved in a murder. Have you called the police yet?"

"No."

"It would be a good idea to call the police. And you might want to be vague about the breaking-and-entering part."

"I might want to be vague about a lot of things."

"Your call," Ranger said.

"You have a rotten attitude!" I yelled at him over the phone. "I'm fed up with this Mysterious Ranger thing. You have a problem sharing, do you know that? One day you have your hands up my shirt, and next day you're telling me nothing's any of my business. I don't even know where you live."

"If you don't know anything, you can't pass anything on."

"Thanks for the vote of confidence."

"It's the way it is," Ranger said.

"And another thing, Morelli wants you to call him. He's been watching somebody for a long time, and now you're involved with this some-body, and Morelli thinks you could be of some help to him."

"Later," Ranger said. And he hung up.

Fine. If that's the way he wants it, then that's just peachy fine.

I huffed off to the kitchen, got my gun out of the cookie jar, grabbed my shoulder bag, and stomped down the hall, down the stairs, through the lobby to the Buick. Joyce was parked in the lot, in the car with the crumpled bumper. She saw me come out of the building and gave me the finger. I gave it back to her and took off for Morelli's house. Joyce was following one car length behind. Okay by me. She could follow me all she wanted today. As far as I was concerned Ranger was on his own. I was taking myself out of the picture.

Morelli and Bob were sitting side by side on the couch, watching ESPN, when I came in. There was an empty Pino's Pizza box on the coffee table, an empty container of ice cream and a couple crushed beer cans.

"Lunch?" I asked.

"Bob was hungry. And don't worry, he didn't get any beer." Morelli patted the seat next to him. "There's room for you, here."

When Morelli was being a cop, his brown eyes were hard and assessing, his face was lean and angular, and the scar that sliced through his right eyebrow gave the correct impression that Morelli had never lived a cautious life. When he was feeling sexy, his brown eyes were molten chocolate, his mouth softened, and the scar gave the mistaken impression that he might need a teensy bit of mothering.

And right now, Morelli was feeling *very* sexy. And I was feeling very *un*sexy. In fact, I was feeling absolutely grumpy. I plopped myself down on the couch and scowled at the empty pizza box, remembering my lunch of olives.

Morelli slid his arm around my shoulders and

nuzzled my neck. "Alone at last," he said.

"I have something to tell you."

Morelli went still.

"I sort of happened on a dead guy today."

He slouched back on the couch. "I have a girl-friend who finds dead guys. Why me?"

"You sound like my mother."

"I feel like your mother."

"Well, don't," I snapped. "I don't even like when my *mother* feels like my mother."

"I suppose you want to tell me about this."

"Hey, if you don't want to hear it, that's no problem. I can just call it in to the station."

He sat up straighter. "You haven't called it in? Oh shit, let me guess: you broke into someone's house and stumbled onto a homicide."

"Hannibal's house."

Morelli was on his feet. *"Hannibal's house?"*

"But I didn't break in. His back door was open."

"What the hell were you doing walking into Hannibal's house?" he yelled. "What were you thinking?"

I was on my feet, too, and I was yelling back. "I was doing my job."

"Breaking and entering isn't your job."

"I told you, it wasn't breaking. It was only en-tering."

"Well, that makes all the difference. Who did you find dead?"

"I don't know. Some guy got whacked in the garage."

Morelli went into the kitchen and dialed dispatch. "I have an anonymous tip here," he said. "Why don't you send someone over to Hannibal Ramos's town house on Fenwood and take a look in the garage. The back door should be open." Morelli hung the phone up and turned to me. "Okay, that's taken care of," he said. "Let's go upstairs."

"Sex, sex, sex," I said. "That's all you ever think about." Although, now that I was rested and had the dead guy off my chest, an orgasm didn't sound like such a bad idea.

Morelli backed me against the wall and leaned into me. "I think about other things besides sex . . . just not lately." He kissed me and put some tongue into it, and the orgasm was sounding better and better.

"Just a quick question about the dead guy," I said. "How long do you think it'll be before they find him?"

"If there's a car in the area, it'll only take five or ten minutes."

Chances were pretty good they'd call Morelli when they took a gander at the guy in the garage. And on my best day, I need more than five minutes. But then probably it would take more than five minutes to get a car to the house, then for the cops to walk to the back and go through to the garage. So, if I didn't waste time taking all my clothes off, and we got right to it, I might be able to do the whole program.

"Why don't we do it here?" I said to Morelli,

popping the top snap on his Levi's. "Kitchens are so sexy."

"Hold on," he said. "I'll pull the blinds."

I kicked my shoes off and shucked my jeans. "No time for that."

Morelli gave me a long look. "I'm not complaining, but I can't help feeling this is too good to be true."

"You've heard of fast food? This is fast sex."

I wrapped my hand around him, and he sucked in a quick breath. "How fast do you want this to be?" he asked.

The phone rang.

Damn!

Morelli had one hand on the phone and the other on my wrist. After a moment on the phone he cut his eyes to me. "It's Costanza. He was in the neighborhood, so he took the call to check on the Ramos house. He says I've got to come over to see for myself. Something about a guy having a bad hair day, waiting for a bus. At least that's what it sounded like, over the laughter."

I gave him a big shrug and a palms-up. Like, well, gosh, I don't know what he's talking about. Just looked like an ordinary ol' dead guy to me.

"Anything you want to tell me about this?" Morelli asked.

"Not without a lawyer present."

We put our clothes back on, gathered our things, and went to the front door. Bob was still sitting on the couch, watching ESPN.

"It's kind of weird," Morelli said, "but I swear

it's like he's following the game."

"Maybe we should just let him keep watching."

Morelli locked the door behind us. "Listen, cupcake, you tell anybody I let that dog watch ESPN, and I'll get even." His eyes drifted to my car, and then to the car parked behind me. "Is that Joyce?"

"She's following me."

"Want me to give her a ticket for something?"

I gave Morelli a fast kiss and drove off to the food store with Joyce close on my bumper. I didn't have a lot of money and my Visa was maxed, so I just got the essentials: peanut butter, potato chips, bread, beer, Oreos, milk, and two scratch-off lottery tickets.

Next stop was Home Depot, where I got a bolt for the front door to replace the broken security chain. The plan was to trade a beer for the bolt-installing expertise of my building super and good buddy Dillan Rudick.

After Home Depot I headed back to my apartment. I parked in the lot, locked Big Blue, and waved bye-bye to Joyce. Joyce inserted her thumbnail behind her two front teeth and gave me a genuine Italian gesture.

I stopped off at Dillan's basement apartment and explained my needs. Dillan grabbed his toolbox and we trooped upstairs. He was my age and lived in the bowels of the building, like a mole. He was a really cool guy, but he didn't do much, and as far as I know he didn't have a girlfriend . . . so, as you might expect, he drank a lot of beer. And since he didn't make a lot of money, free beer was always welcome.

I checked my answering machine while Dillan installed my bolt. Five calls for Grandma Mazur, none for me.

Dillan and I were relaxing in front of the television when Grandma came in.

"Boy, did I have a day," Grandma said. "I drove all over, and I almost got the stopping thing figured out." She squinted at Dillan. "And who's this nice young man?"

I introduced Dillan, and then since it was dinnertime I made all of us peanut-butter-and-potato-chip sandwiches. We ate them in front of the television and between Grandma and Dillan, somehow, the six-pack disappeared. Grandma and Dillan were feeling pretty happy, but I was starting to worry about Bob. I was imagining him alone in Morelli's house with nothing to eat but the cardboard pizza box. And the couch. And the bed. And the curtains and rug and Morelli's favorite chair. Then I imagined Morelli shooting Bob, and that wasn't a good picture.

I called Morelli but there was no answer. Rats. I should never have left Bob alone in the house. I had my keys in my hand and was putting my jacket on when Morelli arrived with Bob in tow.

"Going somewhere?" Morelli asked, taking in the keys and jacket.

"I was worried about Bob. I was going to drive over to your house and see if everything was okay."

"I thought maybe you were leaving the country."

I gave him a big fake smile.

Morelli unhooked Bob's leash, said hello to Grandma and Dillan, and dragged me into the kitchen. "I need to talk to you."

I heard a yelp from Dillan and figured Bob was getting acquainted.

"I'm armed," I said to Morelli, "so you better be careful. I have a gun in my purse."

Morelli took the purse and threw it across the room.

Uh-oh.

"That was Junior Macaroni in Hannibal's garage," Morelli said. "He works for Stolle. Very weird to find him in Hannibal's garage. And it gets even weirder."

I did a mental grimace.

"Macaroni was sitting in a lawn chair."

"It was Lula's idea," I said. "Well, okay, so it was mine too, but he looked so uncomfortable lying on the cement floor."

Morelli cracked a grin. "I should arrest you for tampering with a crime scene, but he was such a vicious bastard, and he looked so fucking stupid."

"How do you know I wasn't the killer?"

"Because you carry a thirty-eight and he was shot with a twenty-two. And more than that, you couldn't hit a barn at five paces. The only time you ever shot anyone, there was divine intervention."

True.

"How many people know I sat him in the lawn chair?"

"Nobody knows, but about a hundred have guessed. No one will tell." Morelli looked at his watch. "I have to go. I have a meeting set up for tonight."

"This isn't a meeting with Ranger, is it?"

"No."

"Liar."

Morelli pulled a pair of bracelets out of his jacket pocket, and before I realized what was happening I was cuffed to the refrigerator.

"Excuse me?" I said.

"You were going to follow me. I'll leave the key in your mailbox downstairs."

Is this a relationship, or what?

"I'm ready to go," Grandma said.

She was dressed in her purple warm-up suit and white tennies. Her hair was neatly curled, and she was wearing pink lipstick. She had her big black leather purse tucked into the crook of her arm. My fear was that she was packing the long-barrel, and might threaten the DMV guy if he didn't give her a license.

"You don't have your gun in there, do you?" I asked.

"Of course not."

I didn't believe her for a second.

When we got downstairs to the lot, Grandma went to the Buick. "I figure I stand a better chance of getting my license if I'm driving the Buick," she said. "I heard they worry about young chicks in sports cars."

Habib and Mitchell pulled into the lot. They were back in the Lincoln.

"Looks good as new," I said.

Mitchell beamed. "Yeah, they did a great job on it. We just got it this morning. We had to wait for the paint to dry." He looked at Grandma, sitting behind the wheel of the Buick. "What's up for today?"

"I'm taking my grandmother to get her driver's license."

"That's real nice of you," Mitchell said. "You're a good granddaughter, but isn't she kind of old?"

Grandma clamped down on her dentures. "Old?" she yelled. "I'll show you old." I heard her purse click open, and Grandma reached down and came up with the long-barrel. "I'm not too old to shoot you in the eye," she said, leveling the gun.

Mitchell and Habib ducked flat on the seat, out of sight.

I glared at Grandma. "I thought you said you didn't have the gun with you."

"Guess I was wrong."

"Put it away. And you better not threaten anyone at the DMV either, or they'll arrest you."

"Crazy old broad," Mitchell said from low in the Lincoln.

"That's better," Grandma said. "I like being a broad."

TWELVE

I had mixed feelings about Grandma getting her license. On the one hand, I thought it was great that she'd be more independent. On the other hand, I didn't want to be on the road with her. She'd run a red light on the way over, snapped me against my seat belt every time she stopped, and parked in a handicapped spot at the DMV, insisting it went along with joining the AARP.

When Grandma stomped into the waiting room after taking her road test, I immediately knew the streets were safe for a little while longer.

"If that don't tear it," she said. "He didn't pass me on hardly anything."

"You can take the test again," I said.

"Darn right, I can. I'm gonna keep taking it until I pass. I got a God-given right to drive a car." She pressed her lips tight together. "Guess I should have gone to church yesterday."

"Wouldn't have hurt," I said.

"Well, I'm pulling out all the stops next time.

I'm lighting a candle. I'm doing the works."

Mitchell and Habib were still following us, but they were about a quarter-mile back. They'd almost plowed into us several times on the way over when Grandma had stopped short, and they weren't taking any chances on the way home.

"Are you still moving out?" I asked Grandma.

"Yep. I already told your mother. And Louise Greeber is coming over this afternoon to help me. So you don't need to worry about a thing. It was nice of you to let me stay. I appreciate it, but I need my shut-eye. I don't know how you get by on so little sleep."

"Well, okay," I said. "I guess your mind is made up." Maybe I'd light a candle, too.

Bob was waiting for us when we walked in.

"Think Bob needs to do you-know-what," Grandma said.

So Bob and I trooped back down to the parking lot. Habib and Mitchell were sitting there, patiently waiting for me to lead them to Ranger, and now Joyce was there, too. I turned around, went back into the building, and exited the front door. Bob and I walked up the street a block and then cut over, back to a residential neighborhood of small single-family houses. Bob did you-know-what about forty or fifty times in the space of five minutes, and we headed home.

A black Mercedes turned the corner two blocks in front of me, and my heart tripped. The Mercedes drew closer, and my heartbeat stayed erratic. There were only two possibilities: drug dealer and Ranger. The car stopped beside me, and Ranger made a slight head movement that meant, "Get in."

I loaded Bob into the backseat and slid in next to Ranger. "There are three people parked in my lot, hoping to get a shot at you," I said. "What are you doing here?"

"I want to talk to you."

It was one thing to have the skill to break into an apartment; it was something else to be able to divine what I was doing at any given moment in the day. "How did you know I was out with Bob? What are you, psychic?"

"Nothing that exotic. I called, and your grandma told me you were walking the dog."

"Gee, that's disappointing. Next thing you'll be telling me you aren't Superman."

Ranger smiled. "You want me to be Superman? Spend the night with me."

"I think I'm flustered," I told him.

"Cute," Ranger said.

"What did you want to talk to me about?"

"I'm terminating your employment."

The fluster disappeared and was replaced with the seed of an ill-defined emotion that settled in the pit of my stomach. "You and Morelli made a deal, didn't you?"

"We have an understanding."

I was being cut out of the program, shoved aside like unnecessary baggage. Or worse, like a liability. I went from hurt disbelief to total fury in three seconds.

"Was this Morelli's idea?"

"It's my idea. Hannibal has seen you. Alexander has seen you. And now half the police in Trenton know you broke into Hannibal's house and found Junior Macaroni in the garage."

"Did you hear that from Morelli?"

"I heard it from *everyone*. My answering machine ran out of space. It's just too dangerous for you to stay on the case. I'm afraid Hannibal will put it together and come after you."

"This is depressing."

"Did you really sit him up in a lawn chair?"

"Yes. And by the way, did you kill him?"

"No. The Porsche wasn't in the garage when I went through the house. And neither was Macaroni."

"How did you get past the alarm system?"

"Same way you did. The alarm wasn't set." He looked at his watch. "I have to go."

I opened the passenger door and turned to leave.

Ranger caught hold of my wrist. "You're not especially good at following instructions, but you're going to listen to me on this, right? You're going to walk away. And you're going to be careful."

I gave a sigh, heaved myself out the door, and extracted Bob from the backseat. "Just make sure you don't let Joyce catch you. That would really ruin my day."

I deposited Bob in the apartment, grabbed my car keys and my shoulder bag, and went back downstairs. I was going somewhere. *Anywhere.* I was too bummed to stay at home. Truth is, I wasn't all that upset about my employment being terminated. I just hated it being terminated for stupidity. I'd fallen out of a tree, for God's sake. And then I'd sat Junior Macaroni in a chair. I mean, how inept can a person get?

I needed food, I thought. Ice cream. And hot fudge. Whipped cream. There was an ice cream parlor at the mall that constructed sundaes for four people. That's what I needed. A mega sundae.

I got into Big Blue, and Mitchell got in with me.

"Excuse me?" I said. "Is this a date?"

"You wish," Mitchell said. "Mr. Stolle wants to talk to you."

"Guess what. I'm not in the mood to talk to Mr. Stolle. I'm not in the mood to talk to *anyone,* you included. So I hope you don't take this personally, but get out of my car."

Mitchell drew his gun. "You should change your mood."

"You'd shoot me?"

"Don't take it personally," Mitchell said.

Art's Carpets is in Hamilton Township, the land of the strip mall. It's on Route 33, not far from Five Points, and is indistinguishable from every other business on that road, save for its glowing chartreuse sign, which can be seen clearly from Rhode Island. The building is a single-story cinder-block with large storefront windows, heralding a year-round sale. I'd been to Art's Carpets many times, along with every other man, woman, and child in New Jersey. I'd never purchased anything, but I'd been tempted. Art's has good prices.

I parked the Buick in front of the store. Habib pulled the Lincoln in alongside the Buick. And Joyce parked beside the Lincoln.

"What does Stolle want?" I asked. "He doesn't want to kill me or anything, does he?"

"Mr. Stolle don't kill people. He hires people to do that stuff. He just wants to talk to you. That's all he told me."

There were a couple women browsing in the store. Looked like mother and daughter. A salesman hovered over them. Mitchell and I walked in together, and Mitchell guided me through the stacks of carpet and displays of broadloom to the office at the back.

Stolle was in his mid-fifties and built solid. He was barrel-chested and had begun to jowl. He was dressed in a flashy sweater and dress slacks. He extended his hand and smiled his best rug-merchant smile.

"I'll be right outside," Mitchell said, and closed the door, leaving me alone with Stolle.

"You're supposed to be a pretty smart girl," Stolle said. "I've heard some things about you."

"Uh-huh."

"So how come you're not having any luck delivering Manoso?"

"I'm not *that* smart. And Ranger's not going to

come near me when Habib and Mitchell are around."

Stolle smiled. "To tell you the truth, I never expected you to hand us Manoso. But hell, nothing ventured, nothing gained, right?"

I didn't say anything.

"Unfortunately, since we couldn't do this the easy way, we're going to have to try something else. We're sending a message to your boyfriend. He doesn't want to talk to me? Fine. He wants to be in the wind? That's okay. You know why? Because we got you. When I run out of patience, and I'm just about there, we're gonna hurt you. And Manoso's gonna know he could have prevented it."

All of a sudden I didn't have any air in my lungs. I hadn't thought of this angle. "He's not my boyfriend," I said. "You're overestimating my importance to him."

"Maybe, but he has a sense of chivalry. Latin temperament, you know." Stolle sat in the chair behind his desk and rocked back. "You should encourage Manoso to talk to us. Mitchell and Habib look like nice guys, but they'll do whatever I tell them. In fact, in the past, they've done some very mean things. You have a dog, don't you?" Stolle leaned forward, hands on desk. "Mitchell's real good at killing dogs. Not that he'd kill *your* dog . . ."

"He's not my dog. I'm baby-sitting."

"I was just giving an example."

"You're wasting your time," I said. "Ranger is

a mercenary. You can't get to him through me. We don't have that kind of relationship. Maybe no one has that kind of relationship with him."

Stolle smiled and shrugged. "Like I said before, nothing ventured, nothing gained. It's worth a try, right?"

I looked at him for a beat, giving him my inscrutable Plum glare, and then I turned and left.

Mitchell and Habib and Joyce were idling when I walked out of the store.

I got in the Buick and discreetly felt my crotch to make sure I hadn't wet my pants. I took a deep breath and put my hands on the wheel. Breathe in, breathe out. Breathe in, breathe out. I wanted to put the key in the ignition, but I couldn't get my hands to unclench the wheel. I did some more breathing. I told myself Arturo Stolle was a big bag of wind. But I didn't believe it. What I believed was that Arturo Stolle was a real piece of crapola. And it didn't look like Habib and Mitchell were all that great, either.

Everyone was watching, waiting to see what I'd do next. I didn't want anyone to know I was scared, so I forced myself to release the wheel and start the car. I very carefully backed out of the parking place, put the car in gear, and drove away. I concentrated on my driving, slow and steady.

While I drove I dialed every number I had for Ranger, leaving a terse message: *Call me. Now.* After I ran through Ranger's numbers I called Carol Zabo.

"I need a favor," I said.

"Anything."

"I'm being followed by Joyce Barnhardt —"

"Evil bitch," Carol said.

"And I'm also being followed by two guys in a Lincoln."

"Hmm."

"Not to worry — they've been following me for days, and so far they haven't shot anybody." So far. "Anyway, I need to discourage them from following me, and I have a plan."

I was about five minutes away from Carol. She lived in the Burg, not far from my parents. She and Lubie had bought a house with their wedding money and had immediately set to work building a family. They'd decided to call it quits after two boys. Good thing for the world. Carol's kids were the scourge of the neighborhood. When they grew up they'd probably be cops.

Burg backyards are long and narrow. Many are enclosed in fencing of some sort. Most back up to an alley. All alleys are one lane wide. The alley servicing the houses on Reed Street, between Beal and Cedar, was especially long. I asked Carol to idle at the juncture of Cedar and the Reed Street alley. The plan was that I'd lead Joyce and the Boobie Boys down the alley, and then as soon as I turned onto Cedar, Carol would ease up and block the alley, feigning car trouble.

I got to the Burg and wandered around for another five minutes, giving Carol some extra time to get into position. Then I turned into the Reed Street alley, sucking Joyce and the goons right along with me. I got to Cedar and sure enough, there was Carol. I wheeled around her, she moved forward and stopped, and everyone was trapped. I glanced back to see what was happening and saw Carol and three other women get out of Carol's car. Monica Kajewski, Gail Wojohowitz, and Angie Bono. Every one of them hated Joyce Barnhardt. Rumble in the Burg!

I went straight to Broad and headed for the shore. I wasn't going to sit around and wait for Mitchell to kill Bob to make a point. Bob today . . . me tomorrow.

I rolled into Deal and slowly drove past the Ramos compound. I tried again to reach Ranger by cell phone. No response. I continued to cruise the street. Come on, Ranger. Look out the window, wherever the hell you are. I was a block past the pink house, getting ready to make a U-turn, when the passenger door was yanked open and Alexander Ramos jumped in.

"Hey, cutie," he said. "Just can't stay away, huh?"

Shit! I didn't want him in my car now!

"Good thing I saw you. I was going nuts in there," he said.

"Jesus," I said. "Why don't you get a patch?"

"I don't want a goddamn patch. I want a cigarette. Drive me to the store. And hurry up, I'm dying."

"There are cigarettes in the glove compartment. You left them here last time."

He pulled the pack out and stuck a cigarette in his mouth.

"Not in the car!"

"Christ, this is like being married without the sex. Go to Sal's."

I didn't want to go to Sal's. I wanted to talk to Ranger. "Aren't you afraid you'll be missed at the house? Are you sure it's safe to go to Sal's?"

"Yeah. There's this problem in Trenton, and everybody's busy trying to fix it."

Like, could the problem be a dead guy in Hannibal's garage? "Must be *some* problem," I said. "Maybe you should be helping."

"I already helped. I'm putting the problem on a boat next week. With any luck, the boat will sink."

Okay, now I'm stumped. I don't know how they're going to get the dead guy on a boat. I don't know why they'd *want* to put the dead guy on a boat.

Since I wasn't having any luck getting Ramos out of my car, I drove the short distance to Sal's, and we went inside and took a table. Ramos slugged back a shot and lit up. "I'm going back to Greece next week," he said. "You want to go back with me? We could get married."

"I thought you were through with marriage."

"I changed my mind."

"I'm flattered, but I don't think so."

He shrugged and poured out another shot. "Suit yourself."

"This problem in Trenton — is it business?"

"Business. Personal. It's all the same for me. Let me give you some advice. Don't have kids. And if you want to make a good living, guns are the way to go. That's all my advice."

My cell phone rang.

"What's going on?" Ranger said.

"I can't talk now."

His voice was unusually tight. "Tell me you're not with Ramos."

"I can't tell you that. Why didn't you return my call?"

"I had to turn my phone off for a while. I just got back, and Tank said he saw you pick Ramos up."

"It wasn't my fault! I was down here looking for you."

"Well, you'd better be well hidden, because three cars just left the compound, and my guess is they're looking for Alexander."

I flipped the phone shut and dropped it into my purse. "I have to go," I told Ramos.

"That was your boyfriend, right? He sounds like a real asshole. I could have him taken care of, if you know what I mean."

I flipped a twenty onto the table and grabbed the bottle of booze. "Come on," I said, "we can take this with us."

Ramos looked over my shoulder to the door. "Oh Christ, look who's here."

I was afraid to look.

"It's my baby-sitters," Alexander said. "Can't

even wipe my ass without an audience."

I turned and almost passed out with relief that it wasn't Hannibal. They were both in their late forties, dressed in suits. They looked like they ate a lot of pasta, and probably didn't refuse dessert either.

"They need you back at the house," one of the men said.

"I'm with my lady friend," Alexander said.

"Yeah, but maybe you could see her some other time. We still can't find that cargo that's going on the boat."

One of them walked Alexander out the door, and the other stayed behind to talk to me.

"Listen," he said, "it's not nice to take advantage of an old man like this. Don't you have any friends your own age?"

"I'm not taking advantage of him. He jumped into my car."

"I know. He does that sometimes." The guy pulled a money clip out of his pocket and peeled off a hundred. "Here, this is for your inconvenience."

I took a step back. "You've got this all wrong."

"Okay, what'll it take?" He peeled off nine more hundreds, folded them together, and dropped them into my bag. "I don't want to hear nothing more from you. And you gotta promise to leave the old man alone. Understand?"

"Hold on here —"

He swept his jacket aside to show me his gun.

"Now I understand," I said.

He turned and walked out the door and got into the Town Car idling at curbside. The car took off.

"Life can be pretty strange," I said to the bartender. Then I left, too. When I was sufficiently far away from Deal to feel safe, I redialed Ranger and told him about Stolle.

"I want you to go home and lock yourself in your apartment," Ranger said. "I'm going to send Tank to pick you up."

"And then what?"

"Then I'm putting you someplace safe until I can straighten this out."

"I don't think so."

"Don't give me a hard time on this," Ranger said. "I've got enough problems."

"Well, solve your damn problems. And solve them fast!" And I disconnected. Okay, so I lost it. I'd had a stressful day.

Mitchell and Habib were waiting for me when I pulled into my parking lot. I gave them a wave, but I didn't get a wave back. I didn't get a smile. No remarks, either. Not a good sign.

I took the stairs to the second floor and hurried to my door. My stomach was uneasy, and my heart felt fluttery. I stepped into my apartment and felt relief wash over me when Bob bounced over. I locked the door behind me and checked Rex to make sure he was okay, too. I had twelve messages on my machine. One was silence. It felt like Ranger's silence. Ten were for

Grandma. The last one was from my mother.

"We're having fried chicken tonight," she said. "Your grandmother thought you might want to come over, since you don't have any food in your house because Bob ate your groceries while your grandmother was cleaning your cupboards. And your grandmother says you might want to walk him when you get home, because he ate two boxes of prunes she'd just bought."

I looked at Bob. His nose was running and his stomach looked like he'd swallowed a beach ball.

"Jeez, Bob," I said, "you don't look too good."

Bob burped and passed gas.

"Maybe we should go for a walk."

Bob started to pant. Drool dripped onto the floor and thunder rumbled in his stomach. He lurched forward and hunched over.

"No!" I shouted. "Not here!" I grabbed his leash and my shoulder bag and dragged him out of the apartment and down the hall. We didn't wait for the elevator. We took the stairs and ran through the lobby. I got him outside and was about to cross the lot when the Lincoln suddenly screeched to a halt in front of us. Mitchell jumped out of the car, shoved me to the ground, and grabbed Bob.

By the time I'd scrambled to my feet, the Lincoln was in motion. I shrieked and ran after it, but the car was already out of the lot, onto St. James Street. Suddenly it stopped short. The doors were thrown open and Habib and Mitchell jumped out.

"Jesus Christ!" Mitchell yelled. "Goddamn! Son of a bitch!"

Habib had his hand to his mouth. "I am going to be sick. Not even in Pakistan have I seen such a thing as this."

Bob leaped out of the car, tail wagging, and ran to me. His stomach looked nice and slim again, and he wasn't drooling and panting. "Feel better now, fella?" I said, scratching behind his ears just the way he liked it. "Good boy. Good Bob!"

Mitchell's eyes were bugged out of his head and his face was purple. "I'm gonna fucking kill that dog. I'm gonna fucking kill him. You know what he did? He did number two in my car. And then he threw up. What are you feeding him? Don't you know nothing about dogs? What kind of a dog watcher are you?"

"He ate Grandma's prunes," I said.

Mitchell had his hands to his head. "No fucking kidding."

I loaded Bob into Big Blue, locked the doors, and drove over the lawn to the street to avoid Habib and Mitchell.

My mother and grandmother were waiting for me, looking through the glass storm door, when I docked the Buick in front of their house.

"We always know when you're coming to visit," Grandma said. "We can hear this car a mile away."

No fucking kidding.

"Where's your jacket?" my mother wanted to

know. "Aren't you cold?"

"I didn't have time to take a jacket," I said. "It's a long story. Probably you don't want to hear it."

"I want to hear it," Grandma said. "I bet it's a pip."

"I need to make a phone call first."

"You can do that while I put the food on the table," my mother said. "Everything's done."

I used the kitchen phone to call Morelli. "I have a favor to ask," I said when he answered.

"Good. I love when you're indebted to me."

"I'd like you to take care of Bob for a while."

"You aren't pulling a Simon, are you?"

"No!"

"So what's this about?"

"You know how you have police business that you can't explain to me?"

"Yeah."

"Well, I can't explain this to *you*. At least not in my mother's kitchen."

Grandma bustled into the kitchen. "Is that Joseph on the phone? Tell him we have plenty of fried chicken, but he'll have to get a move on if he wants some."

"He doesn't like fried chicken."

"I love fried chicken," Joe said. "I'll be right over."

"No!"

Too late. He'd already disconnected. "Set an extra plate," I said.

Grandma was at the table and looked confused. "Is this extra plate for Bob or Joe?"

"Joe. Bob's stomach is on the blink."

"No wonder," Grandma said. "What with all those prunes. And then he ate a box of Frosted Flakes and a bag of marshmallows. I was cleaning your cupboards while I waited for Louise to come over, and I went to use the bathroom, and when I got back there was nothing on the counter."

I stroked Bob's head. He was such a dopey dog. Not nearly as smart as Rex. Not even smart enough to pass on the prunes. Still, he had his moments. He had wonderful big brown eyes. And I was a sucker for brown eyes. And he was good company. He never tried to change my radio station, and he never once mentioned my pimple. All right, so I was sort of attached to Bob. In fact, maybe I'd been ready to rip Mitchell's heart out with my bare hands when he dognapped the big guy. I gave Bob a hug. He was good to hug, too. "You're going home with Joe tonight," I told him. "You'll be safe there."

My mother had the fried chicken on the table, along with biscuits and red cabbage and broccoli. No one would touch the broccoli, but my mother put it out anyway, because it was healthy.

Joe let himself in and took his seat, next to me.

"How'd it go today?" Grandma asked Joe. "Catch any murderers?"

"Not today, but I have hopes for tomorrow."

"Really?" I said.

"Well no, not really."

"How'd it go with Ranger?"

Morelli spooned red cabbage onto his plate. "As expected."

"He told me to butt out. Is that what you want me to do, too?"

"Yeah, but I'm smart enough not to tell you to do it. That's like waving a red flag in front of you." He took a piece of chicken. "Did you declare war?"

"Sort of. I refused his offer of a safe house."

"Are you in enough danger to need a safe house?"

"I don't know. It feels extreme."

Morelli slid his hand along the back of my chair. "My house is safe. You could move in with Bob and me. And besides, you do owe me a favor, you know."

"You want to call in the marker already?"

"The sooner, the better."

The phone rang in the kitchen and Grandma went to answer it. "It's for Stephanie," she yelled. "It's Lula."

"I've been trying to get in touch with you all afternoon," Lula said. "You don't answer nothing. You don't have your cell phone working. And you never answer your pager. What's wrong with the pager?"

"I can't afford both the pager and the cell phone, so I chose the cell phone. What's up?"

"They found Cynthia Lotte sitting in that Porsche, and she was dead as a doorknob. I tell

275

you, you wouldn't get me to sit in that car. You sit in that car, and you end up dead."

"When did this happen? How do you know?"

"They found her this afternoon, in the parking garage on Third Street. Connie and me heard it over the police band. And on top of that, I got a skip for you. Vinnie was total postal on account of you were out of touch, and there's no one else to take this skip."

"What about Joyce? What about Frankie Defrances?"

"We can't raise Joyce either. She's not answering her page. And Frankie just had a hernia operation."

"I'll come in to the office first thing in the morning."

"No way. Vinnie says you gotta get this guy tonight, before he flies. Vinnie knows right where he is. He gave me the papers."

"How much is it worth?"

"It's a hundred-thousand-dollar bond. Vinnie's cutting you ten percent."

Be still, my heart. "I'll pick you up in about twenty minutes."

I went back to the table, wrapped two pieces of chicken in my napkin, and dropped the napkin into my shoulder bag. I gave Bob a hug and Morelli a peck on the cheek. "I've got to go," I said. "I have to pick up a skip."

Morelli didn't look happy. "Will I see you later?"

"Probably. Besides paying off on my debt, I

need to talk to you about Cynthia Lotte."

"I knew you'd get around to that."

Lula was waiting outside when I got to her house. "I got the papers," she said, "and it don't sound too bad. His name's Elwood Steiger, and he's up on a drug charge. He was trying to make meth in his mother's garage, but the whole neighborhood reeked of the P2P. Guess one of the neighbors called the police. Anyway, his mother put her house up as bond, and now she's afraid ol' Elwood's gonna take a trip to Mexico. He missed his court date on Friday, and Mom found plane tickets in his sock drawer. So she ratted on him to Vinnie."

"Where do we find him?"

"According to his mama, he's one of them *Star Trek* fanatics. And there's some *Star Trek* gig going on tonight. She gave me an address."

I looked at the address and groaned. It was Dougie's house. "I know the guy who lives here," I said. "Dougie Kruper."

Lula slapped her head. "I knew that sounded familiar."

"I don't want anyone to get hurt when we make this apprehension," I said.

"Uh-huh."

"We're not going in there like gangbusters with guns drawn."

"Uh-huh."

"In fact, we're not going to use guns at all."

"I hear you."

I looked at the purse in her lap. "You have a gun in there?"

"Hell, yes."

"You have a gun on your hip?"

"Glock."

"Ankle holster?"

"Only sissies use ankle holsters," Lula said.

"I want you to leave the guns in the car."

"These are Trekkies we're dealing with. They could put the Vulcan death grip on us."

"In the car!" I yelled.

"Boy, no need to get PMS over it." Lula looked out the window. "Looks like a party going on at Dougie's."

There were several cars parked in front, and the house lights were blazing. The front door was open and the Mooner was on the stoop. I parked several houses away, and Lula and I walked back to the Mooner.

"Hey, dude," Moon said when he saw me, "welcome to the Trekarama."

"What's going on?"

"This is the Dougster's new business. Trekarama. We thought of it all ourselves. And the Dougster's the Trekmaster. Is that awesome, dude? This is the business of the new millennium. It's gonna be big, you know? We're gonna like, franchise."

"What the hell's a Trekarama?" Lula asked.

"It's a social club, dude. It's a place of worship. It's a shrine to the men and women who went where no man has gone before."

"Before what?"

The Mooner gazed off into space, transfixed. "Before it all."

"Uh-huh."

"It'll cost you five bucks to get inside," the Mooner said.

I gave him ten, and Lula and I pushed through the crush at the door.

"Never saw so many geeks all in one spot in my life," Lula said. "Except for that Klingon over there by the stairs. He ain't half bad."

We scanned the room, looking for Steiger, trying to identify him from his file photo. Problem was, some of the Trekkies were in costume, dressed like their favorite *Star Trek* characters.

Dougie rushed up to us. "Welcome to Trekarama. There's hors d'oeuvres and beverages over in the corner by the Romulan, and we're gonna start showing the films in about ten minutes. The hors d'oeuvres are real good. They're, uh, liquidation stock."

Translation: hijacked goods that were rotting in storage somewhere because he got closed down.

Lula knocked on Dougie's head with her knuckles. "Hello, anybody home in there. Do we look like a couple dumb-ass Trekkies?"

"Uh, well . . ."

"We're just looking around," I said to Dougie.

"Like tourists?"

"Maybe I'll be a tourist over by that fine Klingon," Lula said.

THIRTEEN

Lula and I moved deeper into the room, pushing our way through the crowd, looking for Elwood. He was nineteen years old. My height and slim. Sandy blond hair. Second-time offender. I didn't want to freak him out. I wanted to very quietly move him outside and slip the cuffs on him.

"Hey," Lula said, "you see that little dude in the Captain Kirk suit? What do you think?"

I squinted across the room. "Looks like it could be him," I said.

We worked our way over, and I came up beside him. "Steve?" I said. "Steve Miller?"

Captain Kirk blinked at me. "No. Sorry."

"I'm meeting a blind date here," I said. "He told me he'd be dressed as an officer." I extended my hand. "I'm Stephanie Plum."

He shook my hand. "Elwood Steiger."

Bingo.

"Boy, it's really hot in here," I said. "I'm going outside for some air. Want to join me?"

He looked around, nervous, needing to see if he was missing anything. "I don't know. I don't think so. They said they were showing the films right away."

Lesson number one: no point in coming on to a Trekkie when the films are up. So I had a choice. I could force the issue, or I could wait around until he decided to leave. If he stayed to the end and left en masse with everyone else, it could be a problem.

Mooner ambled over. "Wow, nice to see you two getting it on. Elwood here's fallen on some hard times, you know. He was making some great shit, and they shut him down. It was a real blow to all of us."

Elwood's eyes were darting around like his head was a pinball machine. "Are they gonna do the films soon?" he asked. "I just came for the films."

Mooner sipped his drink. "Elwood was making a good living, saving up to go to college, when he lost his business license. Damn shame. Damn shame."

Elwood gave a small smile. "I didn't actually have a business license," he said.

"You're lucky you know Steph, here," Mooner said. "I don't know what Dougie and me'd do without Steph. Lotta bounty hunters would just drag your bony ass back to jail, but Steph here —"

Elwood looked like someone just hit him with a cattle prod. "Bounty hunter!"

"The best there is," Mooner said.

I leaned forward so I could keep my voice low, and still have Elwood hear me. "Maybe it would be best if we went outside where we could talk."

Elwood backed away. "No! I'm not going! Leave me alone."

I moved to cuff him, but he slapped my hand away.

Lula reached out with her stun gun, Elwood ducked behind the Mooner, and the Mooner went down like a house of cards.

"Oops," Lula said, "think I got the wrong little Trekkie."

"You killed him!" Elwood shrieked.

"Time out," Lula said. "Don't you go yellin' in my ear like that."

I caught one of his hands and slapped the bracelet on him.

"You killed him. You shot him," Elwood said.

Lula was hands on hips. "Did you hear a gun-shot? I don't think so. I don't even have a gun, because Ms. Antiviolence here made me leave my gun in the car. Good thing, too, or I might shoot you just because you're such an annoying little cockroach."

I was still trying to get the other hand in a cuff, and people were pressing in on us. "What's going on?" they wanted to know. "What are you doing to Captain Kirk?"

"We're haulin' his worthless white ass off to the clink," Lula said. "Step back."

In my peripheral vision I caught something fly by and hit Lula on the side of her head.

"Hey!" Lula said. "What's going on?" She put her hand to her head. "This here's one of them smelly cheese ball hors d'oeuvres. Who's throwing cheese balls?"

"Free Captain Kirk," someone yelled.

"The hell we will," Lula said.

Whap! Lula took it in the forehead with a crab puff.

"Now just a minute," she said.

Whap. Whap. Whap. Egg rolls.

The entire room chanted in unison, "Free Captain Kirk. Free Captain Kirk."

"I'm getting out of here," Lula said. "These people are nuts. They been beamed up one time too many."

I yanked Elwood forward, toward the door, getting nailed with a splotch of hot sauce for the egg rolls, plus a couple cheese balls.

"Get them!" someone yelled. "They're kidnapping Captain Kirk."

Lula and I ducked our heads and fought our way through a barrage of hijacked hors d'oeuvres and ugly threats. We reached the front door and bolted outside, hitting the pavement at a run, half dragging Elwood behind us. We threw him into the backseat, and I put the gas pedal to the floor. Any other car would have rocketed away, but the Buick purposefully eased out of its berth and muscled its way down the street.

"You know, when you think about it, those Trekkies were a bunch of pussies," Lula said. "If this had happened in my neighborhood, those cheese balls would have had bullets in them."

Elwood was sullen in the backseat, not saying anything. He'd caught a couple cheese balls and egg rolls by accident, and his Kirk suit wasn't up to Federation standard anymore.

I dropped Lula off and continued on to the police station. Jimmy Neeley was at the desk. "Jesus," he said, "what's that smell?"

"Cheese balls," I told him. "And egg roll."

"You look like you've been in a food fight."

"It was the Romulan who started it," I said. "Damn Romulans."

"Yeah," Neeley said, "you can't trust them Romulans."

I got my body receipt and retrieved my cuffs from Captain Kirk, then I left the police station and walked out into the night air. The police lot was artificially bright, lit by overhead halogens. Beyond the halogens the sky was dark and starless. A light rain had started to fall. It would have been a cozy night if I was over at Morelli's with him and Bob. As it was, I was alone in the rain, smelling like a big crab puff, feeling a little worried that someone had terminated Cynthia Lotte and I might be next. The only good thing about the Lotte murder was that it had temporarily taken my mind off Arturo Stolle.

I didn't feel totally sexually attractive with my sauce-stained shirt and cheese-ball hair, so I went home to change before seeing Morelli. I parked the Buick next to Mr. Weinstein's Cadillac, locked up, and took a step toward the building before I realized Ranger was leaning against the car in front of me.

"You need to be more careful, babe," he said. "You should look around before you get out of your car."

"I was distracted."

"A bullet in the head would distract you permanently."

I made a face and stuck my tongue out.

Ranger smiled. "Trying to get me excited?" He picked a glob of food out of my hair. "Egg roll?"

"It's been a long night."

"Did you learn anything from Ramos?"

"He said they had a problem in Trenton, which I'm supposing is Junior Macaroni. But then he said he'd fixed it so the problem would go on a boat next week. And with any luck the boat would sink. Then the two goons came in to retrieve him, and they said they couldn't find the cargo. Do you know what any of this means?"

"Yes."

"Do you want to tell me?"

"No."

Christ. "You're a real prick. I'm not working for you anymore."

"Too late. I already fired you."

"I mean *ever!*"

"Where's Bob?"

"With Morelli."

"So all I have to worry about is keeping you safe," Ranger said.

"The sentiment is sweet, but not necessary."

"What, are you kidding me? I told you to drop out and be careful and two hours later you've got Ramos back in your car."

"I was looking for you, and he jumped in the Buick."

"You ever hear about door locks?"

I tipped my nose up, trying to pull off looking indignant. "I'm going inside. And just to make you happy I'll *lock* my door."

"Wrong. You're going with me, and I'm going to *lock* you *up.*"

"Are you threatening me?"

"No. I'm flat-out telling you."

"Listen, mister," I said, "this is the twenty-first century. Women aren't property. You just don't go around locking us up. If I want to do something incredibly stupid and put myself in danger, I have the right to do it."

Ranger clapped a bracelet on me. "I don't think so."

"Hey!"

"It'll only be for a couple days."

"I can't believe this! You're actually going to lock me up?"

He reached for my other wrist, and I yanked the cuff out of his hand and jumped away.

"Come here," he said.

I put a car between us. I had his bracelet dangling from my wrist, and in a weird way, which I didn't want to think about, it was sort of erotic. And then in another way, it really pissed me off. I reached into my shoulder bag and came up with my pepper spray. "Come get me," I told him.

He put his hands on the car. "This isn't going well, is it?"

"How did you expect it to go?"

"You're right. I should have known. Nothing is ever simple with you. Men blow themselves up. Cars get flattened by garbage trucks. I've been in full-scale invasions that have been less harrowing than meeting you for coffee." He held the key up for me to see. "Would you like me to take the cuff off?"

"Throw the key over here."

"Uh-unh. You have to come to me."

"No way."

"That pepper spray only works if you get it in my face. Do you think you're good enough to get it in my face?"

"Absolutely."

A junker of a car pulled into the lot. Ranger and I gave it our full attention. Ranger had a gun in his hand, his hand at his side.

The car came to a stop and Mooner and Dougie got out. "Hey, dude," Mooner called to me. "Lucky break finding you here. Me and Dougie need some of your sage advice."

"I have to talk to these guys," I said to Ranger. "Lula and I sort of trashed their house."

"Let me guess, they were serving egg rolls and something yellow."

"Cheese balls. And it wasn't my fault. The Romulan started it."

The corners of his mouth tipped into a small, controlled smile. "I should have guessed it was the Romulan." He holstered his gun. "Go talk to your friends. We'll finish this later."

"The key?"

He smiled and shook his head.

"This is war," I said.

The smile turned grim. "Be careful."

I backed away and moved to the building's back door, Dougie and Mooner following me. I couldn't imagine what they wanted. Restitution for damages? A report on Elwood's future as a drug lord? My opinion of the egg rolls?

I hurried through the lobby and took the stairs. "We can talk in my apartment," I said. "I need to change my shirt."

"Sorry about your shirt, dude. Those Trekkies turned ugly. I'm telling you, they were a mob," Mooner said. "That Federation is in trouble. They're never gonna make a go of it with members like that. They had no regard for Dougie's personal residence."

I opened my apartment door. "Was there much damage?"

Mooner flopped onto the couch. "In the beginning, we thought it was just going to be cheese-ball damage. But then we had trouble with the VCR and had to cut the film portion of the evening short."

"The VCR crapped out right in the middle of 'The Trouble with Tribbles,' and we were lucky to escape with our lives," Dougie said.

"We're, like, afraid to go back there, dude. We were wondering if we could crash here tonight with you and your granny."

"Grandma Mazur moved back to my parents'."

"Too bad. She was happening."

I gave them pillows and blankets.

"Rad bracelet," Mooner said.

I looked at the cuff still locked onto my right wrist. I'd forgotten it was there. I wondered if Ranger was still in the lot. And I wondered if I should have gone with him. I slid the bolt on the door, and then I locked myself in my bedroom, crawled into bed with the cheese gunk still in my hair, and immediately fell asleep.

When I woke up the next morning I realized I'd forgotten about Joe.

Shit.

There was no answer at his house, and I was about to try his pager when the phone rang.

"What the hell's going on?" Joe said. "I just got in to work and heard you got attacked by a Romulan."

"I'm fine. I made an apprehension at a *Star Trek* event, and it sort of got weird."

"Unfortunately, I have some weird news of my own. Your friend Carol Zabo is back on the bridge. It seems she and a whole pack of her friends kidnapped Joyce Barnhardt and left her naked and tied to a tree by the pet cemetery in Hamilton Township."

"Are you kidding me? Carol got arrested for

kidnapping Joyce Barnhardt?"

"No. Joyce didn't press charges. It was a real event, though. Half the force went out to turn her loose. Carol got arrested for being too happy in a public place. I think she and the girls were celebrating with wacky tobaccy. She's only looking at a misdemeanor, but nobody can convince her she's not going to jail. We were wondering if you could go out and talk her off the bridge. She's making a mess out of rush hour."

"I'll be right there." This was all my fault. Boy, when things started to go wrong the whole world turned into a toilet.

I'd gone to bed in my clothes, so I didn't have to bother getting dressed. On my way through the living room, I yelled to Mooner and Dougie that I'd be back. By the time I got to the back door of the building I had my pepper spray in hand, just in case Ranger jumped out at me from behind a bush.

There was no Ranger. And there was no Habib or Mitchell either, so I took off for the bridge. Cops were lucky — they had those big red lights when they needed to get somewhere fast. I didn't have any lights, so I just drove on the sidewalk when the traffic clogged up.

There was a steady rain falling. Temperatures were in the forties, and the entire state's population was on the phone checking airfares to Florida. Except, of course, for the people who were on the bridge, gawking at Carol.

I parked behind a blue-and-white and made

my way on foot to the middle of the bridge, where Carol was perched on the railing, holding an umbrella.

"Thanks for taking care of Joyce," I said. "What are you doing on the bridge?"

"I got arrested again."

"You're charged with a misdemeanor. You won't go to jail for it."

Carol climbed off the railing. "I just wanted to make sure." She squinted at me. "What's in your hair? And what's with the handcuff? You've been with Morelli, right?"

"Not in a while," I said, wistfully.

We went back to our cars. Carol went home. And I went to the office.

"Oh boy," Lula said when she saw me. "Think we got a good story walking in the door, here. What's with the handcuff?"

"I thought it would look good with the cheese balls in my hair. You know, dress up the outfit."

"I hope it was Morelli," Connie said. "I wouldn't mind being cuffed by Morelli."

"Close," I said. "It was Ranger."

"Uh-oh," Lula said. "Think I just wet my pants."

"It wasn't anything sexual," I said. "It was . . . an accident. And then we lost the key."

Connie fanned herself with a manila folder. "I'm having a hot flash."

I gave Connie the body receipt for Elwood Steiger. All things considered, it had been easy money. No one shot at me or set me on fire.

The front door crashed open and Joyce Barnhardt burst in. "You're gonna pay for that," she said to me. "You're gonna be sorry you messed with me!"

Lula and Connie swiveled their heads to me and gave me the "What?" look.

"Carol Zabo and some friends helped me out by leaving Joyce tied to a tree . . . naked."

"I don't want any shooting in here," Connie said to Joyce.

"Shooting's too easy," Joyce said. "I want something better. I want Ranger." She narrowed her eyes at me. "I know you're cozy with him. Well, you better use that as leverage and deliver him to me. Because if you don't deliver him to me in twenty-four hours I'm pressing kidnapping charges against Carol Zabo." Joyce wheeled around on her high-heeled boots and swished out the door.

"Sheee-it," Lula said. "There's that sulfur smell again."

Connie handed me my check for Elwood. "This is a dilemma."

I took the check and dropped it into my bag. "I have so many dilemmas I can't even remember them all."

Old Mrs. Bestler was in the elevator, playing elevator operator. "Going up," she said. "Ladies' handbags, lingerie . . ." She leaned on her walker and looked at me. "Oh dear," she said, "the beauty salon's on the second floor."

"Good," I told her. "That's just where I'm going."

My apartment was quiet when I let myself in. The extra blankets were neatly stacked on the couch. A note had been placed on one of the pillows. Only one word had been written on the paper. "Later."

I dragged myself into the bathroom, stripped, and washed my hair, several times. I got dressed in clean clothes, then blasted my hair with the dryer, and pulled it into a ponytail. I called Morelli to see how Bob was doing, and he said Bob was fine and his neighbor was dog-sitting. Then I went down to the basement and got Dillan to hacksaw through the chain on the cuffs, so I didn't have the second bracelet swinging in the breeze.

Then I didn't have anything to do. I didn't have any FTAs to retrieve. I didn't have a dog to walk. I had no one to watch, no houses to break into. I could have gone to a locksmith to have the cuff opened, but I had hopes of getting the key from Ranger. I was going to turn him over to Joyce tonight. Better to deliver Ranger to Joyce than have to talk Carol off the bridge again. Rescuing Carol from a watery grave was getting old. And it'd be easy to deliver Ranger. All I had to do was arrange a meeting. Tell him I wanted the cuff off, and he'd come to me. Then I'd knock him out with the stun gun and pack him off to Joyce. Of course, after I handed him over I'd have to do something sneaky and rescue him. I certainly wasn't going to have Ranger hauled off to jail.

Since it would appear I didn't have anything on the agenda until tonight, I thought I should clean the hamster cage. And after the hamster cage, maybe I'd do the refrigerator. Hell, I might even get totally carried away and scour the bathroom . . . no, that wasn't likely. I dumped Rex out of his soup can and put him in my big spaghetti pot on the kitchen counter. He sat there, blinking in the sudden light, unhappy to have his sleep interrupted.

"Sorry, little guy," I said. "Gotta clean the ol' hacienda."

Ten minutes later, Rex was back in his cage, frantic because all his buried treasures were now in a big black plastic garbage bag. I gave him a cracked walnut and a raisin. He took the raisin into his new soup can, and that was the last I saw of him.

I looked out my living room window, down into the wet parking lot. Still no sign of Habib and Mitchell. All the cars belonged to tenants. Good deal. It was safe to get rid of my garbage. I shrugged into my jacket, grabbed the bag of hamster bedding, and hustled down the hall.

Mrs. Bestler was still in the elevator. "Oh, you look much better now, dear," she said. "Nothing like spending a relaxing hour at the beauty parlor." The elevator doors opened to the lobby, and I hopped out. "Going up," Mrs. Bestler sang out. "Menswear, third floor." And the doors slid shut.

I crossed the lobby to the rear entrance and paused for a moment to pull my hood up. The rain was steady. Water pooled on the glistening blacktop and beaded on the old folks' freshly waxed cars. I stepped outside, put my head down, and hurried across the lot to the Dumpster.

I pitched the bag inside the bin, turned, and found myself face to face with Habib and Mitchell. They were soaking wet, and they didn't look friendly.

"Where'd you come from?" I asked. "I don't see your car."

"It's parked on the side street," Mitchell said, showing me his gun, "and that's where you're headed. Start walking."

"I don't think so," I said. "If you shoot me, Ranger has no incentive to deal with Stolle."

"Wrong," Mitchell said. "If we *kill* you, Ranger has no incentive."

Good point.

The Dumpster was on the back edge of the lot. I stumbled across a patch of rain-slicked lawn on wobbly legs, too scared to think clearly. Wondering where Ranger was now, when I needed him. Why wasn't he here, insisting on locking me up in a safe house? Now that my hamster's cage was clean, I'd be happy to oblige.

Mitchell was driving the mom-van again. Guess they weren't having a lot of luck cleaning up the Lincoln. And probably I didn't want to choose that as a topic of conversation.

Habib sat beside me in the backseat. He was wearing a raincoat but it looked soaked through. They must have been crouching in the bushes at the edge of the building. He was hatless, and water dripped from his hair, down the back of his neck, and onto his face. He wiped his face with his hand. No one seemed to mind that they were getting the mom-van wet.

"Well," I said, trying to make my voice sound normal. "Now what?"

"Now you do not want to know," Habib said. "You should being quiet now."

Being quiet was bad, since it gave me time to think. And thinking wasn't pleasant. No good was going to come of this ride. I tried to close my emotions down. Fear and regret weren't going to get me anywhere. Didn't want to let my imagination run wild, either. This could just be another meeting with Arturo. No need to go berserk ahead of time. I concentrated on breathing. Nice and steady. Taking in oxygen. I did a mental chant. *Ohhhmm.* I saw someone doing that on television, and she looked like she really got off on it.

Mitchell drove west on Hamilton, toward the river. He crossed Broad and wound around in a part of town that was zoned industrial. The lot he pulled into was next to a three-story brick structure that had been a machine-tool factory but was now sitting unused. A "For Sale" sign had been fixed to the front of the building, but it looked like it had been there for a hundred years.

Mitchell parked the van and got out. He opened my door and waved me out at gunpoint. Habib followed. He unlocked the building's side door, and we all trooped in. It was cold and damp inside. The lighting was dim, coming from open doorways to small offices where the sun filtered through grimy exterior windows. We walked down a short hall and turned into a reception area. The tile was grungy underfoot and the area was bare, with the exception of two metal folding chairs and a small, scarred wood desk. There was a cardboard box on the desk.

"Sit down," Mitchell said to me. "Pick a chair."

He took his coat off and threw it onto the desk. Habib did the same. Their shirts weren't much drier than their coats.

"Okay, here's the plan," Mitchell said. "We're gonna hit you with the stun gun, and then while you're out we're gonna cut off your finger with the shears, here." He picked a pair of bolt cutters out of the cardboard box. "That way we have something to send to Ranger. Then we hang on to you and see what happens. If he wants to trade, we're in business. If he doesn't, I guess we kill you."

There was a loud buzzing in my ears, and I snapped my head to make it go away. "What a minute," I said. "I have some questions."

Mitchell sighed. "Women always have questions."

"Perhaps we could cut out her tongue," Habib

said. "That sometimes works. We have much luck with that in my village."

I was getting the feeling he'd lied about being Pakistani. Sounded to me like his village was in Hell.

"Mr. Stolle didn't say nothing about a tongue," Mitchell said. "He might want to save that for some future time."

"Where are you going to keep me?" I asked Mitchell.

"Here. We're gonna lock you in the bathroom."

"But what about the bleeding?"

"What about it?"

"I could bleed to death. Then how would you trade me to Ranger?"

They looked at each other. They hadn't thought of that. "This is sort of new for me," Mitchell said. "Usually I just beat the shit out of people or pop them."

"You should have some clean bandages and some antiseptic."

"I guess that makes sense," Mitchell said. He looked at his watch. "We haven't got a lot of time. I need to get the van back to my wife to pick the kids up from school. Don't want them to have to wait around in the rain."

"There is a drugstore on Broad Street," Habib said. "We could be getting these things there."

"Get me some Tylenol, too," I said.

I didn't actually want bandages and Tylenol. What I really wanted was time. That's what you always want when a disaster occurs. You want time to hope it's not true. Time for the disaster to go away. Time to find out it was all a mistake. Time for God to intervene.

"Okay," Mitchell said. "Get into the bathroom, over there."

It was a windowless room, about four feet wide and six feet long. One toilet. One sink. That was it. A padlock had been installed on the outside of the door. It didn't look brand-new, so I assumed I wasn't the first person to be held prisoner here.

I went into the little room, and they closed and locked the door. I put my ear to the jamb.

"You know, I'm getting to hate this job," Mitchell said. "Why can't we ever do this kind of stuff on a nice day? One time I had to clip this guy, Alvin Margucci. It was so fucking cold the gun froze up, and we had to beat him to death with the shovel. And then when we went to dig him a hole we couldn't fucking make a dent in the ground. It was all a big Popsicle."

"That sounds like very hard work," Habib said. "It is better in my country, where it is mostly warmer and the ground is soft. Many times we do not even have to dig because Pakistan can be quite rugged, and we can simply throw the freshly dead into a ravine."

"Yeah, well, you know — we got rivers here, but the stiffs bob up to the surface and then that's not so good."

"Just so," Habib said. "I have experienced that myself."

I thought I heard them leave, heard the door at

the end of the hall open and close. I tried the bathroom door. I looked around the room. I did some breathing. I looked around the room some more. I told myself to think. I felt like Pooh Bear, who was a Bear of Little Brain. It was a nasty little room, with a filthy sink and a filthy toilet and dirty linoleum floor. The wall next to the sink was water stained, with a damp spot near the ceiling. Probably a plumbing problem on the floor above. We weren't talking quality construction here. I put my hand to the wall and felt it give. The wallboard was soggy.

I was wearing Caterpillar boots with a hefty lug sole. I put my ass on the sink and gave the wallboard a shot with my Cats, and my foot went clear through to the other side. I started laughing, and then I realized I was crying. No time for hysteria, I told myself. Let's just get the hell out of here.

I clawed at the wall, ripping chunks of board away. I got a good-sized opening made between the studs, and I went to work on the adjoining wall. In a matter of minutes I had both walls destroyed enough to be able to wedge myself between the studs. My nails were broken and my fingers were bleeding, but I was in a small office now with the bathroom behind me. I tried the door. The door was locked. Jesus, I thought, don't tell me I'm going to have to kick my way through this whole fucking building! Wait a minute, fool. The office has a window. I made myself take a breath. I wasn't in top thinking form. I was too panicked. I tried the window, but it wouldn't budge. It had been closed for too long. There'd been numerous paintings over the lock. No furniture in the room. I took my jacket off, wrapped it around my hand, made a fist, and smashed the window. I cleared as much glass away as I could and looked out. It was a long drop, but I could probably do it. I took my boot off and pounded away at the remaining glass in the window, so I wouldn't cut myself any worse than was necessary. I put the shoe back on and swung a leg onto the window ledge.

The window faced front. Please God, don't let Habib and Mitchell drive by when I jump out of the window. I let myself out slowly, back to the street so I could hang by my hands, my toes digging against the brick. When I was fully extended I dropped, landing first on my feet and then falling on my ass. I lay there for a minute, stunned, flat on the sidewalk, rain splattering on my face.

I sucked in some air and got to my feet and started running. I crossed the street and ran through an alley and crossed another street. I had no idea where I was going. I was just putting space between me and the brick building.

FOURTEEN

I stopped to catch my breath, bending at the waist, eyes narrowed against the pain in my lungs. My jeans were torn at the knees, and my knees were scraped from the glass. Both hands were cut. I'd lost my jacket in my rush to escape. It had been wrapped around my hand, and I'd left it behind. I was wearing a T-shirt and a flannel shirt, and I was soaked to the skin. My teeth were chattering from cold and fear. I pressed myself against the side of a building and listened to the rain-muffled sound of cars not far off, on Broad.

I didn't want to go to Broad. I'd feel too exposed. This wasn't a part of town I knew very well. I didn't have too many choices. But I was going to have to go into one of these buildings and get help. There was a gas station–convenience store on the other side of the street. I didn't feel comfortable with that. Too visible. I was next to a building that looked like offices. I slipped in through the front door to a small vestibule. A single elevator sat to the left. A metal fire door leading to stairs was located next to the elevator. The chart on the wall listed the businesses in the building. Five floors of businesses. Didn't recognize any of the tenants. I took the stairs to the first floor and picked a door at random. It opened to a room full of metal shelves, and the shelves were loaded with computers and printers and assorted hardware. A frizzy-haired guy in a T-shirt was working at a table just inside the door. He looked up when I poked my head in.

"What do you do here?" I asked.

"We repair computers."

"I was wondering if I could use your phone to make a local call. My bike slid out from under me in the rain, and I need to call for a ride." Probably the fact that there were men looking to mutilate me was more information than he desired.

He looked me over. "You sure you want to stay with that story?"

"Yeah. I'm sure." When in doubt . . . always lie.

He motioned to the phone at the end of the table. "Help yourself."

I couldn't call my parents. There was no way to explain this to them. And I didn't want to call Joe, because I didn't want him to know how stupid I'd been. I wasn't going to call Ranger, because he'd lock me up, although the idea was gaining in appeal. That left Lula.

"Thanks," I said to the guy, replacing the phone after I'd given Lula the address. "Appreciate it."

He looked sort of horrified at my appearance, so I backed out of the office and went downstairs to wait.

Five minutes later, Lula pulled up in the Firebird. When I got in, she locked the doors and took the gun out of her purse and laid it on the console between us.

"Good call," I said.

"Where are we going?"

I couldn't go home. Habib and Mitchell would eventually look for me there. I could stay with my parents or Joe, but not until I got cleaned up. I was sure Lula would let me stay with her, too, but her apartment was tiny and I didn't want WWIII to start because we were stepping on each other's toes. "Take me to Dougie's house," I said.

"I don't know how you got all those cuts, but you must have got brain damage, too."

I explained it all to Lula. "No one will think to look for me at Dougie's," I said. "Besides, he's got clothes from when he was the Dealer. And he's probably got a car I can use."

"You should page Ranger or Joe," Lula said. "Better one of them than Dougie. They'll keep you safe."

"Can't do that. I have to trade Ranger for Carol tonight."

"Say what?"

"I'm turning Ranger over to Joyce tonight." I punched Joe's office number into Lula's car phone. "I have a huge favor to ask," I said to Morelli.

"Another one?"

"I'm worried someone might break into my apartment, and I can't get home right now. I was wondering if you could get Rex and take him with you."

There was a heavy silence. "How urgent is this?"

"Urgent."

"I hate this," Morelli said.

"And while you're there, maybe you could check the cookie jar and see if my gun is there. And, um, maybe you could also snag my shoulder bag."

"What's going on?"

"Arturo Stolle thinks he can get Ranger to cooperate with him by holding me hostage."

"Are you okay?"

"Peachy fine. It's just that I left the apartment in a hurry."

"I don't suppose you'd want me to pick you up someplace."

"No. Just Rex. I'm with Lula."

"That fills me with confidence."

"I'll try to get over later tonight."

"Try real hard."

Lula came to a stop in front of Dougie's house. The two front windows were boarded over. The shades were drawn in the upstairs windows, but light peeked out from behind. Lula gave me her Glock. "Take this with you. It has a full clip. And call me if you need anything."

"I'll be fine," I said.

"Sure. I know that. I'm gonna wait here until you get in the house and give me the sign to go."

I ran the short distance to Dougie's front door. I'm not sure why. I couldn't have gotten much wetter. I knocked on the door, but no one answered. I imagined Dougie hiding somewhere, afraid a Trekkie had come back to see him.

"Hey, Dougie!" I yelled. "It's Stephanie. Open the door!"

That got results. A shade moved aside and Dougie peeked out. Then the front door was opened.

"Anyone here with you?" I asked.

"Just the Mooner."

I shoved the Glock into the waistband of my jeans and turned and waved to Lula.

"Close and lock the door," I said, stepping into the room.

Dougie was way ahead of me. Not only had he already locked the door, but he was pushing a refrigerator in front of it.

"Do you think that's necessary?" I asked.

"I guess it's overkill," he said. "It's actually been quiet today. It's just that I'm still freaked out from the riot."

"Looks like they broke your windows."

"Only one. The fire department broke the other one when they threw the couch out onto the sidewalk."

I looked at the couch. Half of it was charred. Mooner sat on the uncharred half.

"Hey, dude, you came at the right time," he

said. "We just heated up some crab puffs. We're watching an *I Dream of Jeannie* retrospective on Nick at Nite. It's, like, awesome the way Jeannie does that blinking thing."

"Yeah," Dougie said. "We got lots of crab puffs left. We have to eat them before they expire on Friday."

I thought it was strange that neither of them commented on the fact that I was wet and bleeding and had walked in with a Glock in my hand. But then, maybe people showed up here like that all the time. "I was wondering if you had any dry clothes," I said to Dougie. "Did you get rid of all those jeans you were trying to sell?"

"I have a whole bunch in the bedroom upstairs. Mostly small sizes, so maybe you'll find something. And there's shirts up there, too. You can help yourself to whatever you want."

There were some Band-Aids in the medicine chest in the bathroom. I cleaned myself up as well as I could and picked over Dougie's clothes until I found something that fit.

It was midafternoon, and I hadn't had lunch, so I wolfed down some crab puffs. Then I went into the kitchen and called Morelli on his cell phone.

"Where are you?" he asked.

"Why?"

"I want to know, that's why."

Something was wrong. My God, not Rex. "What's wrong? Is it Rex? Is Rex all right?"

"Rex is fine. He's in a squad car with

Costanza, on his way to my house. I'm still in your apartment. The door was open when I got here, and the place has been ransacked. I don't think anything's destroyed, but it's a real mess. They dumped everything out of your bag, onto the floor. Your wallet and stun gun and pepper spray are still here. Your gun was still in the cookie jar. Looks to me like these guys were more mad than anything. I think they tore through here and didn't even see Rex's cage."

I had my hand to my heart. Rex was okay. That was all I cared about.

"I'm getting ready to lock up," he said. "Tell me where you are."

"I'm at Dougie's."

"Dougie *Kruper?*"

"We're watching *I Dream of Jeannie.*"

"I'll be right there."

"No! I'm perfectly safe. No one would think to look for me here. And I'm helping Dougie clean. Lula and I caused a riot last night, and I feel re-sponsible, and I need to help clean." Liar, liar, pants on fire.

"That sounds reasonable, but I don't believe any of it."

"Listen, I don't interfere with your work, and you can't interfere with mine."

"Yeah, but *I* know what I'm doing."

He had a point. "I'll see you tonight."

"Shit," Morelli said. "I need a drink."

"Check my bedroom closet. Maybe Grandma left a bottle."

I watched *Jeannie* with Dougie and Mooner for three hours. I ate some more crab puffs. And then I called Ranger. He didn't answer his phone, so I tried his pager. Ten minutes later, I got a call back.

"I want to get this bracelet off," I told him.

"You could go to a locksmith."

"I'm having some additional problems with Stolle."

"And?"

"And I need to talk to you."

"And?"

"I'll be in the lot behind the office at nine o'clock. I'll be in a borrowed car. I don't know what kind, yet."

Ranger disconnected. I guess that meant he'd be there.

Now I had a problem. All I had was a Glock. And Ranger wouldn't be afraid of the Glock. He'd know I wouldn't shoot him.

"I need some stuff," I said to Dougie. "I need handcuffs and a stun gun and some pepper spray."

"I don't have any here," Dougie said, "but I could make a phone call. I know a guy."

Half hour later, there was a knock on the door, and we all pushed the refrigerator out of the way. We opened the door, and my upper lip curled back.

"Lenny Gruber," I said. "Haven't seen you since you repossessed my Miata."

"I've been busy."

"Yeah, I know. So many rotten things to do, and so little time."

"Dude!" Mooner said. "Come on in. Have a crab puff."

Gruber and I went to school together. He was the kind of guy who passed gas in class and then yelled out, "Hey, that stinks! Who cut the cheese?" He was missing a molar, and his pants were never completely zipped.

Gruber helped himself to a crab puff and put an aluminum attaché case on the coffee table. He opened the case and inside was a jumble of tasers, stun guns, defense sprays, cuffs, knives, saps, and brass knuckles. Also a box of condoms and a vibrator. I guess he did a good pimp trade.

I picked out a pair of cuffs, a stun gun, and a small can of pepper spray. "How much?" I asked.

His eyes were locked onto my chest. "For you, a special deal."

"Don't do me any favors," I said.

He gave me a price that was fair.

"Deal," I told him. "But you'll have to wait to get paid. I don't have anything on me."

He grinned, and the missing molar looked like the black hole of Calcutta in his mouth. "We could work something out."

"We'll work *nothing* out. I'll get the money to you tomorrow."

"If I don't get paid until tomorrow the price will have to go up."

"Listen, Gruber, I've had a *very bad day*. Don't

310

push me. I'm a woman on the edge." I hit the "on" button on the stun gun. "Is this thing live? Maybe I should test it on someone."

"Women," Gruber said to Mooner. "Can't live with them. Can't live without them."

"Could you move a little to the left?" Mooner asked. "You're blocking the television, dude, and Jeannie's gonna blink Major Nelson."

I borrowed a two-year-old Jeep Cherokee from Dougie. It was one of four cars left unsold because their registration and bill of sale had gotten misplaced. I'd found jeans and a T-shirt that sort of fit. And I'd borrowed a lined denim jacket and clean socks from Mooner. Neither Dougie nor Mooner had a washer or dryer and neither was a cross-dresser, so what I was missing was underwear. I had my cuffs looped over the back of my jeans. The rest of my equipment was stuffed into the jacket's assorted pockets.

I drove to the lot behind Vinnie's office and parked. The rain had stopped and the air felt warm with the promise of spring. It was very dark, no stars or moon showing through the cloud cover. There was room behind the office for four cars to park. So far, mine was the only one there. I was early. Probably not as early as Ranger. He'd undoubtedly seen me arrive and was watching from somewhere to make sure the meeting was safe. Standard operating procedure.

I was watching the alley that led to the small lot when Ranger rapped softly on my window.

"Damn!" I said. "You scared the bejeezus out of me. You shouldn't sneak up on a person like that."

"You should keep your back to the wall, babe." He opened my door. "Take your jacket off."

"I'll be cold."

"Take it off and hand it to me."

"You don't trust me."

He smiled.

I took the jacket off and handed it over.

"Lot of hardware in here," he said.

"The usual."

"Get out of the car."

This wasn't the way it was supposed to happen. I hadn't counted on losing my jacket so soon. "I'd rather you got in. It's warmer in here."

"Get out."

I gave a big sigh and got out.

He put his hand to the small of my back, dipped his fingers below the waistband of my jeans, and removed the cuffs.

"Let's go inside," he said. "I feel safer in there."

"Just out of morbid curiosity, do you know how to get around the alarm, or do you know the security code?"

He opened the back door. "I know the code."

We walked through the short hall to the back room where the guns and office supplies are kept. Ranger opened the door to the front room and ambient light from the street poured in through the plate-glass windows. Standing between the two rooms, he was able to see both doors.

He put my jacket and the cuffs on a file cabinet, out of my reach, and looked down at the hacksawed bracelet on my right wrist. "New design."

"But still annoying."

He took the key out of his pocket, unlocked the cuff, and threw the cuff on top of my jacket. Then he took both my hands in his and turned them palms up. "You're wearing someone else's clothes, you're carrying someone else's gun, your hands are cut, and you're not wearing underwear. What's the deal here?"

I looked down at the outline of breast and protruding nipple, straining against the confines of the T-shirt. "Sometimes I go without underwear."

"You *never* go without underwear."

"How do you know?"

"God-given talent."

He was wearing his usual street clothes — black cargo pants tucked into black boots, a black T-shirt, and a black windbreaker. He took off the windbreaker and wrapped it around me. It was warm from his body heat and smelled very faintly of the ocean.

"Spending a lot of time in Deal?" I asked.

"I should be there now."

"Is someone watching Ramos for you?"

"Tank."

His hands still held the windbreaker, his

knuckles resting lightly on my breasts. An act of intimate possession more than of sexual aggression.

"How are you going to do it?" he asked, his voice soft.

"Do what?"

"Capture me. Isn't that what this is about?"

That had been the original plan, but he'd taken my toys away. And now the air was feeling hot and thick in my lungs, and I was thinking it wasn't any of my beeswax if Carol took a flying leap off the bridge. I put my hands flat to his abdomen, and he watched me carefully. I suspect he was waiting for me to answer his question, but I had a more pressing problem. I didn't know what to feel first. Should I move my hands up? Or should I move my hands down? I wanted to go down, but that might seem too forward. I didn't want him to think I was easy.

"Steph?"

"Huh?"

I still had my hands on his stomach, and I could feel him laughing. "I can smell something burning, babe. You must be thinking."

It wasn't my brain that was on fire. I felt around a little with my fingertips.

He shook his head. "Don't encourage me. This isn't a good time." He removed my hands from his stomach and took another look at the cuts. "How did this happen?"

I told him about Habib and Mitchell and the factory escape.

"Arturo Stolle deserved Homer Ramos," Ranger said.

"I wouldn't know. No one tells me anything!"

"For years, Stolle's cut of the crime pie has been illegal adoption and immigration. He uses his East Asian contacts to bring young girls into the country for prostitution and to produce high-priced adoption babies. Six months ago, Stolle realized he could use those same contacts to smuggle drugs in with the girls. Problem is, drugs aren't part of Stolle's piece of pie. So Stolle hooked up with Homer Ramos, who is known far and wide as a stupid shit always in need of money, and arranged for Ramos to act as bag-man between him and his accounts. Stolle figured the other Mob factions would back off from Alexander Ramos's kid."

"How do you fit into this?"

"Arbitrator. I was acting as a liaison between the factions. Everyone, feds included, would like to avoid a crime war." His pager beeped, and he looked at the readout. "I have to get back to Deal. Do you have any secret weapons in your arsenal? You want to make any last-ditch efforts at apprehension?"

Ugh. He was so smug! "I hate you," I said.

"No, you don't," Ranger said, kissing me lightly on the lips.

"Why did you agree to meet me?"

Our eyes locked for a moment. And then he cuffed me. Both hands behind my back.

"Shit!" I yelled.

"I'm sorry, but you're a real pain in the ass. I can't do my job when I'm worrying about you. I'm turning you over to Tank. He'll take you to a safe house and baby-sit you until things get resolved."

"You can't do that! Carol will be back on the bridge."

Ranger grimaced. "Carol?"

I told him about Carol and Joyce and how Carol didn't want to get caught on *Candid Camera* and how it was all sort of my fault this time.

Ranger thunked his head on the file cabinet. "Why me?" he said.

"I wouldn't have let Joyce keep you," I told him. "I was going to turn you over to her and then figure out a way to get you back."

"I know I'm going to regret this, but I'm going to set you loose so, God forbid, Carol doesn't jump off the bridge. I'm going to give you until nine o'clock tomorrow morning to work things out with Joyce, and then I'm coming after you. And I want you to promise you won't go near Arturo Stolle or *anyone* named Ramos."

"I promise."

I drove across town to Lula's house. She has a second-floor apartment, facing front, and her lights were still on. I didn't have a phone, so I walked up to her door and rang the bell. A window opened above me, and Lula stuck her head out. "What?"

"It's Stephanie."

She dropped a key down, and I let myself in.

Lula met me at the top of the stairs. "Are you spending the night?"

"No. I need some help. You know how I was going to turn Ranger over to Joyce? Well, it didn't exactly work out."

Lula burst out laughing. "Girl, Ranger is the shit. No one's better than Ranger. Not even you." She took in the T-shirt and jeans. "I don't mean to get too personal, but were you wearing a bra when you started the evening, or is this something recent?"

"I started out this way. Dougie and Mooner don't wear my kind of underwear."

"Too bad," Lula said.

It was a two-room apartment. Bedroom with bath attached, and another room that served as living room and dining room and had a small corner kitchen. Lula had placed a little round table and two ladderback chairs at the edge of the kitchen area. I sat on one of the chairs and took a beer from Lula.

"You want a sandwich?" she asked. "I got bologna."

"A sandwich would be great. Dougie just had crab puffs." I took a long pull on the beer. "So this is the problem: what are we going to do about Joyce? I feel responsible for Carol."

"You can't be responsible for someone else's bad judgment," Lula said. "You didn't tell her to tie Joyce to that tree."

True.

"Still," she said, "it'd feel good to screw Joyce over one more time."

"You have any ideas?"

"How well does Joyce know Ranger?"

"She's seen him a couple times."

"Suppose we slip her someone who looks like Ranger, and then we take back the ringer? I know this guy, Morgan, who could pass. Same dark skin. Same build. Maybe not as fine, but he could come close. Especially if it was real dark, and he didn't open his mouth. He got the name Morgan 'cause he's hung like a horse."

"I'd probably need a couple more beers to think it would work."

Lula looked over at the empty beer bottles sitting on her counter. "I got a head start on you. So I'm real optimistic about this plan." She opened a dog-eared address book and thumbed through it. "I know him from my former profession."

"Customer?"

"Pimp. He's a real asshole, but he owes me a favor. And he'd probably get off on passing as Ranger. He probably got a Ranger outfit in his closet, too."

Five minutes later, Morgan answered his page, and Lula and I had ourselves a fake Ranger.

"Here's the plan," Lula said. "We pick the dude up on the corner of Stark and Belmont in a half hour. Only he hasn't got all night, so we gotta get this thing moving."

I called Joyce and told her I had Ranger, and she should meet us in the lot behind the office. It was the darkest spot I could think of.

I finished my sandwich and beer, and Lula and I packed off in the Cherokee. We got to the corner of Stark and Belmont, and I had to do a double-take to make sure the man standing there wasn't Ranger.

When Morgan got closer, the differences were apparent. The skin tone was the same, but his features were more coarse. There was more age around his mouth and eyes, less intelligence in his expression. "Joyce better not look too close," I said to Lula.

"I told you to have another bottle of beer," Lula said. "Anyway, it's real dark behind the office, and if things go right Joyce'll break down before she gets too far."

We cuffed Morgan's hands in front of him, which is a dumb thing to do, but Joyce wasn't a good enough bounty hunter to know it. Then we gave him the key to the cuffs. The deal was that he'd put the key in his mouth when we got to the lot. He'd refuse to talk to Joyce, playing sullen. We'd arrange for her to get a flat, and when she got out to take a look, Morgan would take the cuffs off and escape into the night.

We got to the alley early, so I could drop Lula. We'd decided she would hide behind the small Dumpster that serviced Vinnie and his neighbor, and when Joyce was busy taking Ranger into custody, Lula would drive a spike into Joyce's tire. Déjà vu. I angled the Cherokee so that Joyce would be forced to park next to the Dumpster. Lula jumped out and hid, and almost immediately lights flashed at the corner.

Joyce pulled her SUV in next to me and got out. I got out, too. Morgan was slumped in the backseat, his head down to his chest.

Joyce squinted into the car. "I can't see him. Put your lights on."

"No way," I said. "And you'd be smart to leave yours off, too. He's got a lot of people looking for him."

"Why's he all slumped over?"

"Drugged."

Joyce nodded. "I was wondering how you were gonna do it."

I made a big deal and some noise over pulling Morgan out of the backseat. He collapsed against me, snatching a cheap feel, and Joyce and I half-dragged him over to her car and stuffed him in.

"One last thing," I said to Joyce, handing her a statement I'd prepared at Lula's. "You need to sign this."

"What is it?"

"It's a document attesting to the fact that you willingly went to the pet cemetery with Carol and asked her to tie you to the tree."

"What are you, nuts? I'm not signing that."

"Then I'm hauling Ranger out of your backseat."

Joyce looked at the SUV and her precious cargo. "What the hell," she said, taking the pen and signing her name. "I got what I wanted."

"You take off first," I said to Joyce, pulling my Glock out of my pocket. "I'll make sure you get out of the alley safely."

"I can't believe you did this," Joyce said. "I didn't think you were such a sneaky little shit."

Honey, you don't know the half of it. "It was for Carol," I said.

I stood there with the Glock drawn and watched Joyce drive away. The instant she turned from the alley to the street, Lula jumped into the car, and we took off.

"I give her about a quarter-mile," Lula said. "I'm the queen of the spike-and-run."

I had a visual on Joyce. There was no traffic, and she was a block ahead of me. Her taillights wobbled and the car slowed.

"Good, good, good," Lula said.

Joyce drove another block at reduced speed.

"She'd like to just drive on that tire," Lula said, "but she's worried about her fancy new SUV."

There was another flash of brake lights, and Joyce pulled to the curb. We were a block behind her with our lights killed, looking parked. Joyce had gotten out and turned toward the back of her car when a van swerved around me and skidded to a stop alongside her. Two men jumped out, guns drawn. One trained his gun on

Joyce, and the other grabbed Morgan just as he set foot on the pavement.

"What the hell?" Lula said. "What the fuck?"

It was Habib and Mitchell. They thought they had Ranger.

Morgan got bundled into the mom-van, and the van rocketed off.

Lula and I sat in shocked silence, not sure what to do.

Joyce was yelling and waving her arms. Finally she kicked the flat tire, got into her SUV, and, I assume, made a phone call.

"That worked out pretty good," Lula finally said.

I backed up half a block without lights, turned the corner, and drove away. "Where do you think they picked us up?"

"Must have been at my house," Lula said. "They probably didn't want to make a move when there were two of us. And then they got real lucky when Joyce got that flat."

"They're not going to think they're so lucky when they find out they've got Morgan the Horse."

Dougie and Mooner were playing Monopoly when I got back to Dougie's house. "I thought you worked at Shop & Bag," I said to Mooner. "Why aren't you ever working?"

"I lucked out and got laid off, dude. I'm telling you, this is a great country. Where else could a dude get paid for *not* working?"

I went into the kitchen and dialed Morelli. "I'm at Mooner's house," I told him. "I just had another weird night."

"Yeah, well, it isn't over yet. Your mother's called over here four times in the last hour. You'd better phone home."

"What's wrong?"

"Your grandmother went out on a date, and she isn't back yet, and your mother's losing it."

FIFTEEN

My mother answered on the first ring. "It's midnight," she said, "and your grandmother isn't home. She's out with that turtle man."

"Myron Landowsky?"

"They were supposed to go to dinner. That was at five o'clock. Where could they be? I've called his apartment and there's no answer. I've called all the hospitals —"

"Mom, they're adults. They could be doing lots of stuff. When Grandma was living with me I never knew where she was."

"She's running wild!" my mother said. "Do you know what I found in her room? Condoms! What does she want with condoms?"

"Maybe she makes balloon animals out of them."

"Other women have mothers who get sick and go to nursing homes or die in their beds. Not me. I have a mother who wears spandex. What did I do to deserve this?"

"You should go to bed and stop worrying about Grandma."

"I'm not going to bed until that woman comes home. We're going to have a talk. And your father is here, too."

Oh great. There'll be a big scene, and Grandma will be back, living in my apartment.

"Tell Daddy he can go to bed. I'll come over and sit up with you." Anything to keep Grandma from moving back in with me.

I called Joe and told him I *might* be over later, but he shouldn't wait up. Then I reborrowed the Cherokee and drove to my parents' house.

My mother and I were sleeping on the couch when Grandma came in at two o'clock.

"Where were you?" my mother hollered at her. "We were worried sick."

"I had a night of sin," Grandma said. "Boy, that Myron is some kisser. I think he might even have got an erection, except it was hard to tell what with the way he hikes his pants up.

"My mother made the sign of the cross, and I looked in my purse for some Rolaids.

"Well, I gotta go to bed," Grandma said. "I'm pooped. And I got another driving test tomorrow."

When I woke up I was stretched out on the couch with a quilt over me. The house was filled with the smell of coffee cooking and bacon frying, and my mother was banging pots around in the kitchen.

"Well, at least you're not ironing," I said. When my mother got out the ironing, we knew there was big trouble brewing.

She slammed a lid on the stockpot and looked at me. "Where's your underwear?"

"I got caught in the rain, and I borrowed dry clothes from Dougie Kruper, only he didn't have any underwear. I would have gone home to change, but there are these two guys who want to chop off one of my fingers, and I was afraid they were at my apartment waiting for me."

"Well, thank God," she said. "I was afraid you left your bra in Morelli's car."

"We don't do it in his car. We do it in his bed."

My mother had the big butcher knife in her hand. "I'm going to kill myself."

"You can't fool me," I said, helping myself to coffee. "You'd never kill yourself in the middle of making soup."

Grandma trotted into the kitchen. She was wearing makeup, and her hair was pink.

"Omigod," my mother said. "What next?"

"What do you think of this hair color?" Grandma asked me. "I got one of them rinses at the drugstore. You just shampoo it in."

"It's pink," I said.

"Yeah, that's what I thought, too. It said on the label that it'd be Jezebel Red." She looked at the clock on the wall. "I gotta get a move on. Louise will be here any minute. I got the first appointment for my driving test. Hope you don't mind I asked Louise to take me. I didn't know you were going to be here."

"No sweat," I said. "Knock yourself out."

I made myself some toast and finished my coffee. I heard the toilet flush overhead and knew my father would be down momentarily. My mother looked like she was thinking about ironing.

"Well," I said, jumping up from my seat. "Things to do. Places to go."

"I just washed some grapes. Take some home," my mother said. "And there's ham in the refrigerator for a sandwich."

I didn't see Habib or Mitchell when I pulled into my lot, but I had the Glock in hand, just in case. I parked illegally, next to the back entrance, leaving as little space as possible between me and the door, and went directly to my apartment, taking the stairs. When I got there I realized I didn't have a key, and Joe had locked the door when he left.

Because I was the only one in the entire universe who couldn't open my door without a key, I got the spare from my neighbor Mrs. Karwatt.

"Isn't this a nice day?" she asked. "It feels just like spring."

"I guess everything's been pretty quiet here this morning," I said. "No loud noises or strange men out here in the hall?"

"Not that I've noticed." She looked down at my gun. "What a nice Glock. My sister carries a Glock, and she just loves it. I was thinking about trading in my forty-five, but I couldn't bring myself to do it. My dead husband gave it to me for our first anniversary. Rest his soul."

"What a romantic."

"Of course, I could always use a second gun."

I nodded my head in agreement. "You can never have too many guns."

I said good-bye to Mrs. Karwatt and let myself into my apartment. I went room by room, checking closets, looking under the bed and behind the shower curtain to make sure I was alone. Morelli had been right — the apartment was a wreck, but not too many things looked destroyed. My visitors hadn't taken the time to slash upholstery or put their foot into the television screen.

I took a shower and got dressed in clean jeans and a T-shirt. I put some gel in my hair and worked with the big roller brush so I had a lot of loose curls and looked like a cross between Jersey Girl and *Baywatch* Bimbo. I felt dwarfed by the volume of hair, so I added extra mascara to my lashes to balance things out.

I spent some time straightening the apartment, but then I started to get nervous that I was a sitting duck. Not just for Habib and Mitchell, but for Ranger as well. It was past my nine o'clock deadline.

I called Morelli at the office.

"Did your grandmother ever come home?" he asked.

"Yes. And it wasn't pretty. I need to talk to you. How about meeting me for early lunch at Pino's?"

After I hung up with Morelli I called into the office to see if Lula knew anything about Morgan.

"He's fine," Lula said. "But I don't think those guys Habib and Mitchell are gonna get their Christmas bonus."

I called Dougie and told him I was going to keep the Cherokee for a little longer.

"Keep it forever," he said.

By the time I got to Pino's, Morelli was already at a table, working on breadsticks.

"I'll make a deal with you," I said, shrugging out of my denim jacket. "If you tell me what's going on between you and Ranger, I'll let you keep Bob."

"Oh boy," Morelli said. "How can I pass that up?"

"I have an idea about this Ramos business," I said. "But it's pretty far out. I've been thinking about it for three or four days now."

Morelli grinned. "Woman's intuition?"

I smiled, too, because as it's turned out, intuition is the big gun in my arsenal. I can't shoot, I can't run all that fast, and the only karate I know is from Bruce Lee movies. But I have good intuition. Truth is, most of the time I don't know what the hell I'm doing, but if I follow my instincts things usually work out okay. "How was Homer Ramos identified?" I asked Morelli. "Dental records?"

"He was identified by jewelry and circumstance. There were no dental records. They mysteriously disappeared."

"I've been thinking — maybe it wasn't Homer Ramos who got shot. No one in his family seems upset that he's dead. Even if a father thinks his son is rotten to the core, I find it hard to believe there's no emotion at his death. And then I went snooping and discovered someone was living in Hannibal's guest room. Someone the exact size of Homer Ramos. I think Homer was hiding out in Hannibal's town house, and then Macaroni got clipped and Homer ran."

Morelli paused while the waitress brought us our pizza. "This is what we know. Or at least, what we think we know. Homer was the bagman for Stolle's new drug operation. This whole thing sat real bad with the boys in north Jersey and New York, and people started choosing sides."

"Drug war."

"More than that. If a member of the Ramos family was going to deal drugs, then north Jersey was going to deal guns. And nobody was happy about any of this because it meant boundaries would have to be redrawn. Everyone was feeling nervous. So nervous that it became known a contract was out on Homer Ramos.

"What we think but can't prove is that you're right — Homer Ramos isn't dead. Ranger suspected it right from the beginning, and you reinforced the theory when you told him you saw Ulysses in the doorway of the shore house. Ulysses never left Brazil. We think some other poor schnook got toasted in that building, and Homer's squirreled away someplace, waiting to get moved out of the country."

"And you think he's at the shore now."

"It seemed logical, but I don't know anymore. We have no reason to go in and search. Ranger went in but couldn't find anything."

"What about the gym bag? That was filled with Stolle's money, right?"

"We think when word got back to Hannibal that his little brother was about to start a crime wave, he ordered Homer to stop all activity outside the family business and have no further contact with Stolle. Then Hannibal asked Ranger to transport Stolle's money and tell Stolle he was no longer protected by the Ramos name. Problem is, when Stolle opened the suitcase it was filled with newsprint."

"Didn't Ranger check on the contents before he accepted it?"

"The suitcase was locked when it was turned over to Ranger. That was the way Hannibal Ramos had arranged it."

"He set Ranger up?"

"Yeah, but probably only for the fire and execution. I guess he figured Homer had gone too far this time, and promising to be a good boy and stop selling drugs wasn't going to get the contract removed. So Hannibal arranged to have Homer look dead. Ranger makes a good scapegoat because he doesn't belong to anyone. No reason for any retaliation if Ranger's the killer."

"So who has the money? Hannibal?"

"Hannibal set Ranger up to take the fall for the murder, but it's hard to believe he intended to cheat Stolle. He wanted Stolle pacified, not pissed off." Morelli helped himself to another piece of pizza. "I think it sounds like a stunt Homer would pull. He probably switched bags in the car on the way to the office."

Oh boy. "I don't suppose you know what kind of car he was driving?"

"Silver Porsche. Cynthia Lotte's car."

I guess that could explain Cynthia's death.

"What was that face you just made?" Morelli asked.

"It was a guilt grimace. I sort of helped Cynthia steal that car back from Homer."

I told Morelli about Cynthia walking in on Lula and me, and how Cynthia wanted her car back, and how that entailed getting the dead guy out of it. When I was done Morelli just sat there, looking dazed.

"You know, when you're a cop you get to a point where you think you've heard it all," he finally said. "You think there's nothing left that could surprise you. And then *you* come along, and it's a whole new ball game."

I selected another piece of pizza and thought the conversation was probably going to deteriorate now.

"Probably I don't have to point out that you destroyed a crime scene," Morelli said.

Yep. I was right. It was definitely deteriorating.

"And probably I don't have to point out that you withheld evidence in a homicide investigation."

I nodded affirmative.

"Jesus Christ on a crutch, what the hell were you thinking?" he yelled.

Everyone turned and looked at us.

"It wasn't like I could stop her," I said. "So it seemed like the expedient thing to do was to help her."

"You could have left. You could have walked away. You didn't have to *help!* I thought you just picked him up off the cement floor. I didn't know you dragged him out of a car, for crissake!"

People were staring again.

"They're going to find your prints all over that car," Morelli said.

"Lula and I wore gloves." Lucy and Ethel get clever.

"It used to be I didn't want to get married because I didn't want you sitting home worrying about me. Now I don't want to get married because I don't know if I can handle the stress of being married to *you.*"

"This would never have happened if you or Ranger had confided in me. First I get asked to help in the investigation, and then I get shoved aside. This is all your fault."

Morelli narrowed his eyes.

"Well, maybe not *all* your fault."

"I have to get back to work," Morelli said, calling for the check. "Promise me you'll go home and stay there. Promise me you'll go home and lock your door and not leave until this gets settled. Alexander is scheduled to fly back to Greece tomorrow. We think that means Homer is leaving tonight, and we think we know how he's going to do it."

"By boat."

"Yeah. There's a container ship sailing out of Newark, headed for Greece. And Homer is a weak link. If we can bring him in on a homicide there's a chance he'll plea-bargain and give us Alexander and Stolle."

"Gee, I kind of like Alexander."

Now Morelli grimaced.

"Okay," I said, "I'll go home and stay there. Yeesh."

I didn't have anything to do that afternoon, anyway. And I couldn't get excited about giving Habib and Mitchell another crack at kidnapping me and chopping off my fingers, one by one. Locking myself into my apartment was actually appealing. I could clean up some more, and watch some junky television, and take a nap.

"I have your shoulder bag at my house," Morelli said. "I didn't think to bring it to work with me. Do you need a key to your apartment?"

I nodded. "Yes."

He took a key off his key ring and gave it to me.

The lot to my building was relatively empty. At this time of day the seniors were either off shopping or making maximum use of the Medicare system, which was fine by me because it got me a good parking space. There were no strange cars in the lot. And as far as I could tell, no one was lurking in the bushes. I parked close to the door and got the Glock out of my jacket pocket. I quickly went into the building and took the stairs. The second-floor hall was empty and quiet. My door was locked. Both good signs. I unlocked my door with the Glock still in hand and stepped into the foyer. The apartment looked just as I'd left it. I closed the door behind me but didn't slide the bolt, in case I had to make a fast exit. Then I went room to room, making sure all was secure.

I went from the living room to the bathroom. And when I was in the bathroom a man stepped out of the bedroom and leveled a gun at me. He was average height and build, slimmer and younger than Hannibal Ramos, but the family resemblance was obvious. He was a good-looking man, but the good looks were ruined by lines of dissolution. A month at Betty Ford wouldn't make a dent in this man's problems.

"Homer Ramos?"

"In the flesh."

We both had guns drawn, standing about ten feet apart.

"Drop the gun," I said.

He gave me a humorless smile. "Make me."

Great. "Drop the gun, or I'm going to shoot you."

"Okay, shoot me. Go ahead."

I looked down at the Glock. It was a semiautomatic, and I owned a revolver. I had no idea how to shoot a semiautomatic. I knew I was supposed to slide something back. I pushed a button, and the clip fell out onto the carpet.

Homer Ramos burst out laughing.

I threw the Glock at him, hitting him in the forehead, and he fired at me before I had a chance to take off. The bullet grazed my upper arm and lodged in the wall behind me. I cried out and stumbled back, holding tight to the wound.

"That's a warning," he said. "If you try to run I'll shoot you in the back."

"Why are you here? What do you want?"

"I want the money, of course."

"I don't have the money."

"There's no other possibility, sweetie pie. The money was in the car, and before good ol' Cynthia died she told me you were in the town house when she walked in. So you're the only candidate. I've been all through Cynthia's house. And I tortured her sufficiently to be confident she was telling me everything she knew. She originally gave me this bogus story about throwing the bag away, but not even Cynthia would be that stupid. I've been through your apartment and the apartment of your fat friend. And I haven't found the money."

Harpoon to the brain. Habib and Mitchell weren't the ones who'd ransacked my apartment. It was Homer Ramos, looking for his money.

"Now I want you to tell me where you put it," Homer said. "I want you to tell me where you've hidden my money."

My arm stung and a bloodstain was growing on the torn material of my jacket. Little black dots were dancing in front of my eyes. "I need to sit down."

He waved me to the couch. "Over there."

Getting shot, no matter how minor the wound, is not conducive to clear thinking. Somewhere in the muck of gray matter between my ears I knew I should be forming a plan, but damned if I could do it. My mind was scurrying down blank paths in panic. There were tears pooling behind my eyes, and my nose was running.

"Where's my money?" Ramos repeated when I was seated.

"I gave it to Ranger." Even *I* was surprised when this answer popped out. And clearly neither of us believed it.

"You're lying. I'm going to ask you again. And if I think you're lying I'm going to shoot you in the knee."

He was standing with his back to the small hallway that led to my front door. I looked over his shoulder and saw Ranger move into my line of vision.

"Okay, you got me," I said, louder than was necessary, with just a touch of hysteria. "This is what happened. I had no idea there was money in the car. What I saw was this dead guy. And I don't know, call me crazy, maybe I've seen too many Mafia movies, but I thought to myself, Maybe there's another body in the trunk! I mean, I didn't want to miss out on any bodies, you know? So I opened the trunk and there was this gym bag. Well, I've always been nosy, so of course, I had to see inside the bag —"

"I don't give a flying fuck about your life story," Homer said. "I want to know what you did with the freaking money. I've only got twelve hours before my ship sails. You think you could get to the point before then?"

And that was when Ranger yanked Homer Ramos off his feet and pressed the stun gun to his neck. Homer gave a squeak and collapsed onto the floor. Ranger reached down and took Homer's gun. He patted him down for more weapons, didn't find any, and cuffed his hands behind his back.

He kicked Ramos aside and stood over me. "I thought I told you not to hang out with members of the Ramos family. You never listen."

Ranger humor.

I gave him a weak smile. "I think I'm going to throw up."

He put his hand to the back of my neck and pushed my head down between my legs. "Push against my hand," he said.

The bells stopped clanging and my stomach sort of calmed. Ranger pulled me to my feet and took my jacket off.

I wiped my nose on my T-shirt. "How long were you here?" I asked.

"I came in when he shot you."

We both looked at the gash in my arm.

"Flesh wound," Ranger said. "Can't get much

sympathy on this one." He steered me into the kitchen and pressed some paper toweling to my arm. "Try to clean it up a little, and I'll go look for a Band-Aid."

"Band-Aid! I've been shot!"

He came back with my first-aid kit, used Band-Aids to hold the wound together, put a gauze patch on it, and wrapped my arm with surgical gauze. He stepped back and grinned at me. "You look kind of white."

"I thought I was going to die. He'd have killed me for sure."

"But he didn't," Ranger said.

"Did you ever think you were going to die?"

"Many times."

"And?"

"And I didn't." He used my phone to dial Morelli. "I'm at Steph's apartment. We've got Homer Ramos bagged and waiting for you. And we could use a blue-and-white. Stephanie caught a bullet in the arm. It just sliced through some flesh, but she should have it looked at."

He slid an arm around me and pulled me to him. I rested my head on his chest, and he nuzzled my hair and kissed me just above the ear. "Are you okay?" he asked.

No way was I okay. I was as unokay as I could get. I was in a state. "Sure," I said. "I'm fine."

I could feel him smile. "Liar."

Morelli caught up with me at the hospital. "Are you okay?"

"Ranger asked me that same question fifteen minutes ago and the answer was no. But I'm feeling better now."

"How's the arm?"

"I don't think it's too bad. I'm waiting to see the doctor."

Morelli took my hand and pressed a kiss to the palm. "I think my heart stopped twice on the way over."

The kiss fluttered in my stomach. "I'm fine. Really."

"I had to see for myself."

"You love me," I said.

His smile tightened, and he gave a small nod. "I love you."

Ranger loved me too, but not quite in the same way. Ranger was at a different place in his life.

The doors to the waiting room crashed open, and Connie and Lula barged in.

"We heard you got shot," Lula said. "What's going on?"

"Omigod, it's true," Connie said. "Look at your arm! How did this happen?"

Morelli stood. "I want to be there when they bring Ramos in. And I think I'm excess baggage now that the troops have arrived. Call me as soon as you're done with the doctor."

I decided to go from the hospital to my parents' house. Morelli was still busy interrogating Homer Ramos, and I didn't feel like being alone. I had Lula stop at Dougie's first so I could get a flannel shirt to wear over the T-shirt.

Dougie and Mooner were in the living room, watching a new big-screen TV.

"Hey, dude," Mooner said, "check this television out. Is this excellent, or what?"

"I thought you were done with the hijacking."

"That's the astonishing thing," Mooner said. "This is a newly purchased television. We didn't even steal it, dude. I tell you, God works in mysterious ways. One minute we're thinking our future is in the crapper, and then next thing you know, we come into an inheritance."

"Congratulations," I said. "Who died?"

"That's the miracle," Mooner said. "Our inheritance isn't tainted by tragedy. It was given to us, dude. A present. Can you dig it?

"Dougie and me had the good fortune to make a car sale on Sunday, so we took the car to the car wash to get it all spiffed up for the buyer. And while we're there this blonde comes streaking in, in a silver Porsche. And she, like, cleaned this car to within an inch of its life. We were, like, just watching. And then she took this bag out of the trunk and threw it in the garbage. It was a real genuine bag, so Dougie and me asked if she minded if we took it. And she said it was just a disgusting gym bag, and we could freaking do whatever we wanted with it. So we took the bag home and, like, forgot about it until this morning."

"And when you opened it up and looked inside

this morning, the bag turned out to be filled with money," I said.

"Wow. How did you know that?"

"Just a guess."

My mother was in the kitchen when I got to the house. She was making *toltott kaposzta,* which is stuffed cabbage. Not my favorite thing in the world. But then my favorite thing in the world is probably pineapple upside-down cake with lots of whipped cream, so I guess it's not a fair comparison.

She stopped working and looked at me. "Is something wrong with your arm? You're holding it funny."

"I got shot, but —"

My mother fainted. *Crash,* onto the floor with the big wooden spoon still in her hand.

Shit.

I soaked a dish towel and put it on her forehead until she came around.

"What happened?" she asked.

"You fainted."

"I never faint. You must be mistaken." She sat up and mopped her face with the wet towel. "Oh yeah, now I remember."

I helped her to a kitchen chair and put the water on for tea.

"How bad is it?" she asked.

"It's just a nick. And the guy's in jail now, so everything's fine."

Except I felt a little nauseated, my heart was

skipping a beat once in a while, and I didn't want to go back to my apartment. Otherwise, everything was fine.

I put the cookie jar on the table and gave my mother a cup of tea. I sat opposite her and helped myself to a cookie. Chocolate chip. Very healthy, since she'd put some chopped walnuts in, and walnuts are filled with protein, right?

The front door banged open and closed, and Grandma stormed into the kitchen. "I did it! I passed my driver's test!"

My mother made the sign of the cross and put the wet towel back on her head.

"How come your arm's all puffy under your shirt?" Grandma asked me.

"I'm wearing a bandage. I got shot today."

Grandma's eyes opened wide. "Cool!" She pulled a chair out and joined us at the table. "How did it happen? Who shot you?"

Before I could answer, the phone rang. It was Marge Dembowski reporting that her daughter Debbie, who's a nurse at the hospital, called to say I was shot. Then Julia Kruselli called to say her son, Richard, who's a cop, just gave her the scoop on Homer Ramos.

I moved from the kitchen to the living room and fell asleep in front of the television. Morelli was there when I woke up, the house reeked of stuffed cabbage cooking on the stovetop, and my arm ached.

Morelli had a new jacket for me, one without a bullet hole in it. "Time to go home," he said, gingerly slipping my arm into the jacket.

"I am home."

"I mean *my* home."

Morelli's home. That would be nice. Rex and Bob would be there. Even better, Morelli would be there.

My mother put a big bag on the coffee table in front of us. "There's some stuffed cabbage and a fresh loaf of bread and some cookies."

Morelli took the bag. "I love stuffed cabbage," he said.

My mother looked pleased.

"Do you really like stuffed cabbage?" I asked him when we were in the car.

"I like anything I don't have to cook myself."

"How'd it go with Homer Ramos?"

"Better than our wildest dreams. The man is a worm. He ratted on *everyone*. Alexander Ramos should have killed him at birth. And as a bonus, we picked up Habib and Mitchell and told them they were being charged with kidnapping, and they gave us Arturo Stolle."

"You've had a busy afternoon."

"I've had a very good day. Except for you getting shot."

"Who killed Macaroni?"

"Homer. Stolle sent Macaroni over to get the Porsche. Guess he figured it'd pay off part of the debt. Homer caught him in the car and shot him. Then Homer panicked and ran out of the house."

"Forgetting to put the alarm on?"

Morelli grinned. "Yeah. Homer had gotten into the habit of sampling the wares he carried for Stolle, and he wasn't too with the program. He'd get stoned and go out for munchies and forget to set the alarm. Ranger was able to break in. Macaroni broke in. You broke in. I don't think Hannibal realized the extent of the problem. He thought Homer was sitting tight in the town house."

"But Homer was a wreck."

"Yep. Homer was truly a wreck. After he shot Macaroni, he really freaked. In his drugged-out, deranged state I guess he thought he could hide himself better than Hannibal could, so he went back to the house to get his stash. Only his stash wasn't there."

"And all that time Hannibal had his men out, scouring the state, trying to find Homer."

"Sort of gratifying to know they were scrambling around, looking for the little jerk," Morelli said.

"So what about the stash?" I asked. "Anybody have any idea what happened to the gym bag filled with money?" Anybody besides me, that is.

"One of life's great mysteries," Morelli said. "The prevailing theory is that Homer hid it while in a drug-induced haze and forgot where he put it."

"That sounds logical," I said. "I bet that's it." What the hell, why not let Dougie and Mooner enjoy the money? If it was confiscated it would only go to the federal government, and God only knew what *they*'d do with it.

Morelli parked in front of his row house on Slater Street and helped me out. He opened his front door, and Bob jumped out and smiled at me.

"He's happy to see me," I told Morelli. And the fact that I was holding a bag filled with stuffed cabbage didn't hurt, either. Not that it mattered. Bob gave a terrific welcome.

Morelli had put Rex's aquarium on his kitchen counter. I tapped on the side and there was movement under a pile of bedding. Rex stuck his head out, twitched his whiskers, and blinked his black bead eyes at me.

"Hey, Rex!" I said. "How's it going?"

The whisker twitching stopped for a microsecond, and then Rex retreated under the bedding. It might not seem like much to the casual observer, but in terms of hamsters, that was a terrific welcome, too.

Morelli cracked open a couple beers and set two plates on his small kitchen table. We divided the cabbage rolls between Morelli and Bob and me and dug in. Halfway through my second cabbage roll I noticed Morelli wasn't eating.

"Not hungry?" I asked.

Morelli sent me a tight smile. "I've missed you."

"I've missed you, too."

"How's your arm?"

"It's okay."

He took my hand and kissed my fingertip. "I

hope this conversation counts as foreplay, because I'm feeling a real lack of self-control."

Fine by me. I wasn't seeing much value in self-control *at all* at the moment.

He took the fork out of my hand. "How bad do you want those cabbage rolls?"

"I don't even *like* cabbage rolls."

He pulled me out of my chair and kissed me.

The doorbell rang, and we both jumped apart.

"Shit!" Morelli said. "Now what? It's always something! Grandmothers and murderers and pagers going off. I can't take it anymore." He stormed off to the front of the house and wrenched the door open.

It was his grandma Bella. She was a little lady, dressed in Old Country black. Her white hair was pulled into a knot at the nape of her neck, her face was free of makeup, her thin lips were pressed tight together. Joe's mother stood to the side, larger than Bella, no less scary.

"Well?" Bella said.

Joe looked at her. "Well, what?"

"Aren't you going to invite us in?"

"No."

Bella stiffened. "If you weren't my favorite grandson I'd put the eye on you."

Joe's mother stepped forward. "We can't stay long. We're on our way to Marjorie Soleri's baby shower. We just stopped by with a casserole for you. I know you don't cook."

I came to Joe's side and took the casserole from his mother. "It's nice to see you again, Mrs.

Morelli. And nice to see you, too, Grandma Bella. The casserole smells terrific."

"What's going on here?" Bella said. "You two aren't living in sin again, are you?"

"I'm trying," Morelli said. "I'm just not having any luck."

Bella jumped up and smacked Joe on the head. "Shame on you."

"Maybe I should take this into the kitchen," I said, backing away. "And then I should be running along. I wasn't staying long, either. I just dropped in to say hello." Last thing I needed was for Bella to put the eye on *me*.

Joe grabbed me by my good arm. "You're not going anywhere."

Bella squinted at me, and I flinched. I could feel Joe dig in beside me.

"Stephanie's staying here tonight," he said. "Get used to it."

Bella and Mrs. Morelli sucked in a breath and pressed their lips tight together.

Mrs. Morelli tipped her chin up a half-inch and gave Joe a piercing glare. "Are you going to marry this woman?"

"Yeah, for crying out loud, I'm going to marry her," Joe said. "The sooner, the better."

"Married!" Bella said, clasping her hands together. "My Joseph, getting married." She kissed both of us.

"Wait a minute," I said. "You never asked me to marry you. You're the one who doesn't want to get married."

"I changed my mind," Morelli said. "I want to get married. Hell, I want to get married tonight."

"You just want to have sex," I said.

"Are you kidding? I can't even *remember* sex. I don't even know if I can still *do* it."

His pager beeped. "Damn!" Morelli said. He ripped the pager off his belt and threw it across the street.

Grandma Bella looked down at my hand. "Where's the ring?"

We *all* looked at my hand. No ring.

"You don't need a ring to get married," Morelli said.

Grandma Bella gave her head a sad shake. "He don't know much," she said.

"Hold on here. I'm not going to get railroaded into marriage," I told them.

Grandma Bella stiffened. "You don't want to marry my Joseph?"

Joe's mother made the sign of the cross and rolled her eyes.

"Gosh," Joe said to his mother and Bella, "look at the time. I wouldn't want you to miss the shower."

"I know what you're up to," Bella said. "You want to get rid of us."

"That's true," Joe told them. "Stephanie and I have things to talk about."

Bella's eyes rolled back in her head. "I'm having a vision," she said. "I see grandchildren. Three boys and two girls . . ."

"Don't let her scare you," Joe whispered. "I've

got an entire box of the best protection money can buy upstairs next to the bed."

I chewed on my lower lip. I'd have felt much more comfortable if she'd said she saw a hamster.

"Okay, we're going now," Bella said. "The visions always make me tired. I'll need to take a nap in the car before the shower."

When they drove off, Joe shut and locked the door. He took the casserole from me and set it out of Bob's reach on the dining room table. He carefully slipped my jacket off my shoulders and let it fall to the floor. Then he unsnapped my jeans, hooked a finger into the waistband, and pulled me to him. "About that proposal, cupcake . . ."